Hear My Cry

Hear My Cry

R. G. Wood

RESOURCE *Publications* · Eugene, Oregon

HEAR MY CRY

Resource Publications
An Imprint of Wipf and Stock Publishers
199 W. 8th Ave., Suite 3
Eugene, OR 97401

www.wipfandstock.com

PAPERBACK ISBN: 978-1-7252-6969-9
HARDCOVER ISBN: 978-1-7252-6968-2
EBOOK ISBN: 978-1-7252-6970-5

Manufactured in the U.S.A.   07/13/20

This book is dedicated to my wife Rosi, who suffered through a few million plot revisions. I'm also thankful to Pastor Chris, Carol, and Pam, who read my first (horrendous) drafts and didn't point and snicker. Finally, I'm grateful for about a half dozen Christian men who served as my mentors and role models over the years. You guys know who you are.

1

COLE EVANS RAN HIS finger down the yellow legal pad.

Yeah, this will work.

It's a little short. I need one or two more Scripture references. Better to have more than I need than to have a brain cramp and not be able to wrestle something from memory.

The old Bible's fine paper crinkled.

There. That'll do.

"I wait for the LORD, my whole being waits, and in his word I put my hope," he read aloud.

Yeah. Sounds okay.

He inserted a bookmark and jotted down the reference. Psalm 130:5.

The dull thuds stole into his consciousness like far-off thunder.

What was that? A truck?

No. Closer. Back door. Someone banging. Who in the world—? It's six-thirty a.m.

"Mr. Evans! Mr. Evans!" The voice was high-pitched, almost shrill.

He bounded down the stairs and cracked two slats of the blinds.

The white T-shirt hung like a tent, and the girl's spindly limbs looked like spider legs.

The next-door neighbor kid. What's her name? Autumn? No. Tori? No. Think, dummy. Stormy, Stormy. That's right.

A wave of humidity rolled in when he threw open the door.

"Stormy, what's the matter, sweetie? Come on in. My air conditioner's running."

The girl stood about chest high. A matted mess of untamed straw-blond hair jutted out in spots and hung down in others. She was all elbows and knees, and her collar bones protruded below hollowed-out shoulders. How long had it been since he'd seen her? Was she always so thin?

"Are you all right? Where's your mom?"

"Do you have anything to eat?" Stormy said. Her huge blue eyes pleaded.

Sure, he had food, but not much. And he wouldn't get new milk and meat rations for a week.

"Well, I guess the Lord will provide," he said, more to himself than to Stormy.

She tilted her head, her eyes questioning.

"Where's your mom?" he tried again.

"Working."

"What about your aunt?"

"She's working, too."

What was her aunt's name? Gabby? No, Abby.

He pointed to a chair.

The girl climbed up, exposing black soles.

Clearly, the kid rarely wore shoes.

Her twiggy legs dangled over the edge of the chair.

"Do you know your mom's phone number?" he asked.

Stormy shook her head.

"What about your aunt's?"

Another head shake. The eyes continued to plead.

For the love of Pete. This kid's actually home alone. Do I need to report this?

He'd waved at Stormy and her mom in passing from time to time. Olivia Sandlin was a TV reporter for a local early-morning news show. He'd watched it occasionally. Olivia sometimes pulled into her driveway as Cole was leaving for work. He rarely saw the other woman, Olivia's sister.

He set a heaping bowl of Cheerios and milk in front of Stormy.

Large spoonsful flew from the bowl to her mouth.

Poor kid. Lord, how do you want me to help?

I'll get them some food from the church's food pantry. If Stormy's mom will take it. She might be too proud.

He'd remind her of the truth. The hard times were affecting everyone. The government's meat and milk rations weren't enough. And most people couldn't afford to get food on the black market. Not to mention that selling or trading rations was illegal.

Stormy chewed quickly and swallowed. Then, as quickly as she'd started eating, she stopped.

"Okay, all done. Thanks," she said.

She put a hand to her stomach and grimaced.

Two-thirds of the cereal remained. It made sense. Cole had read that people initially can't eat much after long fasts. He'd experienced as much.

All right, now what? I can't send her home.

"Are you sure your aunt's not home?"

Stormy shook her head.

Cole cracked the slats of the blinds. Wider this time. No cars occupied the driveway, and the house looked dark.

Maybe I should walk over and knock. No, she probably knows whether anyone's home.

"Okay, sweetie, how about we make a deal?" Cole said. "You watch a movie on my tablet for a few minutes, and I'll find someone to come and stay with you until your mom or aunt gets home. Sound good?"

Stormy's smile revealed a crooked canine tooth.

I wonder if Olivia will be able to afford braces. Probably not in the near future. We can't even afford food.

Cole tapped the green dot on his phone and waited. "Hey, Annie, it's Cole. Sorry to call so early. Do you think Michelle would want to make a couple of bucks?"

～

"What do you mean 'creepy pervert?' The kid knocked on my door and asked for food!"

Stormy's mom's voice blasted through the phone. "That doesn't matter! You had no right inviting an eleven-year-old girl into your *house*. *Anything* could've happened in there!"

Cole hadn't thought of it at the time, but she was right.

"Look, Olivia. It's Olivia, right? I get it. The world is full of horrible, creepy people. But what was I supposed to do? Tell her to go play in the highway?"

"What business was it of yours?"

"Stormy *made* it my business when she knocked on my door at dawn and said she was home alone and hungry." His voice carried more venom than he wanted. He needed to dial it back. "What was she doing home alone that early in the morning, anyway?"

The line went quiet. A second. Two seconds.

Well, is she going to say anything? Apparently not.

"There was mass miscommunication over here this morning," Olivia said. The anger had left her voice. "Abby, my sister, got called in to work two hours early, and she was afraid to say no. We need the money, and she needs the job. She thought Stormy would sleep till I got home."

For the love of Pete. This country's a wreck.

"Well, that's not really okay but it's understandable," Cole said. "At least she's not a little, little kid. And everything turned out all right. The church secretary's daughter came and hung out with Stormy. I think they had fun. I can give you her number if you want—in case you ever get in another pinch."

"No, thank you, though," Olivia said.

"I'd even pay for it if you were in a jam. It's better than leaving Stor—"

"I said, 'No, thank you!'" The anger was back.

Okay, Lord, do I broach the next subject? Despite the anger? Yeah, I have to.

"I understand. I certainly didn't mean to offend. At the same time, I know everyone is struggling right now. I just wanted to help. By the way, if you ever need food, our church has—"

"We're *fine*, Mr. Evans."

Cole didn't know how, but she'd ratcheted the anger up a notch.

"If you'd just leave us alone and stop meddling, we'd all be a lot happier."

"Truly, my apol—"

The line went dead.

"Whelp. Another happy customer," Cole said.

Lord, please help her. Provide for her family and draw Olivia to yourself.

He sighed.

Could I have done anything else? Maybe gone next door?

You can't beat yourself up over this. You had to feed the kid.

He ate a spoonful of Stormy's Cheerios.

Eww, lukewarm. And mushy.

But he had to eat them. They'd cost a fortune.

2

———

THE 3-D IMAGE SWAM out of the TV until it surrounded him and filled the living room. Cincinnati's skyline stretched out in the distance. A cluster of office towers and the Bengals stadium stood slightly off to the right, beyond three bridges that spanned the Ohio River. Patriotic swags draped a stage in the foreground, and American flags waved everywhere.

People wearing scarlet T-shirts emblazoned with jagged white lettering that read "Stop the Madness" created a red splotch in the crowd to the left.

Cole turned up the volume.

"Let's review the facts." Roberto Gonzalez stood tall and broad shouldered behind the lectern. Concern etched his rugged Latino features. "The United States produces an astounding seventy-one percent of the world's robots and artificial intelligence circuitry. But our tech industries are struggling. Copper producers in Chile and a few smaller countries are holding them hostage."

Cole put his feet on the coffee table.

"Much like Middle Eastern oil producers stopped selling oil to the United States a few generations ago—in 1973—the Copper Producing Consortium has stopped shipments of copper," Gonzalez said. "And, as I'm sure you've learned since the embargo began, a stable copper supply is critical to our nation's economic health."

The camera cut to the audience. The throng, mostly men in their thirties and forties, wore intense expressions.

"Rising copper prices have had a ripple effect. Not only do robots, computers, and phones cost more, everything costs more."

The camera zoomed in on Gonzalez, his expression somber.

"And President Robertson's response has been a disaster. Inflation is up thirteen percent since the embargo began. Thirteen percent! That's staggering! Prices of milk and bread and vegetables and clothing and transportation and housing are going up almost every week. And our wages aren't keeping up."

A male voice in the audience carried. "That's right!"

"You know it!" another man yelled.

Chatter rippled through the gathering.

The noise swelled for several seconds while Gonzalez waited, his face placid. He raised a hand to quiet the din.

"That's not the America I grew up in, ladies and gentlemen," he said softly. "That's madness! And the time has come to stop the madness!"

At the catchphrase, the crowd erupted. Chants of "Gon-za-lez! Gon-za-lez! Gon-za-lez!" broke out. People jumped up and down and pumped fists. A middle-aged woman with her arms outstretched toward Gonzalez fell to her knees and wailed.

Cole grabbed the remote from the coffee table and switched off the set.

Ridiculous. And scary.

Lord, you know this country's in trouble. Out of your love, please help us, even though we certainly don't deserve your grace. Be with our president, legislature and courts . . .

Cole opened the Bible on the coffee table as he continued to pray.

A row of pickup trucks sat in the gravel parking lot along with a Ford Fusion, its white paint bleached to chalk. Cole eased his old F-150 into a space at the far corner of the lot, the only spot available. The Pitchfork occupied one end of the faded four-unit strip mall. A post office resided at the other end, and a convenience store that sold everything from firewood to lousy pizza anchored the middle. All manner of small businesses had moved into and out of the remaining unit over the past few years. The current business sold wood signs and other trinkets that served only to clutter up the house.

A red-orange neon sign in The Pitchfork's window advertised that the place was "pen," the *o* having been burned out for weeks.

Cole loved the place. Pictures of tractors, barns, and covered bridges adorned the walls along with a few grainy black-and-whites of local graduating classes from the early 1900s. The largest of the classes had fourteen people.

About a half-dozen tables sat in the middle of the room, the wood stain worn off in spots where countless elbows had rested over the years. Almost every time Cole went in, the same six men sat at the same back table. They wore weathered faces, T-shirts, and blue jeans. Their ball caps bore tractor or seed company logos. And snippets of conversation typically centered around crops and livestock.

The aromas of coffee, bacon, and fried onions greeted Cole as he walked in. His stomach grumbled.

"Cole Daniel Evans!" the man in the corner called. Over six-feet tall, stocky, and with shaggy hickory-colored hair, Jake Moore could have been part Wookie.

"Jacob!" Cole replied. He pronounced the name with something of an Eastern European or Hebrew lilt. It sounded more like "Hyakob" than "Jacob."

Cole couldn't remember how the ritual began. It had been part of their Wednesday morning breakfast routine for several years. The breakfasts had been weekly events before the recession. Now, the men could afford to meet only once a month. On the first Wednesday. For the past couple of months, The Pitchfork had been closed on the month's final Wednesday. The place had been out of rations. The owner, Mason, had said he'd go under in another six months if the economy didn't improve. It was one of the reasons Cole continued to make the breakfast meetings, even when money was tight. Mason was a good man, and Cole cared for The Pitchfork's waitresses as well.

Jake stretched out a meaty paw and pulled him in for a quick hug. "How've you been, my brother?" Jake said.

"Awesome, you?"

"Good enough," Jake said. "Have you heard from Tom?"

"He said he'll be right here," Cole said.

As Cole pulled up a chair, the waitress arrived with a coffee pot and set three cups on the table. Melody was tall and broad shouldered. Cole's mom would've said she had big bones, and the platinum in her blond bob was giving way to dull gray.

"Is your friend running late again?" she asked as she poured.

"Are the three of us breathing?" Jake asked.

Melody laughed. "He does live in his own time zone, doesn't he?" An eastern Kentucky twang garnished Melody's speech.

He couldn't get to breakfast on time, but as Cole's assistant pastor, Tom Henderson was invaluable. He walked in as if on cue.

"We're talking bad about you. You better get over here," Cole called, pointing to his wrist.

"Can I help that I need my beauty sleep?" Tom said.

"If that's what you need, you'd better go back home and crawl back in bed," Jake said, giving rise to laughter.

"I'm cuter than you are," Tom said.

Melody poured Tom's coffee. "Now, boys, am I going to have to sit you at different tables?" she asked.

"No, ma'am, I'll try to get these guys to behave," Tom said, causing more laughter and teasing.

When Melody had gone, Tom said, "I stayed up late to watch news coverage of that stupid Gonzalez rally."

"Yeah, I turned that on for a minute. Couldn't stomach it," Cole said.

"You missed it," Tom said. "That blond woman from Channel Twelve got an interview with him."

"Olivia Sandlin?" Cole asked.

"Yeah. Sandlin, I think," Tom said.

"She's my next-door neighbor. I think she thinks I walk on water," Cole said, his voice dripping sarcasm.

"Made another fan, ay?" Tom said.

"Oh, yeah. She'll cheer for me like Red Sox fans cheer for the Yankees."

"That bad, huh," Jake said.

"Well, her interview with Gonzalez was great," Tom said. "She showed that Gonzalez is communist, or at least hard-core socialist."

"What's the difference?" Jake asked.

"It basically comes down to how much control the government has over the economy and people's daily lives. In true communism, the government owns everything, decides what you need, and gives it to you. There's no real need for money. In socialism, you still have to make money and buy stuff. The government just heavily regulates what businesses do. That's over-simplified, but that's more or less it," Tom said.

"Well, look at you, Mr. Smarty Pants!" Cole said.

"Hey, what can I say? I'm handsome *and* brilliant."

"Not to mention humble," Cole said.

"So, what'd Gonzalez say?" Jake said.

"He talked about regulating businesses and setting production levels for stuff. At one point, he even said Karl Marx was 'a very wise man.'" Tom said, making air quotes. "You've gotta see this."

He thumbed his phone and tapped. When the video began, Olivia and Gonzalez sat on a plush leather sofa in what looked like a tour bus. Cream-colored blinds covered the large window behind them.

"You made a good showing right out of the gate in Iowa, South Carolina, and other early primaries, and that success seems to be continuing," Olivia said. "Clearly, your message is striking a chord."

"Well, hopefully," Gonzalez said. "Obviously, we have problems at home and abroad. As you know, Ms. Sandlin, I have extensive international business experience in the area of robotics. And I've had many, many interactions with people in copper industries, as well as with government officials in Chile. I know these people. I know how they think. I know what motivates them. And I believe my experience will allow me to resolve the current dispute."

Tom stopped the video as Melody approached to take their orders, then hit the play arrow again as she headed toward the kitchen.

"So, I've read," Olivia said. "However, some of your critics say your ties to the robotics industry create a conflict of interest. What would you stand to gain personally as a result of improved relations with Chile and copper producers?"

"That's a fair question," Gonzalez said. "And the answer is nothing. I wouldn't benefit personally. I've sold all of my interests in copper-related businesses, and I no longer hold any positions in those companies or on their boards of directors."

Cole hated to admit it, but Gonzalez was smooth. Too smooth. He was so smooth, he was slick.

"Can you go into further detail about how you would foster improved relations?" Olivia asked.

"I can only say we cannot be perceived as weak, so all options will remain on the table."

"It doesn't sound as if you're limiting those options to merely economic measures," Olivia said.

"All options must remain open," Gonzalez said. "I cannot go into further detail."

"Whoa," Jake said. "Is he talking about going to war?"

"Sounds like it," Tom said.

Melody set down their plates while the video continued. Tom muted the sound while the men prayed.

Gonzalez was speaking when Tom turned the volume back up. "We believe the gap between rich and poor has become unacceptable. A relative handful of Wall Street executives make tens of billions of dollars a year while a huge underclass can't afford to put food on their tables. Something needs to be done to spread the wealth. When I become president, I will make that happen."

"And how would you accomplish that?" Olivia asked.

"I'm proposing strict government control over banking, business, and industries in order to set production levels and assure that goods and services are equally distributed."

"So, you're proposing hard-left socialism," Olivia said.

"Let's not get caught up in semantics," Gonzalez said. "I prefer the term 'progressive policies.' I'm proposing a system to more equally distribute wealth and to allow all people to enjoy the necessities of life."

"So, you're taking a page out of Karl Marx's book," Olivia said.

"We cannot deny that Marx was a very smart man," Gonzalez said. "He believed that the government should own all property, and all means of production, essentially that everyone should work for the government. But that didn't work, and that isn't my proposal. I will bring to America a relationship between the common man and companies who produce our goods. Every American will once again be well-fed and relatively prosperous. We deserve better than a system that makes us work impossible hours for a paycheck that doesn't feed our families."

Cole wanted to reach through the phone and smack the guy. "You're right, Tom. This guy is even further left than I realized," he said.

"Yeah. Some of it isn't even that veiled," Tom said.

"Didn't you also say he spewed some kind of anti-Christian rhetoric?" Jake asked.

"He did. I think it was her next question," Tom said.

Melody quietly refilled their coffee cups.

Olivia was midsentence, ". . . a subject that's taboo in this day and age. I would like to briefly discuss your religious views. It's been whispered, although not specifically reported, that you're an avowed atheist. No one who publicly proclaimed atheism has ever served in the Oval Office. How would your views influence the way you carry out the duties of the president?"

"You have to admit, she has guts," Jake said.

"Yeah, I'll give her that," Cole said.

Gonzalez looked like he'd expected the question. "Well, Ms. Sandlin, it's highly unusual, perhaps even offensive, to speak of religion at this point in our nation's history. But I have no secrets. I want the people to know that their president is transparent and worthy of their trust. History shows that Jimmy Carter was a very religious man and outspoken about his Christian beliefs, and yet he was not a successful president. Ronald Reagan, by contrast, who was considered by Republicans to be an outstanding president, was very private about his faith. It is said, in fact, that President Reagan didn't attend church during his presidency because he didn't want his presence in the church building to distract from the service. So, in my mind, a person's religion in no way influences how successful he or she will be as president. But you brought up Karl Marx earlier. He was correct in his belief that religion is of no real help to a suffering people," Gonzalez said. "And honestly, religion is of no real help to me. The point is, what I believe about the existence or nonexistence of God has little to do with my ability to support and defend the Constitution of the United States. My beliefs, in fact, may make me more qualified to hold office than people who have difficulty with the separation of church and state."

"Whoa," Jake said, "this guy is scary."

"We need to be in serious prayer, boys," Cole said.

"Has that pastor's group you're in considered a citywide prayer event of some type?" Jake asked.

"No, but it may not be a bad idea," Cole said.

"I could look into that," Tom said.

"If he's not getting his beauty rest," Jake said to Cole.

A wadded napkin flew Jake's direction.

3

THE TRASH CAN'S PLASTIC wheels rumbled over the concrete.

Great. Perfect timing. Olivia.

His stupid garbage can would give her one more reason to think he was some kind of weirdo. Most people had switched years ago to automatic trash bins they guided to the curb using a remote control. People didn't even come out of their houses. If they did, they got as far as the porch as they watched the cans drive themselves to the curb. The gadgets looked fun in a twelve-year-old-boy sort of way, but Cole couldn't see spending the money on one.

Guess I need to wave. Try to keep the peace.

Her van eased to a stop, and the window whined open.

Well, so much for that. I guess it's on. Here we go.

"Hey, I just wanted to apologize for how I acted the other day," she said.

Wow, I didn't see that coming. Is this the same woman who acted like a madwoman forty-eight hours ago?

Cole forced the words out. "Thanks. I get it. Everybody's stressed."

"Yeah. The whole thing really scared me, and I seriously overreacted. I'm sorry," Olivia said.

Her words sounded genuine.

"It's all good," Cole said. "I would've freaked out a little, too, if I were in your shoes." He wanted to say that he wouldn't have automatically called the person helping him a creepy pervert, but he resisted. "By the way, nice interview with Gonzalez."

Her face brightened. "You watched it?"

"Yeah. I can honestly say I was impressed. How'd you land a sit-down with him?"

"A former boss who moved to CNN arranged it. He owed me a favor. Over the couple years he was here, he called me in to work early or on weekends dozens of times. I hated it then, but I guess it worked out."

"I'd say so," Cole said. "I was glad you asked about religion."

"I thought people would want to know."

Cole wondered where Olivia stood with the Lord. Dare he ask? No, the timing didn't feel right. If the Lord wanted it to happen, he'd get his shot.

"Do you think he has a chance to win?" she asked.

"I know a lot of people are hungry and scared," Cole said.

Should he offer his opinion of Gonzalez? No, probably not. Once again, if he was supposed to, he'd get another opportunity.

"I guess we'll see what happens," she said. "Good talking to you."

He hadn't noticed before, but she was cute. About his age, maybe a little younger. Through the car window, he saw she wore dark slacks, a white blouse, and a dress jacket that had a specific name he couldn't remember. She was slim and toned, and her blond hair, highlighted with streaks of copper, fell to her shoulders.

"Yeah, maybe we should do it again sometime," he said.

"Let me know when you plan to roll out that old trash can, and I'll pull into the driveway," she said, smiling.

"Good plan," Cole said.

He smiled as her window whined upward.

4

"Lord, we now leave this in your hands, trusting that you will do what's right for this nation, and that your will will be done. We pray in your precious and awesome heavenly name," Cole said.

Everyone echoed his amen.

"There are probably people who think there's something seriously wrong with us," Jake said. "But you know what? I don't care."

Chips, dips, a veggie tray, and a meat tray crowded Tom and Janice's counter, and the smell of coffee—decaf at this hour—wafted into the living room. Cole was sure everyone had spent a large chunk of their month's rations on the spread. He had. But he was sure the Lord would give them what they needed. He always did.

With the couch, love seat, and easy chair taken, Cole perched himself on a bar stool and turned toward the TV.

"I think we're just living out our faith," Tom said.

"We've done everything else we could do," Janice said. "We've put up signs, helped with mailers, worked phone banks, stood outside of polling places, and we've voted. All we can do now is wait."

"Yeah, I've never been this involved in a campaign," Jake said. "It was fascinating."

"And exhausting," his wife Tosha said. "I won't be able to stay up until they predict a winner. I'm dead on my feet."

The TV emitted a sounder and a map of Pennsylvania appeared.

"Fox News is now calling Pennsylvania for challenger Roberto Gonzalez," the gray-haired newsman said. "Pennsylvania now goes into the Gonzalez column."

"Oh, not good. That was a big one," Janice said.

"Twenty electoral votes. Ouch," Tom said.

Cole left twenty minutes later. He didn't need to stay until the end. He could see what had happened. America had voted with its stomach.

5

"Yes, I'm aware it's Pride Week," Cole said. "You'd have to live in a cave not to know. But I'm sorry, I just can't do it."

That was a lie, or at least not accurate. He didn't feel sorrow, he felt pity. And he was happy he'd taken a stand. No matter how many rainbow flags flew on Main Street, and even if the government threatened to throw him in jail, he wouldn't perform the ceremony.

"But it's illegal for you to refuse. We have a right," John Porter said. Porter was the taller of the men on the other side of Cole's desk. Fortyish and lean, he wore a tailored dark gray suit, and every strand of his auburn hair lay gelled into submission. Thick eyeglasses enlarged his silver-blue eyes.

"The Supreme Court said you have a right to marry, not that I have to perform the service," Cole said. His gut twisted and he stifled an urge to let out a deep sigh.

"We could take this to court," Porter said.

"You could, but you'd lose," Cole said. He worked to keep his voice even. He didn't want a fight. He just wanted these guys to leave.

Cole knew Porter's so-called fiancé. Trace Johnson had gone to New Hope as a teen but hadn't set foot in the place since high school. His parents still attended.

Trace had his mom's Asian features, and his T-shirt revealed he'd spent plenty of time at the gym. He shot a worried glance at his partner. "Please, John, don't go there," Trace said. "This is about love, not rights." Looking at Cole, he continued, "I just thought that since my parents still go here . . ." Trace said. "Besides, lots of other churches—"

Cole cut him off. "I know some churches perform gay weddings, and some even have gay clergy, but I can't validate that lifestyle. I don't *condemn* gay people. Who am I to throw the first stone? But I also don't have to marry gay folks. And whether your parents worship here or not has no bearing. I'm sure they won't be surprised that I refused."

"But I thought you guys were friends," Trace said.

"We are. I love your folks. But that doesn't mean I'm going to do something unbiblical," Cole said.

Trace rubbed his hands along the thighs of his holey blue jeans.

"Even if it makes them mad, and they leave the church?" Trace asked.

"Even then, although I hope it never comes to that, and I don't think it ever will," Cole said.

"We could force you to do this," Porter said.

"Sure, you could try. But why would you want to? Why would you want a coerced blessing?" Cole said. "Certainly, you don't think you can twist God's arm into blessing this mess, do you?" The word "mess" was out of his mouth before he could reel it back in.

Smooth move, knucklehead. Just throw gas on the fire.

I guess it doesn't matter. It's not like I'm going to try to appease these guys. They'll just have to leave mad.

Porter's brows lowered, and his face darkened.

Trace placed a hand on the older man's arm.

"Let's just go," Trace said. "We can go to another church or to City Hall."

"We're not going anywhere!" Porter's voice thundered. "This homophobic bigot isn't going to push us around!"

"Johnny, please," Trace pleaded. "It would be simpler if we just went to the courthouse."

"Maybe, but this is about principle!"

Porter's glare swept from Cole to Trace and back again. "We can't just let these people blow us off because they believe in some crazy, antiquated fairy tale."

Cole felt his hands beginning to clench. "Trace is right. I think it's time for you fellows to head on out," he said. He wished he had a security person at the church during the week.

Embarrassment flashed in Trace's eyes, and his shoulders rolled forward. "Please, Johnny," he repeated.

Porter launched himself from his chair. He jabbed a finger Cole's direction. Cole could almost feel the digit bore into his chest from three feet away. "Fine. But this isn't over," he said.

The office shook as Porter slammed the door.

～

The names slid up the screen of Cole's phone until Frank Hamilton's appeared.

"I'll probably get voice mail," Cole said into the empty office.

His hands still shook a little, but the knot in his stomach had untangled itself.

"Frank, it's Cole Evans over at New Hope. I think I'm going to need your services."

6

COLE SCANNED THE CROWD, then squeezed through the weaving traffic at the terminal's passenger pickup area.

"Hey, Big Sister!" he called through the open passenger-side window.

"Hey, Little Brother!" Kiley said.

She tossed her suitcase into the truck bed and climbed in.

Cole managed an awkward half hug from behind the wheel.

"How was the flight?"

"Nothing to it. Thanks for picking me up."

"Any time. You know that."

Kiley looked good, rested. She had their mother's chestnut-colored hair and brown eyes. And she'd put on a couple of pounds, another sign that she'd stopped running herself ragged.

"Looks like the new job agrees with you," he said.

"I love it. Less work, more pay."

"You can't complain about that." Cole eased the truck onto the highway.

"How are things at the church?"

Should he tell her? Would it mess up her weekend?

"They're okay," he said. Crap. His voice sounded wrong. The intonation was too flat.

"What do you mean, 'okay?' They don't *sound* okay," Kiley said.

Cole sighed.

There's no use trying to lie. Not to Kiley. She'd see right through me.

As Cole explained, Kiley drew her knees to her chin, feet on the car seat. That had been her go-to position when she was scared since she was little.

"So, what will you do?" she asked.

"Just wait, I guess. Maybe his partner can talk him down."

Kiley's right cheek rested on her knee as she looked at him. Fear shone in her eyes.

"I talked to the church's lawyer."

Kiley wound her arms tighter around her legs. "Oh, Cole, I'm so sorry."

Wavy red lines of brake lights glared through the windshield, and he braked to a stop. The truck's air conditioner hissed. Two tractor trailers screamed past on the opposite side of the interstate.

"It's all good. Whatever happens, God's got this," Cole said.

"I hope you're right. I mean, I know he's got this. I just hope you don't get annihilated before he straightens it out."

"Me, too, but I'm certain things will be okay."

"You're really sure?"

"I'm positive." He hoped he sounded more confident than he felt.

Kiley loosened the death grip on her legs.

He needed to change the subject. "So, who's the baby shower for, again?"

"I *told* you. Stephanie. Adam's sister. You still don't listen to a word I say, do you?" Kiley rolled her eyes.

"Why should I start now?" Cole asked.

She punched him on the arm.

"Ow! Those bony knuckles hurt!"

"Poor baby. Want me to call the *wambulance*?"

Traffic several car lengths ahead started to move.

"I'm glad you're here, Sis," Cole said, smiling.

"Me, too, Little Brother. Where are you taking me to lunch?"

7

Kɪᴍɪ Jᴏʜɴsᴏɴ's ʜᴜɢ ғᴇʟᴛ stiff and wiry, unnatural. She'd said Japanese didn't hug socially, and Cole had gotten the impression she hugged now to fit in with the mushier Midwestern U.S. culture.

"Thank you for coming," she said, gesturing toward a parlor to the right.

Cole had been in the house before, when the Johnsons hosted huge after-church lunches.

He wasn't sure how to describe the décor. Shabby chic fit. The marble mantle and hearth were the parlor's focal point. To his right, antique Queen Anne end tables stood alongside a curved-top sofa with worn upholstery.

Shabby chic. How pretentious. Well, what else are they going to call it? "Dog-eared stuff that looks good?"

Cole smiled as he imagined the advertising campaign. *"Thinking old crap? Think Joe's furniture!"*

He sat in a distressed-looking wingback chair.

Kimi sat on the sofa, crossed her legs and put her hands in her lap. Her tightened lips exposed her stress, and the lines around her eyes looked like they'd deepened in the past week.

Her husband eased into the room and sat beside her. Despite Trace's predominantly Asian features, there was little doubt Mark was his dad. They shared the same jawline and forehead.

"Thanks for coming over, especially on a Saturday," Mark said.

"Not at all. Thanks for initiating this."

"I know you're busy, so I'll get right to the point," Mark said. "I know you think homosexual marriage is wrong, but can't you do *anything* for Trace and John? Even if it isn't an actual marriage ceremony?"

Crud. Well, here we go!

"Sorry, Mark. The Bible is really clear. Marriage is between one man and one woman. To do anything for them would be to condone their union."

Mark sighed and ran a hand through his thinning red hair. "But they can't help they're attracted to men. They were born that way."

Cole's heart broke. He wished he could help but knew he couldn't. "You know, my fiancé had a nephew, and even when he was in early elementary school, he had really feminine mannerisms, and Holly and I said we wouldn't be surprised if he chose a gay lifestyle. But even though I saw that with my own eyes, I just can't buy that being gay or lesbian—or any of the other orientations out there these days—isn't a chosen or learned behavior. People may have genes or things in their childhoods that predispose them or make them more likely to choose a gay lifestyle. But people can be prone to a lot of things. Heck, we've been told forever that alcoholics are genetically predisposed to alcohol abuse. That doesn't make bad behavior related to alcoholism okay. The same thing holds true for gay relationships. Even if there's some type of predisposition, acting on it is wrong."

"C'mon, Cole. Really?" Mark said. "Is that a fair comparison?"

"I think it's a fairer statement than saying people have no choice. If you listen, you hear of people all the time who've decided they're not gay anymore. Besides, straight or gay, you can always choose whether you're going to be sexually active or celibate."

"I disagree, and I don't think it's fair for people who are gay, lesbian or transgendered to be forced to choose celibacy because of their sexual orientation," Mark said. "Besides, what about love?"

"It's great that Trace and John want to treat each other well, but I'm sure homosexuality isn't what the Lord had in mind. Just like he didn't have sleeping around or divorce in mind," Cole said.

"Seriously?"

Cole couldn't budge. There were times you didn't. This was one of them. Cole thought about the scene in Genesis 39:12 when Joseph refused Potiphar's wife and ran. *"She caught him by his cloak and said, 'Come to bed with me!' But he left his cloak in her hand and ran out of the house."*

"As much as our culture wants to say otherwise, being ancient doesn't make what the Bible says wrong," Cole said. "I can't give in on this, Mark."

Cole stood to leave.

Mark looked into his lap. Was he sad? Angry? Both?

"I want so much for Trace to be happy," Mark finally said, standing.

"I know you do," Cole said. "Believe it or not, so do I. But more important than his happiness, I want hm to feel the joy of his salvation."

Mark's expression pleaded. "Fine, the homosexual lifestyle is sin, but I remember when I was a teenager, the church had its shorts in a knot over divorce. Divorced people couldn't do this, and they couldn't do that. And they sure couldn't serve in church leadership. But I'll bet half the pastors in America today are divorced."

"That may be true," Cole said. "But that doesn't mean I'd automatically counsel someone to divorce. And in the case of gay marriage, I can't bless something the Bible clearly says is wrong."

Cole took a step toward the door, but Mark kept talking.

"Yeah, but aren't a lot of Bible passages the church trots out as opposed to homosexuality actually related to homosexual rape? The whole business about Sodom. Didn't that have more to do with the townspeople wanting to rape the angels than the fact that the people were gay?"

Cole sighed. Mark wasn't giving up easily. Well, one more response, and if that didn't settle the matter, Cole would have to just walk out.

"The rape was part of the issue," Cole said. "But there are passages in both the Old and New testaments that make it clear God doesn't condone homosexuality. Leviticus 18:22 is adamant. It calls sex between men detestable. And the passage in Romans 1:26 and 27 in the New Testament doesn't leave any doubt, either. Paul uses the expression 'unnatural.'"

"You know that's homophobic, right?" Mark said.

"Label it what you want," Cole said. "I'm not going there. Just like I'm never going to tell someone it's okay to cheat on a spouse. I'll have to answer to God for what I counsel people to do. Besides, I think it would lead to misery for Trace in the long run. And I don't want that for him. I'm sure you don't, either. If people hate me for taking this position, so be it."

Cole moved toward the door.

"I think John Porter's going to take you to court," Mark said.

"I hope not, but I've already talked to the church's attorney," Cole said. "He said even if this goes sideways, I'm on solid legal footing. The Supreme Court has said pastors can't be forced to do same-sex marriages. Gay rights don't supersede our freedom to practice our religion. At least not yet. A court fight would be a hassle, and expensive, but we'd win."

Mark stood and Kimi followed suit.

"I've tried to talk John down," Kimi said. "I don't think he really wants a court fight."

"I guess we'll see what happens," Cole said. "I'm sorry about all this."

Mark nodded, and the two shook hands.

The disappointment hung on Mark's face, and Kimi's hug felt even colder than usual.

∾

New Hope Church wasn't big. The early twentieth-century redbrick building with a stumpy steeple sat on the corner of First and Main streets in White Pine, a gritty little city a half hour from Cincinnati.

Further down Main Street, nearly empty businesses with faded facades and sun-bleached signs kept a sleepy and ineffective vigil. Drug peddling and prostitution served as the downtown neighborhood's nightly pastime. And as unsavory as the area was, Cole liked New Hope's location. It positioned the church in the center of a mission field. A week didn't go by when New Hope didn't help someone who was hungry or needed clothes, or who was begging to get clean and sober.

The gathering at church the Sunday after John and Trace's visit was larger than Cole had expected, as big as a Christmas or Easter crowd. People wedged themselves into every available space in the polished wood pews, and Don Fisher set up a dozen folding chairs at the back of the room.

I'm glad to see everyone, but why are they here? Did someone spread rumors about that wedding?

Cole had discussed it only with Frank Hamilton, and his Wednesday morning breakfast crew. None of those guys would have said anything.

As he looked across the auditorium, Cole realized for probably the hundredth time how much he loved these guys. He was honored to be their pastor.

But he sensed an uneasiness. Instead of the laughter and chatter that normally carried through the building before services, Cole heard only a low murmur, a sound akin to the air conditioner's muted rumble.

He caught Don's eye and motioned him over.

"I know this is a weird question, but what's everybody doing here? And why are they all acting like long-tailed cats in a room full of rocking chairs?" Cole asked.

"Are you serious? You haven't heard?" Don asked.

"Heard what? I was hanging out with Kiley all day yesterday. I haven't heard anything."

"Oh, man, that's not good," Don said. "It's all over social media."

Don pulled out his phone, tapped and scrolled, and held the screen Cole's direction.

John Porter's visage filled the frame. "We're not going to let those homophobes get away with it!" he said.

Cheers erupted off screen before a new face appeared. A banner at the bottom of the screen identified the short-haired thirty-something man as Morgan Simmons, Gay Rights in Action president. The U.S. Capitol served as Simmons's backdrop.

"The decision by this pastor in Ohio is preposterous, and it calls for immediate and forceful action," Simmons said. "I'm calling on every gay, lesbian, and transgendered person in America, and those who support the LGBTQ cause, to stand up. Write, call and, if possible, march on this church. Don't let this pastor erode the rights we've worked so long and hard for."

"Great. Just great," Cole said.

"Yeah," Don said. "Our church is the epicenter for a gay-rights debate."

"I didn't see anything or anyone this morning when Kiley and I came in," Cole said.

"Don't worry. By the time church is over, I'm sure they'll be there," Don said.

Cole plunked himself at the end of the first pew. "Oh, my word. Lord, please help us."

The small stack of note cards in his shirt pocket felt heavy, and a corner of the yellow legal pad with more detailed notes waved to him from under his Bible on the pulpit.

Do I send these people home? I can't put them in harm's way, can I? Should I save these notes and preach this sermon next week?

No, you can't think like that. Where's your faith? Christianity has always been dangerous. We've just been lucky in America for the past couple of centuries.

Well, I'll ad lib something about the gay issue and then move into my message.

He folded his hands in his lap. *"Lord, please guide me. Let me know what to say."*

His legs felt heavy and his feet seemed stuck in carpet glue as he climbed the two steps and took his spot behind the tiny pulpit. Graveyard silence greeted him.

"Wow, I wish it was this easy to get you guys to settle down every Sunday," he said.

A couple of people smiled. Most wore grim expressions.

"It looks like I'm the last person in the building, or at least one of the last, to know what's going on," he said. He scanned the crowd until he caught Kiley's gaze. Her eyes widened. She probably didn't know specifics, but she understood things weren't good.

Cole continued, "I've been blessed to spend time with my sister and have paid no attention to news for the last twenty-four hours. Given what's apparently happened on social media, I need even more than usual to start this morning with a word of prayer."

Every head bowed.

Please, Lord, help me know what to say and do. Help me take care of your people.

When he finished praying aloud, he had no idea what he'd just said. He hoped it had made sense.

"Okay folks, in case there's anyone else here, besides me, who's unaware of what's happened in our fair little town over the last day or so, let me start with some background," Cole said. "A few days ago, two men showed up at my office and asked me to marry them. I refused."

Several people nodded. A few shot angry glares.

Cole searched the crowd.

Where are Mark and Kimi Johnson? Are they out with the protesters? That doesn't matter right now. Stay focused and keep moving.

"I understand that our government and our culture say they have a right to be married," Cole said. "And I know that some churches and denominations even . . ."

He struggled for the right word. Support? Condone? Tolerate?

"Some churches have gay clergy and perform gay services."

A few heads nodded.

"Now, I think people can try to read things into this book," Cole said as he lifted his Bible from the lectern. "But I think the Lord's intent is crystal clear. God intended marriage to be between one man and one woman."

A woman, a visitor, about halfway back on the right shuffled past the people in her row and headed toward the door. A man in the back left joined her.

Cole waited while they exited. Should he ask if anyone else wanted to leave? No, no need to provoke people. If they were offended by the Word, that was one thing. Purposely agitating folks was another. Being right didn't give him the right to be nasty.

"I believe God loves the LBGTQ community," Cole continued. "The Bible says in 2 Peter 3:9 that he's 'not wanting anyone to perish.' At the same time, I believe the gay lifestyle makes the Lord unhappy. And I'm not going to condone it. If that makes me a homophobe or a bigot, then that's what I am. I'll take my lumps down here and let God sort out the rest later. Jesus said take up your cross. If standing up for something that's clearly explained in Scripture makes a few people mad, then that's how it's going to have to be. As long as I'm your pastor, I'm not going to do anything that is so plainly against the will of God."

A few heads nodded.

Three others had wrapped their arms across their chests.

Well, at least they didn't get up and leave. Okay, what do I say next? Do I belabor this or move on?

He swept his gaze around the room one last time. Yeah, he'd gotten through to everyone. No need to pummel people.

"One last thing," he said. "If protesters do show up, don't engage with them. If at all possible, walk some other way to get to your cars. Do your utmost to just stay away from them."

A murmur ran through the room. Cole waited.

"And above all, treat these people the way you would want to be treated. After all, they're image bearers of a blessed and merciful God."

He caught Kiley's gaze, and she gave him a nod. He was on the right track.

"Okay, enough of that. Let's move on. Let's pray one more time before we get started."

As heads bowed, the sanctuary's main door flew open.

Olivia! For Pete's sake!

A bearded, shaggy-looking guy in jeans and a T-shirt followed the woman into the room, a TV camera affixed to his right shoulder.

Fantastic. Lord, please just help me.

People turned toward the noise.

I need to get people out of here. Under no circumstances do I want to see anyone's face on the news tonight.

He raised a hand and said, "Okay guys, we're going to cut this short this week. Go in peace. Quickly. Unless you want to see yourselves on TV."

≈

Olivia didn't wait for people to leave but instead pushed past an older couple who was trying to move into the center aisle.

While a few people drifted toward the back of the church, most people froze. Some scrutinized the cameraman. Others watched the newswoman stalk toward Cole.

She wore her game face. Intense. Somehow self-righteous. "Mr. Evans? Olivia Sandlin. Channel Twelve News."

Why did she think she needed to introduce herself? Was this part of the schtick? Did she think it would somehow make her seem more objective, even though he knew she already had a negative opinion about Christianity and New Hope?

She stuck out a slender hand with maroon nail polish. Did he really have to shake hands? Ugh. Unfortunately. He had to do whatever he could to influence her reporting. Her touch was a feather, her skin smooth, her eyes the color of the ocean.

Why do the pretty ones always seem to come with a trunk load of trouble?

That's not true. Holly was gorgeous, and she wasn't trouble. Quite the opposite.

Olivia's voice brought him back to the present.

". . . consent to an on-camera interview?"

Halfway across the sanctuary, a tiny bulb on the camera glowed red, and the cameraman pointed the machine at the crowd.

"Hey! You! Camera guy!" Cole called. "I don't care if you shoot video of me but leave these people alone."

The camera swung Cole's direction. He realized he'd sucked in a deep breath and rolled his eyes. Oh, well, being on camera was better than endangering others in the church.

"The court has ruled that gay people have the right to marry. Why shouldn't he video people who agree that it's okay for a clergyman to refuse to obey the Supreme Court?" Olivia's tone was combative, and she'd placed a hand on her hip, like a mother scolding a young child.

Cole felt his teeth clench and his face redden. "Why would you assume that's how anyone in here feels?"

"They're all still here, aren't they? If they were truly supportive of gay people—and in favor of doing what the Supreme Court says—they'd leave. Or not show up in the first place. They might even be outside with the protesters."

"I thought journalists were supposed to get all the facts, not just half of them," Cole said. He heard the hard edge in his voice but didn't care. "The Court said in *Orbergefell vs. Hodges* that states have to issue marriage licenses. It didn't say anything about religious liberties. It also specifically said in the *Masterpiece Cakeshop* case in Colorado that a pastor's religious freedom outweighs a gay couple's right to marry."

The newswoman looked taken aback, as if she hadn't expected a fight. At least not a well-reasoned one.

"Really. I'm telling you the truth," Cole said. "Go read the rulings for yourself. I did." He didn't mention that he hadn't read them until after he'd talked to Frank Hamilton. But that didn't matter.

Olivia's expression moved back to anger.

The camera continued to roll. Had it caught her change in expression?

A few dozen people clustered around them, between the first pew and the stage.

"But still, don't you think it's hateful not to marry these guys?" she asked.

"No more hateful than telling a man he can't cheat on his wife," Cole said. His voice had lost its edge. "Look, Olivia, the Lord has set boundaries in place to protect us, whether we like those boundaries or not."

She rolled her eyes. "So, you plan to continue to spread what the Supreme Court has declared to be hate." It wasn't a question, but more of an accusation.

"Jesus gives us love, joy, healing, and deliverance from suffering, and we try to spread that message," Cole said. "If those things are hateful, then the Christian message is hate speech."

"So, not marrying a couple who wants to marry isn't hateful," she said.

"Not in the least. It may be the most loving thing I've done all week," Cole said. He wanted to add "not that you'd understand why," but restrained himself.

Olivia's mouth fell agape. She nodded to the camera guy, who turned off his equipment.

Cole didn't know how it was possible, but Olivia bristled even more and shoved her way through the crowd. As she stomped down the center aisle, the cameraman shook Cole's hand, and smiled.

"Can I ask you something?" Cole said. "How many protesters are out there?"

"About two dozen when we came in," the cameraman said. "But I'm sure that number will grow. The guy leading this thing—a guy named Porter—tweeted he'd give the first hundred people who showed up free lottery tickets."

People within earshot groaned.

"That wouldn't get me out there, but I'm sure he'll get some takers," Cole said.

Olivia's profanity-laden shriek pierced the room, and she demanded the camera guy move a certain of his body parts to join her.

"Thanks for the info," Cole said, shaking the man's hand again. "What's your name?"

"Just call me Red," the cameraman said, giving Cole a thumbs up.

Olivia's door slam reverberated through the sanctuary. If they'd been in a cartoon, things would've been sucked out the door with her, and papers would've swirled in the sanctuary afterward. Cole couldn't help smiling at the thought.

Red shook his head as he turned to head out.

"Be safe out there," Cole said.

"You, too."

8

SHORT AND ROUND WITH flushed cheeks and intense blue eyes, Reed Bryant resembled a garden gnome. The Lord had knocked off his personality's sharper edges, but Cole often still felt like he needed to wash off some of the cynicism after they talked. At the same time, Reed was zealous, and Cole could see the Lord's hand on his life.

"Yeah, go ahead and look out," Cole said.

Reed cracked open the heavy wooden door and peeked out, then his head shot back inside as something thudded against the door. His face was ashen, his eyes huge.

"Camera dude's right. There's a mob. Some of them have signs. People threw bottles and stuff when I stuck my head out."

"How many?" Cole asked.

"About twenty. Maybe thirty. In the street and on the sidewalk in front of the building," Reed said.

The room erupted. Cole couldn't understand everything being said, but he was sure he heard several words he'd never expected to hear in his own church.

Lord, just let me know what to say. You need to deal with this. I don't know how.

"Whoa, whoa, whoa!" Cole's voice carried over the noise, and people quieted.

"Okay, everybody, okay! Let's quiet down. We can't solve this with everybody talking at once. Let's get organized here. Let's pray."

Cole asked the Lord for discernment and protection, then Tom picked up the thread. A couple of the elders prayed, and when they had run out of steam, Cole wrapped up the petition.

"So, what do we do?" Don Fisher asked. Don, one of the elders, was in his fifties, slender, with thick silver-gray hair. He helped run the sound boards and computers during church services.

"Call the cops," Reed said.

"That won't help," Don said. "They probably think we're the bad guys."

Murmurs rippled.

"We're not breaking the law, but Don's probably right. The police won't help," Cole said. "Let's think this through. So, the front of the church is on First Street, and most of us are parked in the lot on the left side of the building," Cole said.

"We know that." Reed's voice was a machete.

"Yeah, I know, Reed, I'm just thinking out loud here," Cole said. He wanted to add, "And I could use a little grace," but he didn't.

"Yeah, sorry," Reed said. "I guess I'm just a little on edge."

"It'll be okay. If worst comes to worst, we'll hang out in here until most of them get tired and go away. I doubt many people these days would protest for more than a few hours, even for free lottery tickets," Cole said.

Snippets of a side conversation about how the nation's attention span had diminished battered his ability to concentrate.

Lord, help me. I don't know what else to pray.

∾

Buttons, sliders, knobs, and keyboards stretched out like furrowed fields in front of him, and computer screens surrounded him.

"How do you even know what all this stuff is?" Cole asked.

"I'm a genius," Don responded.

"Not to mention modest," Cole said. "Can you show me the view from in front of the church?"

Don clacked a computer keyboard, and live video appeared on one of the screens. Cole studied an area about five car lengths wide. Most of the crowd stood on the sidewalk with part of the mob spilling into the street, as Reed had said. And he'd been right about the signs.

"Too bad there's no audio," Cole said. Mouths moved in unison and fists pumped.

The sounds coming through the building's walls weren't clear enough to understand.

"I can't make it out, either," Don said. "Looks like the middle two words might be 'go home.'"

"I'd love to. If they'd leave, I could," Cole said. "No, wait. It looks like they might be saying 'Stonewall.'"

"What's that?" Don asked.

"It was a riot in New York in the sixties that helped start the gay-rights movement."

"And you know this because . . . ?"

"Mark Johnson mentioned it yesterday. Let's see the side of the building by the parking lot," Cole said.

A few more clacks and a pond of metal and glass appeared. The sun glinted sharply from the windshields. No one moved onto or off the screen.

Cole and Don looked at three more camera angles.

"You can look at these on your phone anytime you want, too. And the system saves video for a week. If you want to save it longer than that, you have to download it," Don said.

He walked Cole through the process.

Kiley met them as they came down from the booth.

"So, how many are out there?" she asked.

"Quite a few, but it isn't a big deal," Don said.

While most people inside the building remained near the front doors, others stood in clumps of threes and fours around the sanctuary. The crowd inside had thinned. About twenty people had ducked out through side or back doors.

"Okay, boys and girls, listen up!" Cole called.

The murmur around him quieted.

"All right, these guys are all right out front," he said, nodding toward the street. "If we're sneaky, most of us can get out of here unnoticed. It looks like several people already have. Who's parked in back, near the doors by Children's Ministry?" he asked.

A dozen hands went up.

"Tom, you're in back, right? Did you drive your van?"

The boxy-looking vehicle was big and ancient, but it looked intimidating. And fifteen people could fit into the thing. It would take a few trips, but it seemed like the safest, most efficient option to get people where they needed to go.

Who's parked right out front?"

Six hands raised.

"You guys will have to go home with others and come back later. Take a second to partner up."

Chuck Sanchez nodded toward Jessica and Dale Wimmers, and Brian and Ellie Lucas whispered with Tim and Hannah Southerland. Stephanie Wright exchanged nods with Jake and Tosha Moore.

"Okay, that leaves the rest of us," Cole said. "You need to go out the emergency doors on this side of the building." He pointed to his left.

Heads nodded.

"I'll go out the fire door on the opposite side of the building, near the front entrance, and shout to the demonstrators to create a diversion," he said.

"I can't let you do that, Cole. You're asking to get hurt." Ed Plowman's voice was emphatic. Ed was another of the elders. In his forties, he had served in the Marines, and he looked like he could still handle himself.

"All due respect, Ed, I can't ask anyone who's not on paid staff to take any additional risk. Liability issues. Besides, I'll be far enough away from the crowd to get back inside if they come after me. And if that happens, I'll hang out in here until our friends get tired and go to collect their gazillion-dollar lottery tickets."

"Are you sure about this?" Kiley sounded worried. "I don't want to make any trips to the emergency room today."

"It'll be okay. Really," Cole said. "I think most of them will be glad to let us leave. Just pull up alongside the building and pick me up."

Kiley said nothing, but her eyes pleaded.

"It'll be okay," Cole repeated. "Give people a couple of minutes to get to their cars, then pull up, but try to stay out of sight as long as possible," he said.

He tossed her his keys.

Tears filled her eyes.

"Are you sure, buddy?" Ed asked.

"Positive. Those of you going with Tom can take off. Reed, do you have your phone?" Cole asked.

Reed held up the device.

"I'll text you when it's time to head to the side lot," Cole said.

Cole turned to his sister. "I'll FaceTime you and leave the line open, so you'll know when to come and get me."

"I still think this is crazy, Cole," Kiley said.

"Probably, but there's no other way."

~

Cole stood next to the metal fire door, unable to decipher the crowd's chatter on the other side. How many people were there? How violent were they?

Lord, protect us. Help get these people home.

He texted Reed a single word: Go. Then he video-phoned Kiley.

The image on his phone tilted crazily. Kiley was climbing into the truck.

"Anyone back there?" he asked.

"Just people from inside the church."

"Okay, here we go," he said.

He shoved the fire door open, and the voices merged into a wall of jumbled angry noise.

The cameraman had found a vantage point to shoot both Cole and the crowd. Olivia walked alongside the building and texted.

Tom's van passed. Was he already on his second trip? Awesome.

Cole counted off three seconds, then whistled, loud and shrill.

Amazing. It worked. Okay, now what?

"You know, no one in this building wants to bother any of you," he said. "No one wants to trouble you."

Should he say the Truth might bother them, but the people in the church wouldn't? No. Probably a bad plan.

"You're violating our rights!" someone shouted.

"I thought you guys were supposed to be loving!" someone else called.

Several other protesters joined in.

To his left, the camera kept rolling.

Behind Red, Mark Johnson watched, his face impassive, hands in his blue-jeans pockets.

Had Mark tried to talk his son down? Or had he encouraged the protest?

"I can understand why some people are mad at the church or don't understand Christians. Historically, the church has been really good at reacting very loudly, very quickly to anything we don't like," Cole said. He had their attention. "Sometimes we've been our own worst enemy."

The seconds dragged. Had people gotten to their cars? Where was Kiley?

Tom's van reappeared, headed back toward the church.

Cole continued, "We don't want—"

"Shut up, you bigot!" It was John Porter. Off to the right.

Uh-oh, he's coming this way. Crap. This is about to get ugly.

Mark Johnson faced the crowd and put his arms out to his sides to try to stop the stampede. To no avail. The mob rushed forward, around Mark.

I need to move. I need to move. Uh-oh, a rock! The reporter. Look up from your phone!

What the heck is her name? Sophia? No. Amelia? Why can't I remember names? Of all the stinking times!

"Head's up!" Cole shouted.

Thank goodness, she sees it.

The woman lifted her left arm, then cried out. The stone glanced off her forearm and struck the side of her forehead. She staggered and fell. Immediately, blood ran from a gash above her left eye, close to the hairline.

Lord, you've got to be kidding me right now. This woman barges into the church, is obnoxious and foul-mouthed, and now I have to help her?

The verses from the Sermon on the Mount played in his mind. *But I tell you, love your enemies and pray for those who persecute you.*

"I don't want to love my enemies," Cole growled and stomped toward the newswoman.

"Huh?" It was Kiley, on FaceTime.

"Go on without me," Cole said. He bent and scooped up the groggy newswoman.

"But, Cole—"

"Just go!" He clicked off the call.

Hands pushed and tugged. Chaotic screaming engulfed him. Ten feet to the door. They'd make it.

9

Olivia sat on the long stainless-steel table in the church kitchen, crimson droplets and streaks on her white blouse. Her feet dangled a few inches off the floor.

Her chest rose and fell, and her breath came in short gasps. Tears pooled in her eyes.

Her left forearm had caught the brunt of the impact. A large purple-red blotch had emerged on its underside. Still, the rock had connected with her head. Blood matted her hair and stained her face.

He'd seen worse. In Afghanistan. Compared to what he'd seen there, she had a scratch.

"Sorry. I tried to get your attention, but I couldn't remember your name."

"It's Olivia, you idiot! Now, hurry up. I'm missing the story."

"Sorry. When people are throwing stuff at me, I tend to forget un-important details."

Ouch!

He wanted to lick his finger, scratch a tick mark in the air and hiss.

"Would you just shut up and let me get back out there?"

"You're bleeding. And if I let you go back out there, you'll probably sue me," Cole said.

"It's a head wound. They bleed. Now, just put something on it so I can leave."

"You should probably be on some type of concussion protocol. I think I'll call an ambulance, and you can wait until they get here." Cole smiled inwardly at the threat.

She picked up a stainless-steel coffee carafe from the counter.

"If you don't put that bandage on my head and get out of my way, *you're* going to need a concussion protocol." She didn't sound like she was kidding.

Sirens wailed and abruptly stopped outside the building. What in the world was going on out there?

Lord, please just keep everybody safe.

"Look, those sounded like ambulances. At least have the paramedics look at you once we get back outside."

"Yeah, yeah, yeah. Just fix it."

Cole gently ran two fingers of his gloved hand across Olivia's forehead. He felt the lump and a small cut. She winced, then squirmed as he applied antibiotic ointment and sterile gauze.

"Could you hurry up? I need to be out there. It didn't hit me that hard."

Cole couldn't help smiling. "Right. You got hit in the head with a giant rock—but not that hard. You're going to sit here until I'm done with you. I'll tell you if and when you go back out. How's your arm?"

"You know this is your fault," she said. "If you would've just married those guys, or if you hadn't held your stupid church service, none of this would've happened."

"You know what, Olivia? You help me understand why some species eat their young. Can you please just sit there for a minute, with your mouth closed?"

She rolled her eyes.

∽

The sun bore down, and lights flashed everywhere as Cole followed Olivia out of the building. A new group of people had replaced the protesters and their signs.

Two cruisers stood in front of the church and another in the parking lot. An ambulance with open back doors prattled loudly at the mouth of the alley. Another stood in the street. Two paramedics led a guy toward the second squad. His broken arm jutted unnaturally toward his body.

A cop wound yellow police tape around the handle of one of the main entrance doors.

"Nice bandage. You okay?" the camera guy said. He continued without waiting for an answer. "You missed it! Some lady tried to drive through the crowd, and a guy got hit in the head with a brick." His voice rang with excitement.

Red pulled the camera from his shoulder and turned a small viewing screen so Cole and Olivia could see.

Behind them, the cop with the tape completed his circuit, closing off the scene.

Cole stared at the tiny monitor. An engine roared somewhere off screen, then the vehicle flashed onto the screen from the right.

"Kiley."

On the screen, his pickup truck screeched to a stop as the mob rushed forward. Stones thumped and clanged against the metal and glass. The first of the protesters reached the truck. From somewhere off-screen to the left, a half-full bottle of aquamarine sports drink hit a demonstrator. The man stumbled into the driver-side window. Cole recognized him as the man paramedics had led to the squad.

Dozens of hands covered the windows on Kiley's side of the truck, and the vehicle began to rock. Someone appeared in the top left corner of the screen. His jet-black hair glistened, and his skin looked almost tawny. His eyeglasses flashed in the sun.

Oh, no. Trace!

V-shaped and quick, he launched himself like a high hurdler from the pavement. His foot landed on the front bumper, and he propelled forward onto the hood. Glaring through the windshield, he screamed profanities at Christians and at God.

"Preach about that, Pastor Evans!" he roared above the crowd.

Oh, my word, he thinks I'm driving. Back up, Kiley. Back up.

Shock spread over the man's face as he looked through the windshield.

Good, he's figured it out. Now get off the truck, Trace. Jump off.

Kiley's right arm moved. The engine screamed but the truck went nowhere.

Neutral. Crap. Put it in a gear, Kiley! Trace, jump off!

Kiley shook.

Trace's mouth hung open.

A chunk of brick, orange-red, appeared on the top right of the screen. About the size of a stick of butter, it hung in the air, neither turning end-over-end, nor spiraling.

That's going to hit the windshield. Move, Trace! Get out of the way!

The man on the hood moved closer to the glass to get a closer look.

His face exploded in pain, and the brick took a new trajectory, away from the truck.

Trace fell forward and then rolled to the left, off the truck. He lay between the pickup and the building across the alley.

Kiley's scream pierced the competing noise.

Oh, no! No, Lord, please don't let this be happening.

Again, Kiley grabbed the gear shift and looked backward.

The engine bellowed, and the car lurched frontward. The vehicle shot through the mob and went around the corner to the right, away from the church.

"Wow, awesome video, Red. You know that's gonna lead tonight," Olivia said.

"Yeah, the network will probably pick that up," Red said, beaming.

Cole tore his eyes from the screen. The cop who'd strung the tape worked crowd control, and another took statements.

Two paramedics hovered over Trace, who still lay on his back in the alley.

Wait a minute. Where was Mark? Cole swept his gaze across the scene. There. The backseat of the cruiser, his head in his hands, shoulders shaking. Had the cops had to restrain him? Had they put him in there to keep him from interfering with the paramedics?

A voice grabbed Cole's attention. "But you just drove in from over there." The cop pointed down First Street, over Kiley's shoulder. He was huge, over six-feet tall and built like an offensive lineman.

Cole strained but couldn't hear well. The cop looked pleasant enough. He nodded. Compassion filled his eyes. He wrote something in a small notebook and nodded again. He spoke again, and Kiley responded. Then something changed, as if someone had flipped a switch. The cop's eyes and body language screamed his suspicion.

What on earth had Kiley said?

The cop said something else.

Kiley's arms crossed over her chest, and she frowned, her eyes huge with fear.

Oh, God, just help her.

Cole hoped the prayer needn't be more elaborate. That was all he had.

"I thought she left," Olivia said to Red.

"She came back," Red said.

"Well, that was stupid," Olivia said.

Part of a passage from the book of Luke flashed through Cole's mind. "Lord, do you want us to call down fire from heaven and destroy them?" The disciples James and John had asked the question, and Jesus had rebuked them. Cole had always imagined Jesus saying something like, "Knock it off, fatheads!" And he was sure the Lord had similar words for him at that moment.

I need to walk away before I smack this woman. I should've used the gauze as a gag.

He moved toward the cop and Kiley, and their conversation became clearer.

"Mobbed. By protesters. Right." The cop's tone made it clear he didn't buy Kiley's story. "Wait right here," he said, then spoke into his radio.

The knot in Cole's stomach grew tighter, and he felt the sweat soaking his brow.

He'd been frightened in front of the church fifteen minutes earlier. But that was different. He'd feared physical harm. Now, his sister was in danger, and there was nothing he could do.

He pulled out his phone and punched up Frank Hamilton's number. *Voice mail. Crap.*

"Hey, Frank. It's Cole. My sister Kiley has had a scrape with the law outside the church building this morning. I'm sure she's headed to the Justice Center. If there's anything you can do . . . Thanks, Frank."

Cole clicked off the phone and walked toward the cop and Kiley. *This is probably a bad idea.*

When he was five feet away, the cop glared. "You can't be here, buddy. This is a crime scene, and I'm interviewing a witness."

"I'm the pastor, and this is my sister."

"I don't care if you think you're God, and she's an angel, step outside the tape."

"Sorry, officer." Cole shifted his gaze to Kiley. Was it illegal to tell her not to say anything? Was there such a thing as interfering with a police investigation? He was sure he'd heard of obstructing justice. Would he be charged with it if he told Kiley to clam up?

"I called Frank Hamilton, the church's attorney," he said. "You probably should wait for him before you say anything else."

The cop turned on Cole and touched his holstered Taser, then pointed. "Stand over there. I'll deal with you later."

"Love you, Sis," Cole mouthed.

"Love you, too," she mouthed back.

Oh, God, please protect and guide her.

From Cole's new spot near the church building, he saw only Trace's legs strapped to a back board. Paramedics kneeled on the alley's cobblestones and worked on his upper half. Based on their positions, it looked like a head injury.

Had he been wrong? Had the brick hit him on the head? It hadn't looked that way in the video. Had he landed on his head when he fell off the car?

Everything took forever. Kiley must be petrified.

He looked at his phone. Only about fifteen minutes had passed since he and Olivia had come back outside. It felt more like a half hour or forty-five minutes.

The cop spoke into his radio, then reached toward Kiley. His hand swallowed her upper arm, and he led her toward a cruiser.

Kiley looked over her shoulder, her eyes pleading.

∾

Cole's jaw clenched under the cop's stare.

"I only saw the video, but people were throwing rocks and stuff as my sister pulled up." He nodded toward the truck, hoping the cop would notice the truck's cracked grill and dents and dings in the roof and hood.

The cop only stared at him.

"After that, a guy jumped on the hood."

The cop raised an eyebrow. This wasn't going well.

Stay calm. Whatever you do, you have to stay calm.

"As my sister tried to leave, I saw a chunk of brick fly toward the truck from over in this general area," Cole said. He pointed toward the front of the church. "The brick hit the guy who was on the hood, and he kind of rolled off of the truck."

"Did you yell to your sister to stop?" the cop asked.

"No, like I said, I was inside the building at that point. I only saw video of what happened when I came back outside. But I know she couldn't stop. The protesters were rocking the truck so badly, I thought they might tip it over. Or somehow get in and drag her out and beat her."

"So, you told your sister to drive forward," the cop said.

"No, I told you, I was inside. I saw a video."

Is this guy not listening on purpose in order to get under my skin, or is he truly unable to understand what I'm telling him? Either way, this isn't good.

"And you claim the man had already fallen off of your truck when your sister stepped on the accelerator."

"I don't *claim* the guy fell off. He fell off. Look at the video for yourself."

You can't use that angry tone, dude. If you do, Kiley's toast.

Lord, please help her. Just please help her.

"So, why would you tell your sister to stop providing information?" the cop asked. "You realize I could charge you with obstructing justice, right?"

I hate this guy, Lord. I know you say I'm not supposed to, but I want to smash my fist into his teeth.

"I didn't tell her not to provide information. I told her to wait till the lawyer got here before she talked to you. There's a difference. Miranda didn't go away, did it? She still has a right not to talk to you, doesn't she?"

Anger flashed in the cop's eyes but vanished as quickly as it had appeared.

Uh-oh, had he gone too far? Was he about to be led to a cruiser? Or did the spark of anger signal the cop's defeat?

"Please wait here," the cop said. He turned and crossed the parking lot and talked to a guy in a cheap brown suit. Some kind of detective.

Trace still lay on the ground, paramedics hovering over him. John Porter stared at the pavement as he paced with his arms crossed, outside the crime scene tape.

Did the brick hit Trace in the head? Was he seriously hurt? Did the cops think Kiley killed the guy?

Kimi Johnson walked up alongside Porter.

I need to reach out. Mark and Kimi need to know I'm here for them.

Me: Kimi, so sorry about everything. I'm about to talk to the cops. Talk later? His phone whooshed as the text disappeared.

Across the parking lot, Kimi looked at her phone. Her body stiffened, and she glared Cole's direction.

Lord, please let me know what to do and say.

A plainclothes cop headed his direction.

The man introduced himself as John Krause. The name fit. With close-cropped blond hair, a square jaw and pale blue eyes, the guy looked like he came to the twenty-first century straight from 1940s Nazi Germany. Sweat beaded on the man's brow.

"You're Pastor Evans?" Krause sounded almost friendly as he stuck out his hand for Cole to shake. "How long have you been the pastor here?"

Something clicked in Cole's mind. Part of a documentary or a scene from a TV show. Maybe something he'd read. Wherever the tidbit originated, Cole realized the cop wanted a baseline. Krause needed to observe Cole telling the truth in order to detect changes in behavior or demeanor if Cole lied later.

He didn't have anything to fear. He and Kiley had done nothing wrong. And to refuse to talk would only raise suspicion.

Cole told the detective everything he'd told the first cop. Like the uniformed officer, Krause jotted notes.

When Cole finished, Krause asked him to go to the station to write out a formal statement. He said Kiley had already agreed to go.

She already agreed. Right. I doubt she had a choice.

∿

Cole prayed as he walked the two blocks to the station. *What are you doing, Lord? I'm freaking out. Please protect Kiley and give me the words to stay out of jail, so I can help her.*

The thought was almost audible. "But when they arrest you, do not worry about what to say or how to say it. At that time, you will be given what to say." Cole had read the verse dozens of times—in the Gospel of Matthew. Jesus gave the instructions before sending out the Twelve to minister in towns and villages in Israel.

So, am I about to be arrested?

If you are, the Lord will take care of you.

"Just take care of Kiley, Lord," Cole said aloud.

∿

In a bizarre way, the bland, windowless chamber looked like those Cole had seen on dozens of old TV cop shows. Glossy gray paint peeled from the walls. Tile floor peaked through holes in worn industrial gray carpet, and an old wooden table abutted one wall, extending into the room like a peninsula.

A comfortable-looking faux leather office chair sat between the table and the door while a matching chair created an obstacle near the end of the table. A folding metal chair inhabited the corner near the wall behind the table. Cole recognized what was about to happen. The Reid Technique. He'd read about it and heard fellow Psy-Ops guys and interrogators talk about it while he was stationed in the Middle East.

First, the cops would jam him into the corner in the crappy chair. With a table and a cop between himself and the door, and another cop at the end of the table to prevent him from moving without permission, they'd hem him in.

They'd start with polite questioning that became more confrontational and accusatory as the interrogation progressed. They would claim to have solid evidence, whether or not that evidence actually existed. They'd act like they didn't believe anything he said in his defense. Then they'd hammer on a theme or rationale for why a person would commit such a crime. Finally, interrogators would suggest a reason for committing the crime that almost seemed socially acceptable. Anyone in the suspect's position might do the same thing.

Cole had read that skilled interrogators could convince weaker-minded people they'd done things they actually hadn't. Suspects felt as if admitting some level of guilt was the only way to stop the interrogation. Some police departments had abandoned the Reid Technique because it produced too many false confessions. The White Pine PD apparently hadn't.

A camera kept watch near the ceiling on the left end of the interrogation room, and a one-way mirror occupied the wall over Cole's left shoulder.

The room stank of rancid cigarette smoke. The odor made sense. Despite society's disdain of tobacco, in this particular room people went to great lengths to calm their nerves.

But he wasn't nervous. He hadn't stopped praying, and the calm he felt surprised him. He'd often read the phrase, "peace of God, which transcends all understanding," but he'd never felt it this intensely. Somehow, he knew he'd walk out of there, and he'd be able to help Kiley.

He'd answer questions for no more than ten minutes. He'd tell the truth and would pray the Lord use it to free Kiley. After telling the story once, he'd lawyer up.

Still, he'd have to control his emotions, tone of voice, and eye gaze. He couldn't remember which direction people supposedly glanced when they lied, not that he believed that theory, but some interrogators did. He'd keep his eyes focused straight forward, if it was possible to control eye movements that supposedly were involuntary. He'd also make sure he didn't fidget.

The detective at the end of the table, a guy named Smith, spoke first. Like the room, Smith looked like he'd come from a TV sound stage. Ruddy, puffy cheeks nearly swallowed his small dark eyes. His button-down shirt, open at the collar, had been laundered from white to a pale gray. His department store dress slacks, likewise, showed their age. Smith wore no necktie or jacket.

Krause, the guy from the church parking lot, took notes on a yellow legal pad while Cole talked. Krause said nothing as he worked but wore an expression that shifted from suspicion to hatred and back every few minutes.

"Did you see who threw the rock?" Smith asked at one point.

"It was a chunk of brick, not a rock, and I didn't see who threw it."

It was clear the cop wanted Cole to tell his story over and over to see if anything changed.

"But your sister kept driving after she moved through the crowd. She didn't remain at the scene," Smith said.

"She was being attacked. She had to move," Cole said. "And she turned around and came right back as soon as she was out of immediate danger."

The detective leaned back and crossed his arms, then leaned forward again and put his hands in front of him.

What are these two guys thinking? What are the interrogators in the other room asking Kiley? How is she holding up?

Cole tried to pray Psalm 43.

Vindicate me, my God,
and plead my cause
against an unfaithful nation.
Rescue me from those who are deceitful and wicked.

His mind returned to Kiley. He prayed they hadn't convinced her she'd done something wrong.

You can't think about that, right now. Kiley's smart. She'll be okay. You have to focus on your own problems right now.

"Mr. Evans, I'm offering you an opportunity here," Smith said. "You can help your sister, and yourself. I'm giving you a chance to tell the truth, to get the load of guilt off your conscience. I know that as a pastor you understand how important it is to confess guilt. I can help if you talk to me right now. But if you don't talk . . ." He let the sentence hang.

Cole needed to verbally punch the guy in the mouth—without further endangering himself or Kiley. "First of all, neither of us did anything wrong," Cole said. "Secondly, it's not your job to help me, it's your job to get a confession. Probably at any cost. The only person you want to help is yourself."

"Mr. Evans, the man your sister struck with her truck is dead," the detective said. "His name was Trace Johnson."

Cole's heart sank. He considered saying he knew Trace but thought that might sound incriminating. Besides, he didn't know if Smith was lying. Struggling to keep his voice even, he said, "She didn't strike him. A brick that someone else threw hit the man."

"Look, Mr. Evans, we really can understand how it happened," Krause said. "You had this church service. And then, all these protesters show up. These hooligans or reprobates or whatever you want to call them, and it makes you mad. It would make anyone mad. So, you say to your sister, 'Let's go out there and teach them a lesson.' Maybe she didn't mean to hit Mr. Johnson with the truck. Maybe she just meant to scare him. But at any rate, she wanted to show these good-for-nothing demonstrators who was boss."

The words were out of his mouth before Cole could stop them. "What drugs have you been smoking? That's the craziest thing I've ever heard."

Krause's eyes widened. "We could bring everyone in that building in here and question them."

Cole felt himself almost wince.

Okay. Now what do I say, Lord? Do I call his bluff? Yeah. He knows bringing people in won't help his case. If this really is a homicide, he's way too busy to waste time.

"Bring them in. If you do, you might learn to recognize the truth when you hear and see it," Cole said. "You might even be saved. If God would even have you."

Now it was Krause who winced. Then, something in Krause's body language changed. He looked less tense, less aggressive, deflated. Almost scared.

Cole recalled the scene in the book of John when soldiers came to arrest Jesus.

Jesus, knowing all that was going to happen to him, went out and
asked them, "Who is it you want?"
  "Jesus of Nazareth," they replied.
  "I am he," Jesus said. (And Judas the traitor was standing
there with them.) When Jesus said, "I am he," they drew back and
fell to the ground.

Smith and Krause exchanged a glance.

Cole wasn't sure how, but he knew the interrogation was over, at least for now. He folded his hands on his abdomen and leaned back in his chair. Smith stared at him. Krause looked at his notepad.

The air conditioner hummed, and muffled voices came from the next room. A light ballast buzzed.

What's happening with Kiley? Please, Lord, bring her home tonight.

The seconds dragged by. Cole had no idea how long he'd held Smith's gaze.

His shoulders tensed. He took a long, quiet breath and exhaled slowly and as silently as possible, hoping to release the tension without Smith becoming any the wiser.

"So, will you make a formal statement, Mr. Evans?" Smith said.

"'Fraid not."

"You realize I can lock you up right now, or bring in your entire church for questioning," Smith said.

"If you had evidence, you would've charged me. And you won't bring in the church because you know it won't help. Unless you just start hauling in Christians to harass them. And if you've done any reading at all, you know that only strengthens the church. So, Detective . . . what was it? Jones?" Cole said, taking a psychological jab. "I suggest you either charge me or let me go. Either way, I'm finished talking."

～

The yellow rank insignia stood out against the crisp whiteness of the sergeant's shirt sleeve. He sat behind a thick pane of glass equipped with a speaker and a pass-through drawer, like at a drive-through teller window.

"She's charged with aggravated vehicular homicide, and no bail has been set." The sergeant relayed the information mechanically, like someone who repeated the same few sentences dozens of times a day. "She'll probably go to court tomorrow for an initial appearance."

Cole wanted to crumple.

"You might want to know that her truck was impounded, too, sir. We had it towed to our garage so our forensics guys can go over it," the sergeant said. He sounded like he thought he was doing Cole a favor by telling him.

"That's *my* truck! Is that even legal for you guys to just seize it?" Cole asked, already knowing the answer.

The sergeant stared at him blankly. He wouldn't be replying.

"When do I get it back?" Cole asked.

"Sorry, sir, I have no way of knowing."

∽

Cole sat in a plastic chair and studied the imitation stone on the walls in the police station lobby while he waited for paperwork. He tried to pray but couldn't concentrate. He was relieved when his phone rang.

Kiley.

"Did they tell you?" she began. Sob followed sob. "Please, just get me out of here."

"What'd they say, Sis?"

"They took me to this interview room, and at first, they were okay, but then they refused to believe anything I said. They said they knew I killed that man on purpose. And they wouldn't let me talk. Every time I tried to say something, they cut me off. And they just kept getting louder and meaner. I was trapped. There was no way out, other than to admit to doing something."

It was classic. Why hadn't she waited for Frank Hamilton? Why had she said anything? She should've known she couldn't outsmart them. They did this every day for a living, and she was alone on their turf.

Yeah, but you did the same thing. You talked without a lawyer. But you also knew a little about interrogation. And they weren't trying to pin the actual death on you.

"Cole, I'm so scared. What's going to happen?"

Cole nearly said he'd have her out in no time but stopped short. The charges would be dropped, but it might take a while, and he didn't want to give her false hope.

"You hang in there, and we'll work as hard as we can on this end."

"Please, Cole. This is really frightening."

"I'm scared, too, Sis, but we've gotten through lots of stuff together before. This is no different."

Cole wished he could hug her. Or even take her place.

Olivia had been right. This was his fault. He hadn't sent people home when he heard about the protest.

"Try not to worry," he said. "I'll talk to you as soon as I can."

He didn't want to tap the screen to end the call, but knew he had to. Kraus and Smith had appeared in the lobby. They'd asked permission to search in the church and had asked for a copy of the computer master file Don used to record the morning's sermon. Cole had granted them permission to look around and he'd told them they could hear the sermon online.

"There might be something on the master that didn't get uploaded to your website," Krause had said.

"Suit yourself," Cole had said.

~

While the detectives snooped around the church, Cole sat in the back pew and fiddled with the thumb drive that held the unedited video of the morning's service.

Oh, my goodness, Mark and Kimi! How could I have forgotten?

He scrolled through the contacts on his phone and tapped Mark's name. Voice mail.

He scrolled again and tapped Kimi's. Same result.

"Hey, Kimi, I'm so sorry about everything. I'm praying for you all. Please know that I'm here for you guys. Give me a call."

Scenes from chili cook-offs and New Year's Eve parties at Mark and Kimi's house paraded through Cole's mind. Mark and Kimi also had been on a tubing expedition to a ski lodge just west of Cincinnati the previous winter.

Lord, please help them. What's up with them, Lord? Maybe they haven't had a minute to call. Maybe they're too grieved to call. Or, maybe they're just mad at me. Whatever's going on, Lord, please be in the middle of it, and bring your comfort and healing to it.

Cole felt the tightness in his chest and across his shoulders. Would it be weird if he went for a run later to dump some of this stress? He was torn between wanting to wad himself into a ball and cry and wanting to walk out of the church shouting his anger at the top of his lungs.

"You mind if we take this?" Krause asked, holding up a pew Bible.

"Knock yourself out," Cole said. He wanted to make a crack about reading it, but he restrained himself.

Don and Teresa Fisher showed up ten minutes later with an SUV Cole could use while his truck was impounded.

"You have no idea how much I appreciate this," Cole said.

"No worries, my brother," Don said. "All of us at New Hope are in this together."

It was cliché, but Cole was glad Don had said it.

10

COLE'S GRANDPA HAD PREACHED, and so had his dad. And Cole knew early on that he wanted to follow in their footsteps. He even told his classmates about his calling during third-grade career day.

He still remembered the classroom. Light gray desks stood in five neat rows. LED lights gleamed off shiny white floor tiles, and a terrarium sat on a shelf behind Mrs. King's desk. The room smelled like a cross between whiteboard marker and cafeteria tacos.

As he stood at the head of the class, Cole scanned his peers' faces. Boys with unruly hair and grass stains on their jeans. Girls with fleece pants and T-shirts.

Mrs. King, who'd folded herself into a student desk, sat in the back, left corner. She wore her typical get-up, a longish dress that partially disguised her barrel-like shape, and gym shoes with reflectorized tape.

Some of the boys had said they wanted to be firemen or to drive bulldozers. Mary Ann wanted to fly in a rocket, and a couple of people wanted to be doctors. All the announcements had been met with fascination, or at least mild interest.

But when Cole said he wanted to be a pastor, the room erupted in laughter.

"You want to *what*?" Trevor Franklin bawled, slapping his knee.

"You know, preach," Cole said, eliciting a fresh round of guffaws.

After what felt like twenty minutes, Mrs. King told the class they'd dished out enough abuse. But even she didn't seem to appreciate the career choice.

"If Cole wants to be a preacher, let him," she'd said. The words were okay, but something felt wrong about their delivery. A note of reproach or derision made Cole feel awkward or ashamed.

Now, as he sat in his empty kitchen and pondered the day's events, he almost wished he'd heeded his classmates' warnings.

You managed to get your own sister thrown in jail because you kept talking, even though you knew there might be trouble.

Okay, shut up, Evans. That thought is from the pit of hell, and it smells like smoke. You're physically and emotionally exhausted and vulnerable. What do you always tell people? Bad things happen to good people because other people have free will. You need to listen to your own sermons, brother.

Cole planted his elbows on the granite countertop and rubbed his brow. The refrigerator chattered to life, and he realized he hadn't eaten. He glanced at the appliance. Holly's shopping list jotted on an envelope hung from a magnet, as it had for the past three years.

Paper pl8s

Buns

H_2O melon

He hadn't had the heart to take it down.

Cole opened the fridge and appraised two small white Styrofoam take-out boxes, remnants of Saturday's dinner. He didn't open them. On second thought, he wasn't hungry.

He went to his study to pray and sat behind the rolltop secretary desk. The antique stretched most of the length of one wall in the converted bedroom. A worn leather Bible lay next to the laptop. Together the two items consumed most of the desk space. The desk was beautiful, but Cole had to admit it wasn't very functional. He constantly needed to lay books on the floor if he had more than a couple open. The books, themselves, were an anomaly, given that most text these days was digital. The books had been his dad's.

"I want you to read as many of these as you can, and I want us to talk about them after you've read them," his dad had said the summer before Cole started college. "You'll find all kinds of ideas in here. Some of them line up closely with what you've heard me preach. Some directly contradict what I've taught. But I want you to read stuff from time to time that you'll disagree with. It'll challenge you to define and defend what you really believe."

Cole perused the author's names: A.W. Tozer, Charles Spurgeon, J.I. Packard, St. Thomas Aquinas, C.S. Lewis, and Thomas Merton took up a shelf. Works by Immanuel Kent, John Dewey, Harry Emerson Fosdick, Washington Gladden Rochester, and Walter Rauschenbusch resided on another.

He swiveled in his office chair, and his eyes fell on a small wood carving. The words had been his dad's motto. "Lord, to whom shall we go? You have the words of eternal life." The verse, John 6:68, was a snippet of conversation between the Apostle Peter and Jesus when people were deserting the Lord. Cole had liked the verse for as long as he could remember, but when the cops loaded Kiley into the back of the cruiser earlier that day, Peter's question took on deeper meaning.

Cole got on his knees, closed his eyes and rested his head against his chair. His mind churned but nothing he considered legitimate prayer formed in his thoughts. Long seconds dragged past before part of a verse in Romans came to mind. "We do not know what we ought to pray for, but the Spirit himself intercedes for us through wordless groans." Cole had no prayers left. He was exhausted, and he asked the Spirit to intercede.

His phone vibrated in his pocket.

"Cole? Frank Hamilton. Sorry to call so late."

Cole glanced at a clock on the desk. 8:47. He was about to say it was no problem when Frank Hamilton continued.

"I talked to the cops. There's nothing we can do tonight. Kiley's being held without bond. She's charged with aggravated vehicular homicide," Hamilton said. "She'll probably be arraigned on Tuesday. I doubt she'll be on tomorrow's docket."

Why did she have to wait a day? Cole wanted to ask but decided he probably shouldn't. It was probably nothing he or Frank Hamilton could control.

"Can you stop by my office at eight tomorrow morning? I need to see any security video you have," the lawyer said.

Cole agreed and thanked him.

"Now, I know you'll think I'm crazy, but try not to worry," Hamilton said. "This thing isn't over."

Cole felt the beginnings of hope. Maybe Hamilton could actually beat this.

Cole thanked Hamilton again and hung up.

He stared at his phone and debated calling his mom. It was early evening in Phoenix. She'd still be up. He didn't want to worry her, but he knew if he didn't tell her, she'd hear the news somewhere, maybe even on TV, and that would scare her.

"I'm so sorry you're going through this, son," the woman said a few minutes later, her voice aged and gravelly.

"I am, too, Mom."

"You know, I always said it would come to this in this country. I knew it in my knower."

Cole and his dad had always poked fun at her for using the made-up word. But more often than not, her predictions came to pass. And she always knew weird stuff. She knew Valerie Fleming, a woman at church, would miscarry. She told Cole's dad as much the day they heard Valerie was pregnant. She told Jason Tanner he'd come into an inheritance. He did, a month later, from an uncle who died of a heart attack. Cole couldn't explain it, but he believed his mom heard from the Lord.

"It's not surprising. It fits right in with Second Timothy." Cole was sure his mom knew the passage. His dad had quoted it often, and, despite its length, Cole had memorized it. He saw it every day growing up. The verses were emblazoned on a scary picture stuck on the side of the refrigerator. In his teenage years, he'd thought the passage was harsh. Now he understood it.

2 Timothy 3:1–4:

But mark this: There will be terrible times in the last days. People will be lovers of themselves, lovers of money, boastful, proud, abusive, disobedient to their parents, ungrateful, unholy, without love, unforgiving, slanderous, without self-control, brutal, not lovers of the good, treacherous, rash, conceited, lovers of pleasure rather than lovers of God.

"Just keep praying for us, Mom," Cole said.
"You know I will."

～

He sat on the edge of the bed, ready to climb in, when his phone rang again.

Now what? I've got nothing left to give today. Lord, please help me.

He didn't recognize the number.

I should just ignore this. You're a pastor, you need to answer.

He recognized the voice. Olivia Whoever-She-Was. "Pastor Evans, it's Olivia Sandlin. My producer wants to do a story for the eleven o'clock newscast on Kiley. Would you mind answering a few questions?"

You must be kidding me. This woman has some hutzpah.

"Sorry, Olivia, I don't think it would be appropriate for me to say anything. I'm sure she wants privacy right now."

"But she's in jail under some very unusual circumstances. Don't you think people want to know more about her?"

Cole tried to keep his tone matter of fact. "They might, but my duty is to her and to the rest of our family, not to your viewers or your producer. Besides, I'm not sure I can trust a TV station not to make her out to be some kind of nut."

Had he really said that? He needed to shut his mouth and go to bed before he said something that further endangered Kiley. Would his comments be taken out of context and twisted to imply something he hadn't intended? It was too late. He'd already opened his big, fat mouth.

"We really try to be fair, Pastor Evans. Most of the people who don't like our reporting have done things they shouldn't have."

"Well, I'll concede that. But you have to admit the media hasn't treated the church well over the past few decades."

"Fair enough," Olivia said. "Even though I don't totally agree, I can understand why you'd think that."

She sounded almost pleasant. Was this the same woman who'd been a raging psychopath only a few hours earlier?

"By the way, thanks for patching me up today," she said.

Cole barricaded the dozens of sarcastic comments that surged toward his mouth. "You're welcome," he said. "How are the wing and the noggin?"

"They hurt, but I'll survive. Why'd you doctor me up, anyway? I mean after I'd acted so crazy in the church this morning?"

Did he dare tell her his thoughts? Would they end up on the eleven o'clock news? If they did, would it matter?

"Have you ever had someone do something for you that was so awesome and such a sacrifice that you couldn't even wrap your head around it?" Cole asked.

The line was quiet for a second. "Maybe not for me, but for my mom and dad," Olivia said. "The man across the street came and helped us to move once."

"I know you're probably on some sort of deadline but tell me about it if you have a second."

"He and his son just showed up and asked my dad if we needed help. My dad knew the guy's name, and they'd waved at each other from opposite sides of the street over the years, but that was about it."

"Yeah, that's about as well as we get to know our neighbors these days," Cole said.

"And my mom had so much stuff. She wasn't a hoarder. She got rid of things. She just replaced them with different stuff. Every closet and every hidden corner were packed to exploding. So, this guy and his son offered to help. And we moved stuff and moved stuff and moved stuff into that truck. It took at least three trips across town to the new place. And at about ten o'clock that night, we got into the last closet at the old house. And it was packed as full as the rest of the closets had been. I knew it would take at least another half hour to get the stuff onto that truck. And the guy, his name was Bill, looked absolutely exhausted. His face and his shirt were soaked in sweat. But he just looked at my dad, and said, 'I must really like you, man,' and he picked up a box and headed for the truck. I could never grasp why he would sacrifice so much time and energy for people he hardly knew."

At that, Olivia fell silent.

Wow. That was perfect. Thank you, Lord.

"I know this morning you made it pretty clear you weren't interested in hearing about Jesus," he said, "but if you could indulge me for just a minute, I think the way you feel about the guy who helped you move is a lot like how I feel about Jesus. Jesus loved me so much and sacrificed so much for me, I can't even begin to understand it. It's not just that he died, it's *how* he died. It was beyond painful. Sure, I think about the whip ripping the skin off his back, and the soldiers driving spikes through his hands and feet. And I understand that the position he was in on the cross essentially suffocated him. And all those things are horrible. But you know what hurts me the deepest and amazes me the most? He let them pull out his beard and spit in his face. They didn't just kill him. They did everything they could to humiliate him. And he could've stopped it. He spoke the entire universe into existence, for crying out loud. But he chose to bear that torture and humiliation. And he did that for me. When I had more or less ignored him and done things to betray him." Cole paused for effect. "He loved me anyway. And now he wants me to pass that love on to others. That's why I bandaged you up."

Olivia was quiet for a beat.

"I'd never really thought about all of that." Her voice was soft, pensive.

"Sorry, I didn't mean to launch into a sermon. See what happens when you ask a preacher a simple question?"

"I expected nothing less," she said.

"I'm just a little curious. Why are you still working? You walked into the church ten or eleven hours ago. Doesn't Channel Twelve have other reporters?" Cole said.

"Yeah, the girl who was supposed to work tonight called off with a bad stomach bug."

"Sorry to hear that. I'll remember her in my prayers."

"Thanks, I guess," Olivia said.

He resisted the urge to tell her to stop rolling her eyes. "You're welcome," he said, "Have a good night."

Cole set his phone on his nightstand, then looked across the room to his dresser. Holly's face gazed at him from a picture frame. Her eyes twinkled and she held out her left hand, the diamond gleaming in the sunlight.

Cole smiled at the picture, then sank into bed and turned off the light.

11

COLE BLINKED HIMSELF AWAKE.

Where . . . ? Oh, living room. Guess I never went back to bed. What time was that? Three? Four? Why's it so bright? What time is it?

His eyes travelled around the room until he found his phone. Face-down on the floor next to the couch.

It's 7:18, wow.

Cole clicked his phone open. *Whoa! A hundred and thirty-two texts and seventeen phone calls? What in the world's going on?*

He clicked on the top text.

Mark: Got ur msgs. Pls don't contact us again. Obviously, we'll get someone else to do the funeral.

"Oh, man. I am so sorry."

He sighed deeply and rubbed his hand across his forehead. *Why do people rub their foreheads? It doesn't help anything.*

Should I call later? No, he specifically said not to. Lord, please help us all. What a mess.

He scrolled to the next text.

Jake: You okay, buddy? If you need to talk, I'm here.

He didn't recognize the next texter's number. Not even the area code. It was a profanity-laden rant.

What in the world? I guess I'll look at one more.

Tom: Hang in there, dude. The media trucks will eventually leave. Need anything?

Media trucks? What media trucks?

Cole went to the window. The SUV Don Fisher had loaned him sat in the driveway. Three media trucks with their antennae hoisted lined his side of the street. Had Olivia called them? Was she that angry and vindictive? She hadn't sounded it. Had someone else called?

It doesn't matter who called. There's nothing you can do about it at this point.

Wait a minute! It's seven-thirty! I have to get to Frank Hamilton's!

The reporters' shouts buffeted him ten minutes later as he walked from the garage to the driveway. Their timbre changed—became more muffled, as if all the reporters had socks in their mouths—as he backed the SUV and swung into the street.

◌

Pictures of Cincinnati's skyline adorned the waiting room walls, and a TV in the corner mumbled about the various legal services Hamilton's firm offered.

Cole thumbed his phone and read his newsfeed.

> Inflation down a fourth straight month
>> The Federal Reserve announced today that inflation has hit an eighteen-month low at 5.6 percent.
>> President Gonzalez attributed the drop to improved relations with Chile.

Well, at least inflation's headed the right direction, if we can believe what they're saying.

Kiley was the second story in his feed.

Fabulous. The entire nation thinks my sister is a murderous zealot.

The previous day's events seemed even worse in print and video.

Lord, I just don't even know what to pray.

Frank Hamilton's voice yanked him out of his daze.

"Sorry to see you under these circumstances," the lawyer said.

◌

The fifteenth-floor window looked down on the Cincinnati Reds and Bengals stadiums and across the Ohio River into Kentucky.

Nice little dump they've got here. I wonder what this place costs.

Everything about the office looked expensive. A thick Asian rug. Heavy-looking leather furniture. And Hamilton's massive mahogany desk.

Those antique bookcases are cool.

Scores of matching embossed leather law books stood in neat formation behind glass doors in the twin cases. Although Cole was sure no one used hard-copy law books anymore, the volumes lent an air of learnedness to the room.

Hamilton looked like he belonged in the surroundings. Tall and lanky, with swept-back silver-gray hair, and an expensive suit, he towered from behind his desk like a monolith.

"Okay, so Kiley is charged with aggravated vehicular homicide," Hamilton said as he gestured to a chair.

"It's a third-degree felony because she's also charged with reckless operation. She could get one to five years."

Cole's guts twisted. His breathing quickened.

He hoped Hamilton hadn't noticed. But why? Was he really that proud? Wasn't Kiley's safety the only thing that mattered?

"I saw the story. National news. I'm not sure if that's fortunate or unfortunate," Hamilton continued, "and I saw the video of the rock-throwing and Johnson. Do you have any security video from the church that shows the same thing?"

Cole punched up the security camera app on his phone and found the video. Hamilton stared intently at the phone and nodded. Although Cole had watched it three or four times already, he couldn't pull his eyes away.

"This is good. It will be helpful. If we can get the news video to use along with this, we might be able to get this whole thing thrown out immediately," Hamilton said.

Please, Lord, let it be so. Get Kiley out of there and get her back home.

Cole realized he wasn't listening. Hamilton was saying something about a court appearance Thursday or Friday.

"It's called a preliminary hearing or a probable cause hearing," Hamilton said. "It's like a mini trial, where the prosecutor has to prove it's reasonable to believe a crime was committed. We can present the news video and the church security video then. It might not even get that far if the prosecution sees the video and realizes what actually happened."

Cole let out a breath he didn't realize he'd been holding.

He didn't know if there was such a thing as a typical brother-sister relationship, but if there was, his and Kiley's had been one. His mom had said he had idolized Kiley, and she'd doted on him when they were small. But by the time Cole was in elementary school, he wasn't always the best brother.

He never harbored evil intent. Things just happened. When he was seven, he melted Kiley's doll house when he put lit candles inside while playing with his fire trucks. Afterward, his dad heated up Cole's backside. Pops didn't talk about grace that day. A few years later, Cole had to help with yard work for four straight weeks to earn money to buy Kiley a new tea set. His explanation that the tiny plates and saucers were good BB gun targets didn't work. Nor did the argument that Kiley didn't play with them anymore.

He remembered a day when he was about nine when he acquiesced and allowed Kiley's Barbie to marry his G.I. Joe on the condition that Kiley dry the dishes that night.

But Kiley remained loyal, no matter how rotten Cole was.

In high school, they watched out for one another. Cole once threatened to beat up a kid named Ryan Martin if he didn't stop stalking Kiley, and Kiley watched out for Cole, as well. She somehow knew what everyone in the school was saying about everyone else, and on the rare occasions when Cole's name was dragged into the fray, she let him know and defended him.

After their dad died, Kiley was his rock. Their mom had wanted to deal with the loss by purging the house of any reminder of their dad. She put away pictures, gave away clothes and donated everything in the garage that had belonged to Pops. But Cole wanted to do everything in his power to keep their dad's memory alive. And Kiley helped. They'd talked late into the night and looked at pictures and videos of their Pops. Kiley had even snagged one of the old man's coffee cups that their mom had earmarked for Goodwill.

When Cole lost Holly, he understood the desire to run from the pain, but Kiley again was there, encouraging him to remember the good times. She stayed up late for months while Cole poured out his pain.

He didn't know how to ask Hamilton the next question. He felt guilty for bringing it up.

"You haven't said what this will cost. If this goes to trial—"

Hamilton cut him off. "Don't worry about that, my friend. Christian legal defense organizations exist to help out in cases like these. Besides, even if I have to do this *pro bono*, I'm sure the Lord will work things out somehow. He always does."

≈

Cole was at the justice center ten minutes later. The building's twin ten-story towers reminded Cole of stacks of brown Kleenex boxes, with tiny slits for windows near the top of each rectangular box.

The municipal court occupied the left side of the building. The jail entrance lay to the right. In the jailhouse lobby, benches bolted to the floor created hunter-green islands in a sea of gleaming white floor tiles. The business windows testified to the morning's sleepiness, their metal security doors rolled down and locked. Records. Inmate Property. Commissary Accounts.

A lone deputy, sandy-haired and baby-faced with a sour expression, sat behind a window to the left of the front entrance. Was the guy's attitude a requirement for dealing with inmates and angry family members? Or had the man been a smiling, jovial person a couple of years earlier, before he took his job?

"I know I can't visit today, but is there a way I can receive calls from my sister?" Cole said. His voice bounced off the concrete walls and high ceiling. "She was brought in yesterday afternoon."

Hamilton had told Cole he could visit twice a week for fifteen minutes at a time. That meant he couldn't visit until at least Wednesday.

"Inmate's name?" The question was a three-syllable grunt.

"Kiley Ev—"

"The pastor's sister," the deputy said, softening. "You can't call her, but she can call you. Here's what you need to do, pastor."

~

The CNN logo disappeared, and an image of New Hope flashed onto the screen.

"The leader of the national gay-rights organization Pride Now is calling for demonstrations after a man died in a protest near Cincinnati yesterday," the newswoman said.

A man in a blue polo shirt and a crew cut appeared on the screen. "We, as a community, have to stand in solidarity." The text box at the bottom of the screen identified the speaker as Clyde French, Pride Now president. "Yesterday's tragic events would not have happened if hypocritical Christians had shown the love they claim to embrace."

The news anchor reappeared. "The violence erupted outside this church about twenty miles northwest of Cincinnati. One man died when a pickup truck driven by the pastor's sister rammed the crowd of demonstrators."

Kiley's mugshot flashed onto the screen.

Lord, I can't believe they're doing this. Please help us.

When Cole opened his eyes, Red's video of Trace Johnson falling from the hood played, before the picture showed the inside of the church.

"So, not marrying a couple who wants to marry isn't hateful," Olivia said.

The statement sounded even angrier on TV than it did in person.

"Not in the least. It may be the most loving thing I've done all week." The screen flashed to an image of Cole that made him look confused and stupid.

Cole sighed.

"What else did you expect?" he said into the empty house.

The news anchor chattered on for several more seconds about New Hope before moving to the next story.

"The Agriculture Department announced today that the disease affecting cattle production in the United States appears to have been eradicated," the newswoman said. "All infected animals have been slaughtered, and disinfection processes are complete."

"Well, I guess that's one piece of good news," Cole said.

He clicked off the TV and closed his eyes. His head pounded.

～

The ringing phone jarred him from his reverie.

"Sis! How're you holding up?"

"As well as can be expected, I guess. What's the lawyer say?" She sounded good, hopeful.

"He says we may be able to get the whole thing thrown out."

"Well, that's good news. I hope he's right," she said.

"Me, too. Keep praying."

～

Jake Moore ran his finger down the screen. "I think you should delete this."

The gray band marked the sentence, and it disappeared.

Jake read the message aloud:

Friends, as you likely have heard, the head of a gay-rights organization has called for additional protests in the wake of the horrible events that happened outside our church yesterday. I implore you, for your own safety and for sake of the name of Christ, please stay away from the New Hope building until further notice. Be assured God is still on his throne, and this situation will work out according to his plan. At the same time, we do not want to do anything to further inflame this situation. Pray diligently for those who would seek to do us harm, and try to follow Jesus's command in the book of Matthew to be shrewd as snakes and innocent as doves. Above all, know that you are loved.

Blessings,
Pastor Cole.

"Are you sure you want to do this?" Jake asked. "Are you inadvertently encouraging people to get involved in whatever goes on over there tonight?"

"I doubt there's anyone from the church who hasn't already heard about this. I'm sure we're all glued to the news."

"I don't know, Cole. Maybe you should run this past the elders," Jake said.

"There's no time," Cole said. "This needs to be hitting people's phones and emails ASAP."

The cursor climbed the screen, and he clicked SEND. The message disappeared. There was no turning back.

～

Cole eased Don's SUV into a space on Main Street, about halfway between the church and the police station. He rolled down the windows. Despite the early evening hour, the mid-summer sun blazed. It would be another ninety minutes until darkness fell. Maybe that was good. Maybe the daylight and the heat would dissuade protesters from coming out.

He sipped his water and waited. The sweat soaked his shirt and glued the hair to his forehead.

I don't understand any of this, Lord, but I thank you and praise you. No matter what happens, you're God, and I'm not. You're perfect and glorious and awesome, and I deserve none of the goodness and blessings you've showered on me throughout my life . . .

The noise approaching from behind him drew his mind back to the present.

What were they chanting? Something . . . something . . . something . . . *now*!

In the rearview mirror, a few dozen people jammed the sidewalk in front of the police station and marched his direction. One man carried a large sign with a picture of two men kissing.

Gross.

Well, here we go. Lord, please keep everyone safe.

Who's that in front of the church?

"Reed, for crying out loud. Get out of there."

Cole opened his phone, pushed the home button, and spoke. "Call Reed Bryant."

"Pastor Cole! You comin' down? A buncha freaks is comin this way right now." His voice brimmed with excitement.

"Reed, get out of there! Please. We've had enough trouble."

As it passed his truck, the mob broke into the gospel song "We Shall Overcome."

Whoever wrote that is rolling over in his grave.

"No, pastor, we need to stick up for ourselves."

"Reed! No!"

The crowd blocked Reed from view.

Do I need to go down there? Please, no. No, no, no.

Cole turned the key and a few seconds later crept into the crowd. People shoved one another. Where was Reed? There, on the ground.

No, no, no, don't kick him.

Cole jumped from the SUV.

Ow. I'd forgotten how much it hurts to be punched.

The fist had come from somewhere off to Cole's left. He couldn't worry about that. The guy in front of him was big, brawny.

It'll be okay. You have the element of surprise.

A sneakered foot rocked Reed's head sideward.

Cole charged and plowed his shoulder into Reed's assailant and grabbed Reed by the belt. Reed wobbled to his feet.

New pain exploded in the side of Cole's head. Was that a fist or did someone throw something?

The SUV stood running in the middle of the street.

Three more steps. Pain shot through Cole's torso as a fist connected with his ribs. Cole heard himself gasp. Reed tottered.

Why is he so heavy? He's five-feet-six, for crying out loud.

Cole grabbed the door handle and launched Reed into the front seat. A new explosion of pain. Something hit his back.

Something else hit the SUV as Cole drove away.

Cole's hands shook on the steering wheel. "Reed, I love you, man, but you're a moron."

Blood trickled from Reed's nose, and he breathed heavily.

"How are your ribs?" Cole asked.

Reed gasped the words. "Can't. Breathe."

Hopefully he hadn't broken a rib and punctured a lung.

Cole's head and back throbbed. Sweat bathed his face. The SUV's tires squealed.

The morning sun revealed three broken windows and bright red lettering across the front of the church. "Biggits."

"Well, clearly the artist didn't win his fifth-grade spelling bee," Don said.

A bolt of pain shot through Cole's head and back. "Don't make me laugh. It hurts."

"I'm just glad no one was seriously hurt," Don said.

"Yeah, Reed'll be okay, and this knot on my head will eventually go away."

"Does that mean I have to stop calling you knothead?" Don asked.

Cole groaned. "Droll, Don. Very droll. I wonder if we can pray that out of you."

"I doubt it."

"Yeah, an entire exorcism might be in order."

Don smiled.

"Did you say they have stuff at the hardware store to get this paint off?" Cole asked.

"Yeah. Don't worry about this. Get over to Kiley's hearing. I'll clean this up."

Cole wanted to hug him.

"You been to sleep yet?" Don asked.

"A couple of hours in a hospital chair, waiting on Reed."

Don clapped him on the shoulder. "Maybe you can get an hour of sleep before court."

12

PANES OF BULLETPROOF GLASS separated spectators from the courtroom's active participants. The gallery was dimly lit, while brighter lights bathed the judge's bench, attorneys' tables, and jury box.

This is bizarre. I feel like a voyeur. It's like watching some kind of creepy peep show.

His skin crawled.

Clumps of people dotted seven pews that stretched across the gallery in front of him. Kimi and Mark Johnson sat toward the front to the left. John Porter sat on the right.

Not surprising. Kimi and Mark may be blaming him for what happened.

Where was Frank Hamilton?

A woman in a business suit slid into the pew next to Cole. He checked his phone. 8:53.

The stranger looked relaxed, approachable. Should he ask? Sure, why not? What could it hurt?

"Can I ask you a question?" Cole said. "What's up with the glass?"

"This is an old building. The glass was put in before they had metal detectors."

Her voice was neither friendly, nor unfriendly just matter of fact. It'd be okay to ask one more question.

"Weird. So, who are all these people?"

"There are several cases on the docket. Most of us are attorneys," the woman said.

"I guess it's not like TV, is it?"

"Not at all."

He checked his phone again. 8:57.

As if by instinct people on both sides of the glass drifted toward their places. Some continued to chat.

Frank Hamilton appeared behind the glass, talking with a sheriff's deputy.

The chatter stopped when the bailiff entered through a door near the judge's bench.

Seconds later, the door directly behind the bench opened, and the bailiff ordered everyone to rise.

The judge, who possessed a mop of unruly gray hair and bushy eyebrows, spoke in clipped tones. "Call the first case."

A man named Jamison and his attorney moved to a podium in front of the bench.

The judge read a list of charges. The man was accused of kicking in the door to his ex-wife's house and punching her.

The man's lawyer entered a not-guilty plea, and the prosecutor requested a high bail.

Less than a minute later, Jamison was headed back to jail, and a new defendant and his attorney stood behind the podium.

For the next hour, the judge moved the cases along like cogs on a sad assembly line.

About twenty people remained in the gallery when Kiley's case was called.

A sheriff's deputy led Kiley into the courtroom from a door to the right. Cole felt like he'd swallowed a golf ball, and he felt his eyes moisten. Kiley's hair hung limp and dingy brown, and gray-green pouches hung under her eyes. With her hands cuffed in front of her and lost in an oversized orange jump suit, she shuffled across the room in her jail-issue flip flops. Cole knew the flip flops added insult to injury. Kiley had always hated them.

Five minutes later, the hearing was over.

~

As Cole pulled into the driveway, Olivia bent at the waist, panting, hands on hips. Her skin glistened.

Turn your head. Don't notice the running shorts and teeny top. Or the cute ponytail sticking out of the back of the pink ball cap. Treat her like you'd treat Kiley.

He raised his hand in a quick wave and shut the SUV's door.

"Hey, sorry about your sister," Olivia called.

She knows already? That was quick.

"Noah Maines texted from the justice center," she said.

Maines was one of Channel Twelve's other reporters. Cole hadn't noticed him in the courtroom, but obviously he'd been there.

"Yeah. She's still locked up. Preliminary hearing's set for Thursday."

"It may not seem like it, but that's actually pretty quick," Olivia said. "I heard about your building, too. That really sucks."

Did she mean that? She sounded sincere enough.

"Thanks," he said. "We'll get it cleaned up."

"Did you hear about Chicago and Atlanta?"

"No, what about 'em?"

"Three dead in Atlanta and two in Chicago."

"In protests? You're kidding."

Her look told him she wasn't.

How could one conversation have such far-reaching consequences? Lord, I'm so sorry.

"Yeah, even I didn't see that coming, and I'm usually pretty good at reading the tea leaves," Olivia said.

"The whole thing just rips my heart out."

"You know, I'm a newswoman and make my living reporting this stuff, but it still makes me sad," she said.

Good. At least she's still human.

"Yeah. Me, too. I guess someone from your station will be at Kiley's hearing on Thursday," Cole said.

"Yeah, I've asked to cover it, myself."

Should he ask her to be kind or just leave things in the Lord's hands?

"Guess I'll see you there," he said.

"Yup." She waved and turned toward the house.

Cole planted his elbows on the granite countertop and held his head in his hands.

Lord, I praise you and thank you, but I absolutely do not understand you. Please, please stop all this violence. I feel responsible for all of this.

He thought about a day when Trace Johnson was about ten and burst into the sanctuary after the service wielding a papier-mâché "sword of the Spirit" he'd made in Sunday School. "Look out, Enemy, here I come," Trace shouted, his preteen voice strident. Cole plucked a used church bulletin from a pew and had rolled it into a tube, and the sword fight ensued in the middle aisle. Cole backed down the aisle until Trace landed a lethal blow in front of the stage, and Cole crumpled. Laughter and applause burst out all around the sanctuary.

"I think he got you, pastor," Mark Johnson had said.

I really love those guys. Is it really my business who Trace has sex with? Yes and no.

A verse came to mind, 1 Corinthians 6:18. *Flee from sexual immorality. All other sins a person commits are outside the body, but whoever sins sexually, sins against their own body.*

Oh, Mark, don't you see I'm really not trying to judge or condemn Trace? Who am I to throw the first stone? I honestly just want what's best for him.

I wish I could wave a magic wand and make this mess go away. Lord, isn't there anything I can do? Isn't there some way to fix this?

The next thought seemed to come from nowhere. *Don's right. You're a knothead. You can only make your own choices and do what the Bible says. You can't control others' reactions.*

Yeah, but—.

Stop yeah-butting. You can only control yourself. Unless you think you want to start running the entire universe.

Cole sighed.

Just guide me, Lord. Help me to hear you and to do what you say.

13

THE PROCEEDINGS HAD MOVED from the bizarre room where the arraignment was held, into a normal-looking courtroom. The Johnsons and John Porter again sat on opposite sides of the chamber.

Cole didn't recognize the prosecutor. It wasn't Mike Davis. Cole had seen Davis dozens of times on TV and online.

An assistant? Is that good or bad? Does it mean Davis thinks the case is a slam dunk and Kiley's doomed, or does he think it's a lost cause for the prosecution and not worth spending his own time on?

Assistant Prosecutor Andrew Winston looked about thirty, with an average build and thick dark hair. Every hair lay in place, and his suit, shirt and tie, looked razor sharp. His black oxfords gleamed.

Did the exaggerated attention to neatness mean anything? Was Winston trying to prove something? Maybe to himself?

With the preface to the day's proceeding concluded, Winston called Brady Hanson to the stand.

This guy looks familiar. Where've I seen him? Was he outside the church the Sunday Kiley was arrested? Wait, a cast. This is the guy who was hit with the sports drink bottle. He looks different. Cleans up well.

Hanson was a twig. About six feet tall, bony and haggard looking, he was probably in his midforties, although Cole suspected a hard life may have caused him to look older than he was. The prosecution had clearly spent money sprucing him up. His salt-and-pepper hair and beard were neatly trimmed, and he wore gray dress slacks, with a white button-down shirt, open at the collar.

Winston started slowly, establishing Hanson's whereabouts on the morning in question.

"And did anything unusual happen that morning?" he asked.

"There was about twenty or thirty people there, and we was yellin' that people shouldn't be in the church because of what the Supreme Court said."

Step by step, Winston led Hanson through the morning's events.

"And what did you see as the last of the people left the church?"

"This lady come barreling through the alley in her truck," Hanson said.

"How do you know it was a lady?"

"I seen her in the car. She looked crazy or somethin'"

"Do you see that person in the courtroom, today?" Winston asked.

"Her, over there."

"Let the record reflect Mr. Hanson has identified the defendant."

Over the next ten minutes Hanson testified that Kiley hit Trace with the vehicle.

Then Hamilton started his cross-examination.

"So, you got a good look at the defendant, is that correct, Mr. Hanson?"

"Yeah, she stopped at one point."

"Did she come to a complete stop?"

"She had to stop. People started runnin' in front of the truck."

"So, if she was stopped, she wasn't going very fast," Hamilton said.

Laughter rippled through the courtroom.

"And had anything happened to you at that point?" Hamilton asked. "Had you been hurt?"

"No."

"What were the people around you doing?"

"We was all runnin' toward the pickup. Some people was throwing stuff."

"What did you do next, Mr. Hanson?"

"Something hit me in the back of the head, and I stumbled into the side of the truck."

"Was the truck moving at that point?"

"I ain't sure. Things was happening pretty quick."

"What had you been doing before you went to the church?" Hamilton asked.

"Irrelevant, Your Honor!" The prosecutor was on his feet, his voice angry.

"It goes to the witness's ability to clearly recall the morning's events, Your Honor." Hamilton's tone was matter of fact.

"Sustained."

Hamilton didn't seem fazed. He looked like he had a Plan B.

"You went to the hospital after you were hurt, didn't you, Mr. Hanson?" Hamilton's voice remained controlled.

"Yeah, I broke my arm when I fell."

Hamilton walked from behind the podium to the defense table and retrieved some stapled pages.

"May I approach the witness, Your Honor?"

"Proceed."

He told Hanson they were a copy of medical records and asked that they be admitted into evidence. The judge agreed. A minute later, Hanson identified his name and the date on the medical report.

Hamilton flipped a couple of pages.

"I'd like you to read the words highlighted in yellow toward the bottom of the page," the lawyer said.

"Levels consistent with recent or heavy cocaine use."

Cole could see just enough of Kiley's profile to tell that she was smiling. He couldn't help smiling, himself.

Hamilton flipped a page.

"And these words right here, Mr. Hanson."

"BAC 0.201."

"Mr. Hanson, do you know what BAC stands for?"

Another objection from Winston. "The witness isn't competent to answer the question, Your Honor."

"The abbreviation is common knowledge. You may answer, Mr. Hanson." The judge's tone was authoritative and firm.

"Blood-alcohol level."

Yes! If things go this way all morning, Kiley will be out of jail by noon.

Mark Johnson's shoulders rolled forward.

I can't imagine what you're going through, Mark.

Winston called a half-dozen witnesses, and Hamilton, on cross-examination, manipulated them into poking holes in the prosecutor's case.

Hamilton began putting his own witnesses on the stand after lunch.

"The defense calls Davonte Bloom," Hamilton said.

Who's this guy? Hamilton didn't mention him.

Tall, African American, shaven headed and probably in his sixties, the man strode confidently into the room. He wore a polo shirt and khakis and looked comfortable in his surroundings. There was no question, Bloom had been on the stand before.

Hamilton took several minutes to establish his credentials. Retired Cleveland police officer, now a private investigator.

"You went back and reexamined the scene, didn't you, Mr. Bloom?" Hamilton asked.

"I did."

"And what of note, if anything, did you find?"

"I found a chunk of brick that measured four and one-sixteenth inches, by two and three-eighths inches, by exactly three inches."

Hamilton introduced photos into evidence as well as the brick, then spent ten minutes having Bloom describe where he found the brick.

"Given the statement from Ms. Evans that the man on her truck was hit with a brick, would you have expected crime scene investigators to collect this as they processed the scene?" Hamilton asked.

"I have no idea why they didn't."

When the judge turned Bloom over for cross-examination, Winston shot out of his chair like a rocket.

"We have no idea where this brick actually came from, do we, Mr. Bloom?" he began.

"If you're suggesting it came from somewhere other than the alley, I think the photos already introduced into evidence clearly show where it was found."

"Did you have the brick tested for the presence of DNA?" Winston asked.

"No. I might ask the state the same thing. Given Ms. Evans's statement to the police, if the state truly was interested in finding out the truth, investigators would have collected the brick and had it tested."

Bloom and Winston sparred for the next five minutes.

Cole tried to read the judge's expression. He couldn't. Surely the judge wouldn't be swayed, would he?

When Winston insinuated a third time the brick hadn't come from the crime scene, Hamilton objected. "He's badgering the witness, Your Honor!" Hamilton's face was flushed, his tone irritated.

Before the judge ruled on the objection, Winston sat down and said he had nothing further.

This isn't good. He knew Hamilton would object and knew the judge would sustain the objection, but he was able to plant the idea in the judge's mind, anyway. Surely, the judge is smart enough to see what's going on. Surely, he doesn't think Hamilton stooped to something as egregious as planting evidence. Lord, please help the judge see the truth.

His heart leapt when Hamilton called his next witness. Jeremy Timmons. The shaggy TV camera guy who'd introduced himself as Red.

I don't know where this man stands with you, Lord, but in the church, he didn't seem hostile. Please give him words to help Kiley.

As he had with Bloom, Hamilton took several minutes to establish the cameraman's credentials before he moved on to what the man had seen.

"As news people, it's important to be truthful, isn't it, Mr. Timmons?" Hamilton asked.

Why had he asked that? Was he trying to convince the judge of the guy's truthfulness or playing to the cameraman's ego in order to get his cooperation?

"Absolutely," Timmons said. "Our credibility is everything."

Hamilton introduced the news footage into evidence then ran a minute or two of video. On the screen, people stood outside of New Hope Church, their shouts a cacophony.

"Does this appear to be the video you shot on the morning in question?" Hamilton asked.

"It does."

Hamilton fast-forwarded to a spot several minutes into the video.

The chunk of brick arced through the air like a rainbow, striking Johnson near the center of the back of the head. Hamilton ran only about three seconds of video.

"Is this an accurate depiction of what happened?" Hamilton asked.

"It is."

"Now, I want to back up the video for just a few seconds."

Cole's truck came into the frame, Kiley behind the wheel. The vehicle lurched to a stop, and Johnson scampered onto the hood.

"The truck is stopped at this point, isn't it, Mr. Timmons?"

"Yes."

Hamilton backed up the video a few seconds again. The truck came onto the screen and stopped. The brick hit Johnson, and he fell off the vehicle.

"The car isn't moving, is it, Mr. Timmons?"

"No."

Hamilton backed up the video a third time. Truck stopped. Man on hood. Brick. Man on ground. Truck moving.

The color drained from the prosecutor's face, and his eyes grew huge. Clearly, he hadn't carefully examined the video. Cole didn't know if he'd zoomed past it or if he simply hadn't watched it closely.

Yes! Yes, yes, yes!

Kiley sat up straighter.

"Your video clearly shows that the vehicle did not move until after Mr. Johnson was on the ground. Isn't that right, Mr. Timmons?"

"That's correct."

"Nothing further, Your Honor."

Silence hung in the courtroom, with every eye riveted to the screen.

Winston sighed deeply and let his shoulders roll forward. He didn't cross-examine.

Five minutes later, the judge ruled.

"The purpose of these proceedings was to determine if there was probable cause to believe the defendant could have committed a felony. While the video evidence clearly shows that a crime was committed against Mr. Johnson, the footage just as plainly demonstrates that the vehicle operated by Ms. Evans was not in motion when Mr. Johnson sustained his injury. I find no probable cause in this case. Case dismissed. You can release the defendant."

Kimi Johnson gasped as the judge tapped his gavel. Her husband quietly wrapped an arm around her.

Kiley turned toward Cole and beamed. A silent tear rolled down her right cheek. A deputy moved toward her, handcuff key in hand.

Hamilton gathered items into his briefcase, and Winston, attaché case already dangling at his left side, moved toward the defense table, his hand outstretched.

Before the men could shake hands, another man stood and spoke loudly from the gallery.

"Your Honor, if I may approach the bar," the man said.

Every head turned.

The man towered above the crowd like a pillar. He wore a dark sport jacket, gray shirt, and dark blue necktie. A badge in a plastic sleeve hung from a lanyard around his neck.

From his seat, Cole couldn't see what type of badge it was.

"And who might you be, sir?" the judge asked.

"Deputy Marshal Connor Sampson, Your Honor. U.S. Marshals Service."

"You can approach," the judge said.

"We have an arrest warrant on federal charges for Ms. Evans," the marshal said, as he hauled neatly folded papers from the inside of his jacket. "We had requested a meeting with local authorities this morning to discuss turning over the case. Your ruling simplifies things."

As Sampson spoke, the judge motioned with his fingers, and the bailiff retrieved the papers.

No one in the courtroom stirred while the judge read. Muffled voices drifted into the courtroom from some other part of the building. The judge remained expressionless as his eyes traveled down the page. Satisfied, he handed the papers back to the bailiff.

"She's all yours," the judge told the marshal.

With that, another man in the gallery stood, probably another deputy marshal.

"Ten-minute recess, while the marshal collects his prisoner," the judge said with another light tap of his gavel. "Bailiff, as soon as they're done here, bring out the next defendant."

Cole struggled to hold back tears. *Now, what, Lord? Where are they taking her?*

~

Hamilton's jaw clenched as he handed the papers back to the deputy marshal, slammed his briefcase shut and shoved his way through the small gate. He pointed toward the door, and Cole followed. They were in a nook in the hallway a moment later, voices echoing crazily from the marble floors and walls.

Hamilton spoke in a loud whisper. "She's charged under the federal hate crime statute."

Anger flashed in Hamilton's eyes. His lips had thinned, and his jaw remained set.

"She'll go across town to the federal courthouse, probably at some point later today, for an initial appearance."

Cole sighed deeply. *Why? This just doesn't seem fair!*

Hamilton continued. "The good news is Kiley will stay here, in Hamilton County, not a federal facility somewhere far away, while the federal process moves forward."

Cole wanted to say that was a small consolation, but he knew he couldn't take his anger out on Hamilton, especially not with everything the lawyer was doing for Kiley.

A vein protruded angry and purple in Hamilton's neck.

"Since it's a federal religious freedom case now, I need to get another attorney involved," Hamilton continued. "Her name's Jennifer Michaels. She's good. She's argued in front of the Supreme Court, and she knows these religious liberty cases backward and forward."

"I truly appreciate what you're doing, Frank. I hope you know I'm willing to pay what I can," Cole said.

"I appreciate that, Cole. But this isn't about money," he said. "The government has twisted the meaning of separation of church and state to ridiculous extremes. The Founding Fathers' original idea was to prevent the establishment of a state church. The Supreme Court has been using the Establishment Clause as club against the faithful for decades." He listed several court cases. "Now it's finding any excuse it can to harass Christians. Arresting the faithful without probable cause is the last straw," Hamilton said.

"It's funny," Cole said. "I don't think people start out intending to become activists. I think life just happens, and it dawns on us at some point we have to do something to help set things right."

Hamilton nodded.

"I never gave gay rights much thought," Cole said. "It was one of those things that would never effect me."

"Yeah, I get it," Hamilton said. "I don't think I really became aware of it until I read about Matthew Shepard back in the late 1990s."

Cole knew the case. Shepard was a gay college student from Wyoming. He was beaten, tortured, tied to a fence and left to die in near-freezing temperatures. He was found alive but died several days later. Two men were convicted of murdering him.

"I remember thinking how horrible that was," Cole said. "The news reports said he was beaten beyond recognition. I remember thinking that no one has a right to mistreat people just because they're gay—or however they identify. They're still made in God's image. And when that *Obergefell* decision was announced a few years ago, legalizing gay marriage, I thought it was unbiblical, but I still never thought it would directly touch my life."

"I guess it's human nature to think nothing bad is actually going to happen," Hamilton said.

Cole nodded and they were silent for a beat.

"It's ironic, isn't it?" Hamilton said. "They're using the law that grew out of the Shepard case to go after Kiley."

"Yeah. That irony isn't lost on me," Cole said. He pressed his lips together and shook his head.

"As much as you read, I figured it wouldn't be," Hamilton said. "But you know what? As bad as this is, we can be sure of one thing. This opposition is going to bring more people to Jesus. In the long run, opposition always has."

At that moment, the thought brought Cole little solace.

Thanks, Lord. Thanks for letting me be your servant. His mental tone gushed sarcasm, and sadness immediately pierced his heart. *I'm sorry for the attitude, Lord. Please help me, and Kiley, of course. Help us to cling to you and not give the devil a foothold.*

~

The initial appearance in federal court took ten minutes. A magistrate explained Kiley's rights and read the charges against her. Hamilton entered a not guilty plea, and Kiley shuffled out, head down, without looking Cole's direction.

14

A NEW CROP OF weeds had sprouted in a flower bed at the house across the street. Were the pink and fuchsia flowers petunias or begonias? Whatever they were, tall, grassy-looking spikes had sprouted in a few spots in the strip between the building and the sidewalk.

That woman really should pull those.

Wow, dude, you're messed up. With everything you have going on, you're worried about a couple of weeds in someone else's yard. You need to get a grip.

"Riots broke out for a fifth straight night in Chicago and Atlanta," the CNN newswoman said. "Three people died in Chicago's violence."

The scene on the screen shifted, and Pride Now President Clyde French stood at a lectern. "The deaths, of course, are unfortunate, but we in the LGBTQ community must make sure our hard-won rights are upheld. While we don't condone violence and don't wish to consider Christians as our enemies, they, time and again, have abridged our rights and mistreated us. We must stay the course."

Cole grabbed the remote from the dining room table. The screen went black.

Lord, I don't even know how to pray.

A cardinal flew from a neighbor's split rail fence to the limb of an ornamental cheery tree.

Such freedom, and not worried about a thing.

What was Kiley doing? Was she in her cell? Sitting in some common area? How was she getting along? Were the other inmates hassling her?

~

Dozens of voices echoed through the jail's cavernous lobby, merging into a shapeless wad of noise. Cole hadn't seen Kiley in six days and hadn't experienced a full night's sleep since she was arrested.

He fumbled for the word to describe the three people in line in front of him. Two women and a man. All three were bony, especially the one woman, whose gleaming black hair fell to the middle of her back. The woman's flamingo-like legs were thinner than his forearms. All three visitors had hardened, almost gaunt facial features. Their clothes were worn and faded.

One thing's certain, no one in this line is rolling in money.

Then a new, seemingly unrelated thought arrived.

What if Kiley blames me for this? What if she's angry? Or she thinks I should do more than I can?

No, you can't let yourself think that way. You know where those thoughts come from. Knock it off. Hasn't the enemy used the same tactic since the beginning to get people to stop believing what the Lord has said? The Lord said he'd be with us always, and he will.

Cole stood with his arms spread like wings. The deputy was huge. A large square head on broad square shoulders. Cole looked the man directly in the Adam's apple.

As the wand passed over him, it squealed at his belt buckle and then again at his left front pants pocket.

"Empty your pockets again, sir." The deputy's tone was harsh, accusing.

Cole felt like he was about to be sent to the principal's office.

As he dug into his pocket, he felt the paper clip and pulled it out.

"You can't have that, sir. If you try to bring contraband into the facility again, your visiting privileges will be suspended."

It wasn't like I brought it on purpose, you big jerk. Besides, what was Kiley going to do with it? Pick the lock to her cell?

Cole opened his mouth to speak but lassoed his retort before it could cause further trouble.

After the wand passed over him a second time, squawking only at his belt buckle, another deputy stamped his hand and pointed to a gray steel door. A buzzer wailed, sending Cole's hands to his ears. Cole didn't miss the disdain in the deputy's chuckle as the cop motioned him forward.

The visiting area's near-perfect symmetry impressed Cole. Low stainless-steel stools bolted to the concrete floor stood in a perfect line in front of evenly spaced cubbies. Rear ends spilled over the edges of each of the stools, which looked big enough to comfortably accommodate only people under twelve.

Old-fashioned phone receivers snaked from the same spot in each cubicle. Everyone talked at once, with many of the conversations lively and filled with banter and laughter.

A toddler affixed to his mother's hip in one of the cubicles howled that he wanted to get down. Cole wondered why someone would bring a small child to a jail but then decided the woman probably had no one else to care for the boy.

As soon as Cole sat, a deputy motioned Kiley to her seat behind the glass partition. Her smile was tired but genuine. As Cole picked up the phone, he had no idea why, but he didn't know what to say. What do you say to a loved one in jail?

Kiley broke the ice. "You're a sight for sore eyes."

"You, too. How are you holding up?"

"Okay, I guess. I'm just kind of waiting. What have you been doing?"

"Sitting around mostly. Thinking a lot," Cole said.

Man, could this conversation get any more awkward?

"I thought today about the time you said I wasn't a defendant in a murder trial," Kiley said.

"Why would I have said something like that?" Cole asked with a laugh.

"It was the day I spilled mom's nail polish."

Cole smiled. Kiley was thirteen or fourteen. Their mom was in the living room watching *Jeopardy!* when Kiley ushered him into the kitchen to whisper her admission. She'd committed the crime in her bedroom.

"You have to help me get it out of the rug," she'd pleaded.

Cole had refused and told Kiley to just go explain what happened. "It's not like you killed somebody," he said.

"Yeah, but I used it without permission."

"Well, you shouldn't have. It's best you just take your lumps and move on. Don't try to cover it up. The coverup is always worse than the crime."

"Yeah, you're right," Kiley had said with a sigh, then said she needed to do a couple of things before confessing. With that, she washed and dried a dish, grabbed a bag of cat food from a closet and dumped some into a bowl, then zoomed to the laundry room for her bookbag.

As she sped back toward the kitchen, Cole intercepted her. Putting his hands on her shoulders, he said, "Stop. Just get in there and get it over with. You're just a petty thief, not on trial for murder. If she threatens you with the electric chair, I'll come to your defense."

Loud talking in one of the adjoining stalls reminded Cole of his surroundings.

"I wish this mess was as easy to clean up," she said.

"Frank Hamilton's working really hard to get you out," he said.

A deputy approached Kiley from behind.

"Time's up, Evans," the shaven-headed man said.

Kiley teared up, and Cole swallowed hard to force the lump back down his own throat.

"Whatever happens, don't forget I love you, Sis."

They each touched the partition. With that, the deputy led Kiley away.

15

You've gotta be kidding me.

Cole turned up the old SUV's radio.

"The ban on gatherings at houses of worship is indefinite," the newsman said. "President Gonzalez said the executive order was necessary to stem the violence that erupted after an Ohio pastor's refusal to marry a gay couple. Thirty-four people have died in seven cities."

"Our First Amendment is alive and well," Gonzalez's voice came through the speakers. "This action I am taking today is aimed at protecting life and restoring the national calm."

Can he do that? No way. He can't just suspend the First Amendment.

"I am calling up reserve units from all four branches of our nation's military forces to assure the ban is enforced, and to serve as a deterrent against further aggression on the part of people of religion."

Cole slammed his palm into the steering wheel, then rubbed his forehead.

The entire world's gone nuts.

"In other news, the White House reported progress today in negotiations with Chile and the Copper Producing Consortium. Wall Street is reacting positively . . ."

Cole clicked off the radio.

~

The hood of Abby's old Toyota Carola was raised when Cole pulled into the driveway. The vehicle had probably been maroon when it came off the assembly line. Its color now reminded Cole of dried blood, a dull reddish-brown.

"Is it dead?" he called as he slammed the SUV's door.

"As a doornail. And I have to be at class in an hour." Abby resembled her sister. Same gold- and copper-colored hair. The same gray-green eyes. Abby's face was more angular than Olivia's, but there was no mistaking they were related.

"I'm not a mechanic, but I can take a look."

"I think it's the battery," Abby said

Cole slid into the driver's seat and turned the key. The engine elicited a few small clicks, then gave up the ghost.

"I could jump it," he said.

"That would be awesome."

A few minutes later, he cranked the Toyota's engine, and it sprang to life.

"Thank you so much!" Abby said. "You have no idea what this means. I have an exam today, and I was starting to panic."

"Glad to do it," Cole said. "This may only be a short-term fix, though. You might have the same problem tonight after class."

"Oh, no. I really can't afford a new battery."

"Well, my church has something we call an Agape Fund. It's a petty cash fund for helping people when they get into a jam. We had to use quite a bit of it when our building was damaged a few days ago, but I can see if we have enough in there to cover a battery."

"I can't ask you to do that," Abby said.

"But you can ask God to do it."

Abby tightened her lips and sighed in resignation. "Fine, from where I sit, he owes me one, anyway."

Dare I ask? Sure, why not? She doesn't seem as angry as her sister. I might even learn something useful.

"Does your sister feel the same way? About God, I mean."

Abby tilted her head. "You know, I'm not sure, but I wouldn't be surprised. Things definitely haven't been going her way lately."

Wow, I wonder what's going on. No, I can't ask. Something in her non-verbals isn't right. I'd be prying.

"Is there anything I can help with?"

"No, I don't think so," Abby said.

"Well, I don't want to insinuate myself into her business. But if you don't think it will upset her, let her know I pray for you guys often."

The surprise on Abby's face was genuine. "You do?"

"How could you not pray for Stormy?" Cole said with a smile.

Abby smiled as Cole pulled his door shut.

⁓

Cole used a small open-ended wrench to tighten the nut that held the second battery cable in place.

"So, what classes are you taking?" he asked.

"Nursing," Abby replied. "I'm trying to get a BSN."

"Awesome, you should always have a job when you're done."

"Yeah, it should be pretty recession proof."

"I think you're all set," Cole said, slamming the car's hood.

"I really appreciate this," Abby said.

"Nothing to it. What are neighbors for?" Cole asked.

"Well, you really went out of your way. And when the time is right, I'll tell Olivia you've been praying for us."

"Well, if all else fails, blame it on Stormy."

Abby smiled and cranked the engine.

⁓

Cole slid into the first-row pew in the empty federal courtroom, thirty minutes early. Kiley's was the first case on the docket.

With his head turned to Cole's left, his white face gleaming, the bald eagle on the Great Seal above the judge's bench kept fierce watch. One talon held thirteen arrows. The other offered an olive branch.

To Cole, the two courthouses couldn't have been more different. While the late twentieth-century architecture and décor of the municipal justice center gave the place a dingy worn-out look, the federal courthouse felt new, glossy, progressive.

Three-D monitors equipped the attorneys' tables, judge's bench, and jury box, and with subdued lighting tucked into illuminated channels around the perimeter of a curved ceiling, the room resembled the cabin of a luxury jetliner. Even the people in the federal building seemed different. The federal court employees weren't exactly scripted, but they were definitely more polished than the folks in municipal and county court. They also wore fancier clothes and had more-expensive-looking haircuts.

The appearances meant nothing. The only thing that mattered was what was about to happen to his sister.

Lord, please be with Kiley and the others who've been arrested for standing up for you. Protect them and send your angels to minister to their hearts. Let their arrests somehow bring people back to you, and help America understand you are Lord, a God who sometimes chastens but always loves.

Cole had lost track of the number of arrests. He thought there'd been seventeen in the last week, mostly during protests in Bible Belt states.

A middle-aged woman wearing a federal court ID on a lanyard came through the courtroom's main doors. She strode past and booted a computer at a desk near the judge's bench. A moment later, Cole heard voices. One was Hamilton's. He didn't recognize the other.

"Look, she's accused of killing a man. My guy testifies."

The man talking with Hamilton passed through the rail that separated the gallery from the well—the area where the attorneys sat. He turned right and took a seat at the U.S. Attorney's table, the one nearest the jury box.

Hamilton went the opposite direction but turned around to face Cole, with the rail between them.

"Okay, Cole, Peters over here is going to try to get the video thrown out," he said, nodding toward the prosecutor's table. "I expected as much. We're just going to have to see how the judge rules. I'll do everything I can."

The courtroom door swung open. The woman's butter-blond hair was pulled into a low bun, and she wore crisp high-end office attire. Black pants, white blouse, black blazer. She carried an expensive-looking black leather briefcase. Smooth skin and a fresh manicure completed the declaration that she was well paid and close to the top of the food chain in whatever world she belonged to.

Hamilton's face registered recognition.

"Jennifer. Thanks for doing this," Hamilton said as he reached to shake the woman's hand. "Cole, this is Jennifer Michaels."

The woman's handshake was business-like, and her brown eyes bored into him.

"Hopefully, this will get thrown out today," she said, "but honestly, Pastor Evans, we'll probably be back in here a few times before this is over."

Cole simultaneously appreciated the honesty and worried for his sister.

~

Kiley looked better. She still wore no makeup and had circles under her eyes, but she was better-kempt, the shackles were gone, and she wore a business suit.

Her eyes glistened with fear as a deputy marshal led her across the courtroom. Cole tried to give her his most confident smile as she moved to her seat next to Hamilton. The corners of her mouth turned up, but the worry never left her eyes.

Kiley sat up straight but not stiff, with her gaze aimed at the person speaking. Hamilton had coached her, no doubt.

Long and lean, Peters glided to the podium in three easy strides. His receding black hair was combed straight back, creating an Eddie Munster widow's peak at the top of his forehead. Cole stifled a chuckle.

In a matter of minutes, Peters laid out his case. Trace Johnson, a gay man, died because Kiley purposely drove a pickup truck into a crowd of gay-rights supporters, hoping she would strike and kill at least one of them.

Hamilton studied Peters and the witness, and he took careful notes. He didn't cross-examine. Shoulders back, gaze steady, swept back silver hair gleaming, he radiated a quiet certainty. When the government rested its case, Frank Hamilton eased to the podium, his yellow legal pad in hand.

"What was the nature of the conversation following the church service on June twenty-seventh?" he asked Reed Bryant, the fireplug who'd confirmed to the rest of the church that a mob had gathered.

Reed was all business, his tone assured, but his posture and delivery respectful. Gone was the sarcastic demeanor that normally emanated from him.

"Ms. Evans didn't want to get behind the wheel. She was afraid Pastor Evans might be hurt if he went out and talked with the crowd. She begged him to find some other way out of the situation, but Pastor Evans said more people could get to their cars safely if he created a diversion," Reed testified.

"Did she say or do anything that led you to believe she was angry at the protesters?" Hamilton asked.

"No, if anything, she looked frightened."

Hamilton called Tom Henderson, who testified to the same things.

Hamilton then called the Jeremy Timmons, the TV cameraman.

Although he still wore long hair and a beard, the man had cleaned up. The beard was neat, and the wavy red hair was trimmed and fell to the collar of a button-down white shirt and sport jacket.

As he had in the state proceeding, Hamilton took the newsman frame by frame through the video.

"Does the video appear to show that the truck was at a complete stop when Mr. Johnson was hit with the brick?"

"It does," Timmons said. "The truck doesn't move until well after the man is on the ground."

Yes, Lord, please let this work. Let me leave this courthouse arm-in-arm with Kiley.

Peters, the government's attorney, wore an almost cocky expression when he got back behind the podium.

"You said you've been a videographer for several years, isn't that correct, Mr. Timmons?" Peters asked.

"Yes."

"Have you had occasion to edit things out of videos during that time?"

"Yes, videos can be edited," Timmons said.

"Is it possible to edit things *into* video footage?" Peters asked.

"It is possible? Yes, but—"

"Nothing further, Your Honor," the prosecutor said, cutting Timmons off.

Cole's insides turned to liquid.

When Hamilton finished putting on his defense, Peters called a rebuttal witness. Liam Brody looked like he'd been plucked out of the halls of the nearest high school. Tall and lanky, with dark eyes and pitch-black hair that he wore spiked straight up, he swaggered toward the witness stand.

Does this guy even shave, yet? He's too young to be an expert in much of anything, isn't he?

Most annoying was an enthusiasm and exuberance that came across when he spoke.

"Certainly, the videos could have been doctored," he said. "Anybody can make anything look like anything else."

"If it please the court, I'd like to admit the following video into evidence," the prosecutor said.

Hamilton was out of his chair. "Objection! Wait a minute, Your Honor, I haven't seen this video."

"My apologies, Your Honor, I just came into possession of it this morning," Peters said.

"How long is it?" the judge asked Peters.

Peters looked at Brody.

"About thirty seconds, Your Honor," Brody said.

"Ten-minute recess while defense counsel looks at the video." The judge tapped the gavel, and people in the gallery began to stir. Three people squeezed past Cole and moved to the aisle. Hamilton, the judge, and Peters, carrying a flash drive, left through a door to the right of the judge's bench.

~

Hamilton looked grim faced. A vertical line creased the center of his deeply lined brow.

This can't be good. Lord, please help Kiley. Please don't let this go to trial.

Brody climbed back onto the stand.

"You created this video, is that correct, Mr. Brody?" Peters asked.

"Yes, sir."

"And why did you create it?"

"It just shows that you can make a video that seems to show anything."

"Did I, or anyone else, ask you to make this video?"

"No, sir, I just thought it would be a good illustration."

"So, you took it upon yourself," Peters said.

"Yes, sir."

"One last question, Mr. Brody. Had you ever seen the judge in person before today's proceedings?" Peters asked.

"No, sir, not in person."

"Go ahead and play the video," Peters said.

The video began with the robed judge putting a coin into a parking meter with the federal courthouse in the background. An animated hot pink pig appeared in the top right corner of the screen, performed a barrel roll, then swooped to the sidewalk. The Fifth Street traffic ignored the animal. The stone-faced judge hopped astride the chubby creature, like a cowboy in a 1930s comedy. He then pointed toward the building. The scene shifted to the inside of a courtroom. The video ended when the pig flew in through an open window and gently deposited the judge behind the bench.

Laughter rippled through the courtroom.

Cole smiled, even as his heart sank.

"It beats taking the elevator," the judge said, sending more boisterous laughter through the courtroom.

Five minutes later, the hearing ended.

"I find probable cause to believe a crime was committed. The prosecution will move forward. Ms. Evans will remain in custody of the Hamilton County Sheriff's Office without bail, awaiting transfer to the U.S. Marshals Service."

Cole couldn't breathe. He wanted to double over as spasms ravaged his stomach.

~

The gaggle of reporters at the bottom of the courthouse stairs began shouting questions as soon as Cole exited the building.

Great, I have to deal with these lunkheads. You guys want my reaction? I'd like to shove a microphone down someone's throat. How's that for a reaction?

Cole stood straighter and walked with purpose.

If they try to block my path, I swear I'll crash into them and knock them out of the way.

The Red Sea parted, and the shouting reporters let him pass.

One reporter's question rang above the rest. "Are you going to close your church?"

The words shot out of his mouth before he could stop them. "No. As long as Jesus allows New Hope to exist, we're going to keep talking about him, whether the government likes it or not. And we're going to lovingly point out sin, whether the government likes it or not. And, believe me, we're not being mean. We just trust that doing things God's way will result in joy and peace in the long run, even if things get tough on this side of eternity."

"Do you think gay people deserve to go to hell?" a reporter called out.

"Everybody deserves to go to hell. Fortunately, Jesus gave us a way to avoid that."

Way to go, Cole. They'll have a heyday with that. When will you learn to keep your big mouth shut?

He pushed through the crowd.

Olivia stood at the end of the throng. She said nothing, a trace of compassion in her eyes. She held out a sheet of reporter's notebook paper folded in half.

Do I take that? If I do, will every reporter in the county thrust notes at me every time I walk by? If she just wants an interview, I'm going to be even angrier. Maybe Abby said something about the whole prayer business. Who knows?

The space between them was closing rapidly. He had to decide. He reached out, took the slip of paper, and kept walking.

He was in Don's borrowed SUV a few moments later. He cranked the key to turn on the air conditioning, then he unfolded the note.

"I just wanted to say I'm sorry and thank you again. Give me a call some time. Off the record. I'm sure you have my number, but just in case . . ." Olivia's number stretched neatly across the bottom of the page.

What does she really want? Her last two news stories were fair enough. She stuck to the facts and didn't twist anything around.

He read the note again.

"Off the record." Okay, maybe. Does that mean she doesn't report anything I say, or does it mean she reports it but doesn't attribute it to me?

Okay, do I trust her? Maybe a little but not fully.

I could call. I'd just have to be careful. If all else fails, we could always talk about Jesus.

16

WHEN COLE THUMBED THROUGH his phone for a 5 a.m. news fix, his tirade at the bottom of the courthouse steps had gone viral. The female news anchor, with a sandy-haired feather cut and stern blue eyes, said more than a million people had watched the video.

"But do this pastor's words constitute hate speech?" asked the middle-aged man with a shock of wavy dark hair. A text box at the bottom of the screen identified him as William Hunt, ABC News legal analyst.

"If it does, what can the government do about it?" the news anchor asked.

He turned off the TV. When Cole looked out his living room window, media trucks lined his street, and camera people and reporters shot stand-ups on his front sidewalk. When he went to the website for one of the nation's more liberal news organizations, the headline, "Preaching in America: Legal or not?" blazed across the screen.

An ACLU spokesman was among those quoted. "This guy can say whatever he wants, even if what he says is ridiculous. If people are stupid enough to go listen to him, that's their problem."

Cole drew his blinds, put on a pot of coffee, and cracked open *Lord of the Rings*. He'd be holed up a while. The news crews wouldn't leave until something more interesting came along. Fortunately, given America's short attention span, he'd probably be able to leave the following day.

Cole had read Tolkien's trilogy four times since he was a teenager. He couldn't wait to re-immerse himself in the world of Frodo, Samwise, and Merry. He smiled as he studied the book's dog-eared cover and yellowing pages.

Prologue

1. Concerning Hobbits

This book is largely concerned with Hobbits, and from its pages a reader may discover much of their character and a little of their history.

His phone vibrated a second later. Olivia's name stood out in white letters on the screen.

Great, I have to refuse to comment again. Well, I suppose she's just doing her job.

"Hey, Olivia."

"I figured you'd be up."

"Why, have you been stalking me?"

"Absolutely. When you have nothing better to do, you spy on your neighbors."

Cole smiled at the sarcasm.

"I'm just calling to see if you have any comment. Looks like you're a rock star."

"I don't really want to say anything about it," Cole said.

"Okay. Just needed to check," she said. "Have a good day."

Okay, was that sarcastic, too, or does she really hope I have a good day?

Cole watched Olivia's news story a half hour later. She didn't sensationalize, but why would she need to? The facts themselves were sensational enough.

Had her attitude changed? At least to one of neutrality? She'd apologized for acting like a madwoman at church that morning, and she'd sounded sincere. Plus, she hadn't taken part in the reporters' feeding frenzy at the courthouse the previous afternoon. Had Abby said something to her that had won her over?

Cole unfolded the note and stared at it. He smiled at the occasional cursive mixed in with the strand of block letters.

Looks a little like Holly's. Do her shopping lists include words like pl8s and H_2O melon?

More importantly, Lord, do I call her when she's off the clock?

God was silent.

～

The microwave clock read 5:01 p.m. Two media trucks remained on the street.

It probably wouldn't hurt to reach out. You can always end the conversation. Who knows, the Lord may have something in mind.

She answered on the second ring.

"I wondered if you'd call," she said.

"I debated for a minute and decided I could pray the Lord send a lightning bolt or something if you got snarky."

Olivia chuckled. "Thanks. I love you, too." She was quiet for a beat and then continued. "Hey, I wanted to apologize and thank you again for a few weeks ago at the church."

"You already thanked me and apologized, but you're welcome, and apology accepted."

"I guess I just kind of want to make amends. God's been showing me some stuff. A few days ago, I actually prayed. It was the first time in years. Maybe decades. And it was like God said, 'Hi, Olivia! Do you need a do-over?' So, here I am."

"I sure didn't see that coming. Can I ask what happened?"

"What didn't? I had about three weeks that were off-the-hook crazy. Do you remember seeing that old red Chevy parked down the street some mornings right before all this stuff started with your sister?" Olivia asked.

Red Chevy. Red Chevy.

"Oh, yeah, I remember!" Cole said.

"Well, that was my ex. He suddenly decided he was going to start stalking me."

"That's awful. What happened? He actually stalked you?"

"Yeah, he'd hang out on our street and then, at one point, he showed up at the TV station. I thought about taking out a restraining order but didn't think it would do any good. The only thing Ty understands is violence."

"Oh. Not good. But I haven't seen him around lately. What happened?"

"I had my boss threaten to kick his—beat him up. Which was a mistake. Because my boss thought since he ran off my ex, he could start hitting on me. Which was disgusting. While all that was going on, I wrecked my car—"

"Yeah, I remember seeing the crumpled fender. I meant to ask you what happened—"

"And to top it all off, for a couple of weeks after the protest, I still had really bad headaches from getting hit in the head with that rock."

Cole couldn't stifle a sad chuckle. "Sounds like you had your own personal black cloud."

"Yeah, my whole world felt like it unraveled. But, do you know what? I remember the exact minute when things started to change. I had taken Stormy to my older sister's in Louisville, and I was sleeping over at a friend's house because I was afraid my ex might show up again. And I was lying there on the living room sofa. It was the middle of the night, and my friend was in the bedroom having loud sex with this revolting guy she's been hanging around with. And I just couldn't take it anymore. I lay there on that couch and stared up at the ceiling and thought, 'What in the world am I doing here, and how did I get here? Better yet, how do I leave?' Finally, I just prayed, 'God, if you're really there, help me.' And somehow, a peace came over me. I got up, went to get Stormy, and went back home. I've been at peace ever since. My situation hasn't changed that much. My ex could show up at any minute, and my boss is still a jerk, but something inside me has changed. I know that whatever happens, Jesus will get me through it."

"Wow, that's awesome! God is good," Cole said.

"You know what else? That stupid bandage you put on my head played a part in everything."

"How's that?"

"At first, I hated it because it looked stupid, and I had to make sure my hair covered it while I was working. And I hated you for putting it there because you were a Christian, and Christians were supposed to be evil. But for several days after the protest, I thought about what you'd said that night, that you thought Jesus was a lot like the guy who helped us move. And the more I thought about it, the more it seemed like *God* put the bandage there because *he* wanted to bandage me up."

"That's a neat thing to realize."

"I went to church as a kid but stopped during college. Lying there on my friend's couch that night, I realized I'd left him. He'd never left me. I somehow understood there's a connection between the rotten stuff that happens in life and our free will. I grasped that God gives us free will so we can choose to love him."

"That's true," Cole said. "That would preach."

"Then, Abby told me you've been praying for us. Even though I haven't exactly done anything to endear myself to you. So, I was wondering if you'd be interested in grabbing a coffee some time. Maybe you can give me some advice about where in the Bible to start reading."

Do I have a couple bucks? Probably. If not, I'll trust the Lord to help me figure it out. He seems to be in the middle of this.

"You understand reading the Bible is politically incorrect, don't you?" Cole said.

"Well, you're not living right if you don't honk someone off every now and then."

Cole laughed. "That's for sure. How about Tuesday afternoon?"

Olivia agreed.

"But before then, if you want to understand how much Jesus loves us, start reading the book of John."

"I will," Olivia said. "Do you know that coffee shop on MLK, just off UC's campus?"

∽

Before his eyes had fully adjusted to the dim lighting in the rustic old place—with its creaky wood floors and painted wood paneling—Cole saw her. Olivia looked mortified. A weird-looking guy stood next to her table. The guy was shaven headed, except for one long circular clump of pink and bright yellow hair that was somehow arranged in a six-inch-tall spike. The mess looked like some kind of psychedelic antenna coming out of the top of his head.

Cole didn't know what the guy had said, but Olivia looked like she was ready to ram her fingers down her throat in order to hurl on him.

He needed to get there quickly.

"Hey, thanks for the invite. Did you get a good story?" he asked.

Olivia's eyes softened in relief, and the tension in her face eased.

"Better get right to it, huh," Cole said. Hopefully, Antenna Head would get the hint.

"Yeah. Can you just jump right in?" Olivia said as she pulled a reporter's notebook from her purse.

Okay, so what do I say now? Is that notebook part of Olivia's spiel to get rid of Antenna Head, or is she going to take notes?

This guy looks high as a kite. I need to start talking about something. Anything.

"What did you think about the court case the other day?" he asked.

"Honestly, I was surprised the news video got thrown out," Olivia said.

Antenna Head didn't get the hint and wanted to start speaking, but Olivia didn't give him the chance. Turning toward the intruder, she said, "Like I said a minute ago, no, thanks, it's just not my thing. Maybe you could go crash someplace for a while until you come down."

Olivia had spoken in a caring and pleasant tone, but her efforts were lost on Antenna Head. He bristled, shoved an empty chair into one side of the table, and hurled a string of profanities, generally aimed at Olivia.

Olivia looked like she wanted to rake her fingernails across his eyeballs.

Okay, what do I do? This guy's irrational, maybe even delusional. He might also be on some kind of adrenaline rush due to whatever he's using. Choose your words carefully, Cole. You can tangle with the guy if you need to, but let's try to avoid it.

"Dude," Cole said. "When I came in, I thought you might be a pretty cool guy. But, now, seriously? Do you want to be *that* guy?"

For a second, Cole thought Antenna Head would get even more violent. The man's body tensed, and he glared.

Cole stood up, every muscle tight. He and Antenna Head were about the same height, but Cole was more muscular.

Every eye in the coffee shop turned toward Cole and Antenna Head. The background clatter ceased.

Antenna Head shifted his glare from Cole to Olivia and back again. Then, his shoulders slumped, and he stomped toward the door.

When the door closed behind him, Olivia let out a huge sigh.

Brief applause broke out.

"Oh, my gosh! What was that?" Cole asked.

"Thanks," Olivia said. "For a second, I thought I would have to use my pepper spray."

"Good thing you didn't, you would've ruined his hair," Cole said.

They both laughed.

"I thought you were going to punch the guy," Olivia said.

"I didn't know what I was going to do, but for a second I thought he was about to take a swing," Cole said.

"It would've made a great news teaser. Pastor punches punk. More at eleven."

"I see a pattern here. Every time I get near you, someone in the vicinity goes berserk."

"It's a special gift, I guess," she said.

"Oh, is that what you call it?"

Cole excused himself to grab a coffee and asked Olivia if she needed anything else. She declined.

When he returned, Olivia thanked him for meeting her.

"So, what's up with you and Jesus these days?" he asked.

"I'm not mad at God, anymore, but we still have a few things to work out," she said.

"Ugh, mad at God. Been there. That's a lousy place to be. When I've gotten to that spot, I've always felt so helpless. Which made me even madder."

"Well, I've worked through a lot of anger, I think. I'm just trying to understand why things happened the way they did."

"You might not find out on this side of heaven," Cole said. "Can I ask what happened that put you and God on the outs? You don't have to tell me if you don't want to. I'm just curious."

"My parents took us to church when my sisters and I were little, but then my mom died in a car wreck eleven years ago. I was seventeen, my sister Abby was fourteen, and my oldest sister Janna was nineteen. She was at college when the wreck happened.

"I was so angry afterward. I just couldn't understand why a God who's supposed to be so good would let that happen."

"I'm so sorry. I'd be lying if I said I understood his ways all the time," Cole said. "And even in instances when I do understand, it doesn't always make some situations easy to endure. I just try to remind myself that Romans 8:28 is still true and that he works all things together for good for those who love him. He even uses the bad stuff."

"Yeah, I guess so," she said, but she didn't sound convinced.

"I think Anne Graham Lotz, Billy Graham's daughter, said it best," Cole said. "In writing about watching her mother suffer on her deathbed, Anne said, 'During the times when you and I can't trace God's hand of purpose, we must trust his heart of love.'"

Olivia looked pensive for a moment then shook her head. "I guess you're right," she said. "In the end we have no choice but to decide God's good or he isn't."

They sat for a moment in comfortable silence. Cole sipped his coffee. "Are you and your older sister close?" he asked.

"I'd say we're still pretty close. She's in Kentucky, about ninety minutes away. She trains horses. Even trains thoroughbreds sometimes."

"Wow, sounds like big bucks."

"She does okay. Stormy loves to go down there. That's where she was the night I cried out to Jesus."

Cole took a sip of his coffee.

"So, tell me about your family," Olivia said. "Any other siblings?"

"No, just me and my sister. My mom lives in Arizona now, and my dad passed away seven years ago. He was sixty-two."

"Wow. Young. I'm sorry for your loss."

"Thanks. My Pops and I were close, even when I was a teenager."

Olivia nodded.

"So, why'd you choose journalism?" Cole asked. "Seems like a hard way to make a living these days."

"My grandpa told me about this White House scandal called Watergate, way back in the 1970s. He said these two journalists exposed the whole thing, and that the president resigned, but that it was their work that helped clean up the government. I thought they did a good thing."

Even if the media had moved further left politically than Cole liked, he had to admit Olivia's heart was in the right place.

"I'll bet you've seen a little bit of everything," Cole said.

"You can say that again!"

"What's the craziest story you've ever been assigned to?"

"It wasn't the story, it was what happened afterward," Olivia said. "The story was just this ground-breaking where an old industrial park was going to be cleaned up and repurposed. Out where that Little League and driving range complex is on the east side."

"I know the place, the one with the sports bars and stuff attached to it," Cole said.

"Yeah. Well, we were just wrapping up the story, and I'd just finished my stand-up when this scrawny half-starved girl came running around the corner of one of those big metal buildings and pretty much collapsed right in front of the whole group of us. Turns out she was a sex slave who was being held in one of those buildings."

"I remember that story!" Cole said. "How long ago was that?"

"It's been about three years."

"Whatever happened with that?"

"The guy who was holding them is in prison. Seventy-five years without parole, I think. And the girls are all doing well, as far as I know. The girl who got loose and alerted us, Manuela, actually has started writing a book."

"Amazing," Cole said.

"It's a nice happy ending," Olivia said. She sipped her coffee. "But I bet you hear some pretty weird stuff, too."

"Kind of. Pastors hear people's darkest secrets. After a while, you recognize a theme. We're all broken and hurting, and we all need Jesus. We just express our brokenness in different ways."

"So, when did you know you wanted to be a pastor?"

"I'm not sure. It seems like I always knew. My grandpa had preached, and so had my dad, and when I was little, I just knew that's what God had for me. He even confirmed it with a dream."

Olivia raised an eyebrow. "You're serious?" she said. "That stuff really happens? Okay, I'll bite. Let's hear it."

"We're still totally off the record, right? Nothing I say gets reported."

Olivia nodded. "Yes. I'm off the clock."

"Good. I can just imagine this story on the news, making me look like a nutcase."

Olivia laughed. "If I think you're a nutcase I'll just keep it between the two of us. Or maybe post it on Facebook," she said playfully.

"Gee, thanks."

Cole started with the story about his third-grade career day and the abuse he took at the hands of his classmates.

"When I got home that night, I told my parents what happened . . ."

17

THE PICNIC AT JAKE Moore's house had been planned for weeks, and Cole saw no reason to skip it. If anything, Gonzalez's attempt to ban worship made meeting even more necessary.

When Cole walked through the back gate, Jake manned the grill, his baseball cap turned backward, a flowery apron covering his T-shirt and shorts. Sweat beaded on his brow, and his forearms shone. The stainless-steel box in front of him belched tiny puffs of smoke.

"You're a sight in that apron, dude. I should post a picture."

"Never mess with a man who wields power over the welfare of your burger," Jake warned.

"Okay, you win."

"Medium rare, right?"

"Yup."

Cole inhaled deeply to savor the aroma.

He thought of Kiley. At the previous year's picnic, she'd helped Jake's wife Tosha with the salad. They'd come out of the kitchen with Kiley laughing so hard, she'd nearly doubled over. Despite Cole's best efforts, she'd never told him why.

Lord, just give her as good a day as she can have. Give her strength. Keep her safe.

As Cole shook Jake's hand, Don and Teresa Fisher hauled food from the house to the picnic table.

Tom Henderson came through the gate and set a cooler of soft drinks in a shady spot on the deck.

"What's up, fellas!" Tom called with a wave.

Somehow it didn't seem right. Everything seemed too normal. People ate, drank, and laughed. TVs babbled, advertisers tried to separate viewers from their money, and kids had their faces glued to video games.

In that vein, the chatter during lunch was typical. Don spun a tale about how his dog ate one of his work boots. Teresa and Tom's wife Janice talked about Halloween sales already starting where Teresa worked. Don and Cole talked about why the Cincinnati Reds should fire their manager. And Teresa and Tosha talked about a couple's new baby.

When they retired to the cool dark-green shade of a grove of oak trees a half hour later, the conversation became more serious.

"Okay guys, Frank Hamilton says the Christian Liberties Council has already filed a lawsuit, and he's pretty sure a federal judge will stop this worship ban from taking effect. There's a hearing somewhere in Alabama tomorrow. Hamilton expects some type of emergency order. But this situation does give us an idea of what's coming, and it might not be a bad idea for New Hope to look for some kind of hideout," Cole said.

"Yeah, you're probably right," Tom said. "But how do we hide an entire church?"

"We'd have to find someplace where a couple hundred people can get together without being noticed. How do you do that?" Teresa asked.

"How do you feed five thousand people with five barley loaves and two fish?" Don asked.

"Touché," Teresa said.

"Aren't we getting ahead of ourselves?" Jake asked. "This whole ban thing will go away. Gonzalez just put it in place because people were killing each other."

"Maybe, but I think he might've been using the violence as an excuse to achieve his long-term goal. I'd rather have a plan and never need it than to need a hiding spot and have no idea where to find one," Cole said.

Murmurs of assent went around the circle, and the group prayed.

"So, do we hide in plain sight or try to find some spot in the middle of nowhere?" Tosha asked.

"I'm probably not much of a criminal, but I don't think hiding in plain sight works," Cole said. "It might if the government weren't already looking at churches, but if Gonzalez is willing to call up reserves to enforce his so-called temporary ban, who knows what he'd do? He probably has a plan to form some sort of Bible gestapo. I think we find someplace off the grid, or at least some isolated place way out in the country."

They talked for twenty minutes. In the end, they agreed to start looking for hiding places.

∼

Cole climbed the two steps to the pulpit a few days later and looked over the crowd. It was much sparser than it had been two weeks earlier, on the day of the protest.

"Well, I'm glad we're all here" he began. "At least for the moment, sanity has prevailed in the courts, and I'm aware of no gay people and Christians fighting. Let's have church."

18

JEM AND SCOUT HAD just snuck into the courthouse when Cole's phone pulled him away from *To Kill A Mockingbird* and Harper Lee's Depression-era Macomb.

Olivia's name adorned the screen.

Kiley's case is going to go on for a while. Maybe I should add a picture to Olivia's contact.

Seriously? Dude, you haven't even decided if you want a distant relationship with her.

"Hey there, don't tell me," he said. "A legion of Antenna Heads has invaded your newsroom."

Olivia laughed. "No, not yet. Our intelligence tells us they're hibernating."

"Well, that's good," Cole said. "I wouldn't want to have to go over there with hair clippers."

"Hey, as much as I hate to ask, my bosses want me to check whether you'll talk about Kiley."

"No, I don't think so. I'm sure she wouldn't appreciate it. Besides, I might say something that could expose the rest of the church."

"I think you know me well enough by now to know I'd never do that," Olivia said.

"I agree. I don't think you would on purpose, but you might use something I say, and people might somehow put two and two together. I just don't want to take the risk."

"I promise I'll be really careful," Olivia said.

"I know you would. I trust you. But the risk is just too great. The less said the better."

"Okay, fair enough. I can honestly tell my news director I tried," Olivia said. "How's your day?"

"It's awesome. I'm reading *To Kill a Mockingbird* and eating a big bowl of popcorn."

Okay, should he ask the next question? Sure, what could it hurt, except his pride if she said no?

"I was just wondering," Cole said, "would you want to have dinner with a hatemongering Christian?"

"Only if no one throws rocks or badgers me to go get high."

"It's settled, then. You leave the chaos at home, and I'll leave my Taser."

~

Olivia emerged from the house next door the following night before Cole had even locked his front door. She wore a pastel yellow sundress that accented her tan and fell a few inches below the knee. Her gold-and-copper-colored hair flowed past her shoulders.

At the car, she slid into his arms for a loose hug.

Yeah, I could hang out here for a very long time.

Ten minutes later, the aromas of garlic, oregano, and basil wafted into the street.

Tucked into a cranny in the middle of the block, Leone's was the real deal. Luca and Valentina Leone had immigrated from Italy about twenty years earlier. Neither fit the roly-poly image of the Italian chef portrayed on Italian food packaging when Cole was a child. Both were tall and lean, and God had blessed them with swarthy good looks. Luca typically worse all black, including a necktie, while Valentina usually sported something with a plunging neckline and tight fashion jeans.

As soon as Cole and Olivia walked in, Luca strode around the host's podium. "Cole, my boy! Come in! Let me look at you." He held Cole by the upper arms, stepped back, and looked him up and down. "You're too skinny. You need to get in here and eat."

Cole laughed. "I'm sure I won't succumb before I get to the table. How's Valentina?"

"She's good. Excited about becoming a *nonna*."

"Yes, I heard your daughter's expecting! I'm so happy for you guys! When is she due?"

"In six weeks. We can't wait!"

"Where is she, again?"

"Des Moines. We're taking a week off to see her—and her husband, of course—and the baby."

"That's great. Are you closing the place for the week?" Cole gestured toward the dining room.

"No, Tony can handle it. It will be good for him. You know, he's said he wants to take over when we're ready to retire."

"I hadn't heard that. It will be good to keep it in the family." Cole turned toward Olivia. "Tony's Luca and Valentina's son."

"What in the world is the matter with me?" Luca said. "I'm rambling on like an old man. Who is this beautiful woman?" Luca said.

"This beautiful woman is my friend Olivia," Cole said.

Immediately, Luca's arm was around her shoulder.

"*Bella donna!* Welcome! Come on in. So sorry you had to come with this guy," he said, laughing and casting a thumb Cole's direction.

Olivia laughed. "Sounds like you have the goods on him."

"We'll talk later, and I'll fill you in," Luca kidded.

Cole and Olivia's table occupied a small alcove near the back of the room. Soft instrumental music whispered through the speakers, and the crystal and silver gleamed in the low light atop the burgundy table linens.

The candlelight accented Olivia's features, and her eyes shone.

"Luca was right. You do look beautiful tonight," Cole said.

Olivia smiled, blushed slightly and gave him a flirtatious sideward glance, "You aren't so bad-looking yourself. Why hasn't someone already snatched you up?"

∼

Her hand felt small and smooth, their fingers interlocked as they strolled toward the ice cream shop.

"You never answered my question at dinner. Why hasn't someone snatched you up, yet?" Olivia asked.

"It almost happened once. We were engaged," Cole said.

"So, what happened?" Olivia asked.

"Cancer."

Olivia stopped, faced him and put a hand on his arm. "I'm so sorry," she said. "I had no idea." Pity emanated from her eyes.

"Thanks, it's fine. You couldn't have known. I lost her three years ago."

"That must have been hard," Olivia said.

"I'd never felt such pain. My whole world felt like it ended." He searched Olivia's face. Had he scared her? No, it looked like she appreciated the openness.

"I felt that way when my mom died," Olivia said.

"For a while, it was almost like I had to remind myself to breathe," Cole said. "At first, getting through each hour was a chore. Then an hour became an afternoon, and an afternoon a day. I didn't realize it until I met you, but slowly, day by day, I've been healing."

"What was her name?" Olivia asked.

"Holly."

"That's pretty."

"It is, and it suited her. But I realize, I need to move on."

Olivia nodded silently. She gently squeezed his hand.

He was quiet for a beat.

She squeezed his hand again, and they resumed their stroll.

"It makes you think when someone dies that young," she said.

"It does. We're not guaranteed tomorrow, are we?" Cole fell silent for a second, then continued. "But it made me a better pastor—made me more empathetic."

They strolled in comfortable silence for a few seconds.

"So, what's on your bucket list?" Cole said.

"Maybe the Great Wall or the Pyramids. Maybe a place in the country."

"What if a big-city news job comes your way?"

"A month ago, I'd have jumped on it," Olivia said. "Now, I'm not so sure. Hopefully, I'd try to do what I thought the Lord wanted. Hopefully, I'd listen. Once I get my mind set on something, I can be hardheaded."

"Really?" Cole said, his voice playful. "Like when you want to go cover a story even though you got hit in the head with a rock?"

Olivia hit him on the arm and laughed. "Stop it. You're rotten." Her eyes twinkled.

"I can't be rotten. I'm a pastor," Cole said.

Another playful swat landed on his bicep.

A few minutes later they sat at a table under the ice cream shop's bright lights and dug plastic spoons into a banana split.

"What about you? What's on your bucket list?" Olivia said.

"Honestly, I don't know anymore. A few years ago, I would've said the same things you did, but with the world as crazy as it is, I think I'd just

like to pastor New Hope as long as possible. It may sound lame, or like I
have an overexaggerated sense of my own importance, but I'm absolutely
passionate about helping people understand how much God loves them."

A tiny dab of whipped cream had affixed itself to Olivia's left cheek.
He felt the smile reach his eyes.

"What? Why are you looking at me like that?" Olivia said.

"It's all good. I can take care of it," he said. He reached across the
table and gently ran his thumb across her cheek.

Olivia blushed, then beamed.

The porch light cast delicate shadows across Olivia's face.

She's absolutely beautiful. So, now what? Hug? Peck on the cheek?
What are pastors supposed to do at the end of first dates?

He looked into her eyes. What would her body feel like against his?
Would her kiss be gentle? Insistent? Both?

Her arms wrapped around his neck as she melted into him.

His heart thumped.

When she broke the embrace, he held her hand for a few extra beats,
lost in her gaze.

"I had a really great time tonight," she said.

"Me, too."

So, do I kiss her. Clearly, she wants me to.

Cole moved in. And the front door flew open.

"Mom! Aunt Abby made popcorn, and she bought me a Coke!"
Stormy's voice was almost a squeal.

Her excitement was understandable. Popcorn and Coke were true
luxuries these days.

Cole smiled at her excitement. "Wow, that's cool. What else did you
do?"

"We watched *The Little Mermaid*, and Aunt Abby painted my toes."

Cobalt blue polish covered the tiny toenails.

"Nice! Do you think she would do mine, too?" Cole said.

"Gross, Mr. Evans," Stormy said, giggling. "Boys don't paint their
toes!"

"Hey, it never hurts to ask," Cole said.

Stormy rolled her eyes, producing an uncanny resemblance to
Olivia.

"Did you remember my poster board, Mom?" Stormy asked.

"It's in the car. Now why don't you go back inside and give me and Cole some privacy?

"Eww. Disgusting!"

"No peeking from between the blinds," Cole kidded.

"Eww." The door slammed behind her.

"I'm not sure she knows what to make of this," Olivia said.

"I'm not sure I do either, but I sure hope to figure it out. Call you later this week?" he asked.

"You'd better."

He pulled himself away and floated next door.

~

Cole stared at the picture and looked into Holly's eyes.

"It's time, isn't it?" he said into the quiet.

She's watching over you. She wants you to be happy.

He held the picture in both hands. "I loved you with all my heart," he said. He gently placed the picture in his top dresser drawer. He'd put it with the rest of the old photos tomorrow.

19

Cole pulled up a stool at the counter that ran along most of the left side of the room. Like the tables at The Pitchfork, the sheen on the white speckled countertop had worn off or been wiped away in spots from decades of use and cleaning.

As Cole waited for Don Fisher, a waitress named Chandra waved from across the room. Melody, the woman who waited on Cole and his posse on Wednesday mornings, hadn't spoken to him since she realized Cole had refused to do Trace Johnson's wedding.

"Trina will be right there," Chandra said.

Trina emerged from the kitchen with a pot of coffee as if on cue.

"Hey, Cole, how are things going? I saw on the news what happened with your sister. I'm really sorry," she said.

Trina Sommers had waitressed at The Pitchfork for the six years Cole had been coming in. She was a couple of years younger than he was. They'd gone to high school together. She'd been pretty, a cheerleader. Predictably, she married a football jock, a guy named Jerry. They were still together and had a couple of young kids. A few shallow crow's feet had etched themselves around her liquid brown eyes, but she was still attractive. Slim with chiseled features, she wore a black tank top and jeans, and she'd pulled her dark auburn hair into a ponytail.

"Things are a long way from over, sweetie," she said. "You hang in there."

She patted his hand twice and poured the coffee. Her touch was light and delicate.

"Thanks, Trina."

"Anybody else coming?"

"Just one."

She set down another eggshell-colored stoneware mug.

Cole wished he could call his dad. He'd know what to do.

His dad had died two weeks after his sixty-second birthday. Cole hadn't even gotten to say good-bye. When the nurse led him through the emergency room to the bay where his father lay, his mom sat in a hard, plastic chair, silent tears streaming down her cheeks.

"The doctor called it a widow-maker," she said. "He was gone before he hit the ground. He was outside grilling."

A fresh round of sobs cut off her explanation.

Cole had been devastated. Pops was his hero, a status that became permanent on Thanksgiving Day when Cole was seven. It was warm for November, and Cole and his cousin Ethan had become superheroes. Cole had donned a mask from his toy box and a towel as a cape and transformed himself into Batman. Ethan, with a white paper star pinned to his chest and a saucer-shaped plastic sled as his "mighty shield," had morphed into Captain America.

They'd vanquished several arch villains in the empty lot next door and were ready to round up the Riddler when the neighbor's dog appeared. Part Rottweiler and part Lab, the huge black beast came to the edge of the lot where they were playing and stared. Then he growled and bared yellow teeth and spotted gums. The fur on his neck stood on end.

Neither boy said a word. Ethan just dropped his mighty shield and ran. Terror-filled screams pierced the afternoon calm a second later. As the boys neared Cole's house, Cole stumbled and fell to one knee. Ethan zoomed past, his bobbing mop of strawberry blond hair keeping rhythm with his strides. The front door slammed a second later.

By then, the dog had latched onto Cole's cape.

Cole didn't see his dad come out. He just heard his shouts and saw the old man spring over the white-spindled porch rail. In a single fluid motion, Pops bent, scooped up a golf-ball-sized rock and flung it. Side-arm, like a shortstop playing a slow roller.

A hollow clunk and a yelp followed.

Cole pressed his tear-stained face into his dad's chest a few seconds later. He could smell his cologne.

"Life can be hard sometimes," his dad told the boys a few minutes later when everyone had calmed down. "We need to love each other and help each other. And never abandon one another," he'd said, looking at Ethan.

The episode became fodder for Thanksgiving merriment for years to come. The dog came to be known as Diablo, and somewhere in the retellings, Pops always said, "I knew at that moment that Ethan wasn't cut out to protect and serve." Pops was also fond of recounting that Cole had to use his own money to replace the towel that Diablo had shredded. The story always ended with good-natured teasing, especially if Ethan was in the room.

Even as Cole moved into his teenage years, with what he assumed were normal spats with his dad from time to time, he deeply respected the man. Pops usually had the answers. And if he didn't, he wasn't afraid to admit it.

Don Fisher reminded Cole a lot of his dad. Don and Pops looked a little alike. And like his dad, Don had a gentle yet no-nonsense way of dispensing wisdom. Don was a robotic engineer. He made sure old robots that built new robots worked efficiently. He'd talked about the job in some detail once, but Cole thought his brain would explode.

Through The Pitchfork's serving window, Cole watched Mason, the owner, glide from one end of the griddle to the other, his wide shoulders encased in a white T-shirt. Steam rose from the gridle, and Mason whistled "Jingle Bells" over and over as he cooked.

Mason, dude. Christmas is two months away. I like Christmas songs as much as the next guy, but can you whistle something else? "Twinkle, Twinkle Little Star" or something . . . at least it's not "Grandma Got Run Over by a Reindeer."

The bell above the restaurant's front door jingled as Don walked in.

"Wow, man, you look rough," he said as he straddled the stool next to Cole. "Sorry to hear about Kiley. Is there anything I can do?"

"Just pray."

"*Just* pray?" Don asked.

"No, I didn't mean it like that. I meant there's nothing humanly possible left to do. Just pray that God moves soon."

Don unwrapped his silverware from the napkin.

What do I say next? Do I mention Olivia? I like her, but the timing seems wrong. Kiley's sitting in a jail cell, and I'm out laughing it up with someone who, until a few weeks ago, was Satan's Little Helper.

Trina came around the corner, and Cole decided to postpone his confession until after she'd taken their orders.

When she left, he began. "Okay, I need to tell you this. I think I might like a woman."

Don's expression brightened. "Good for you! Where'd you meet her?"

"Well, this is the tough part. It's the reporter who came to church the day of the protest."

Don's brows knit together. "The shrill, obnoxious one?" He grimaced as he realized what he'd said. "Oh, sorry."

"Uh, yeah." Cole felt his lips tighten. "The Lord's been working on her."

"Well, I certainly hope so. How'd all this come about?" Don asked.

Cole relayed the events of the past few days. He talked for several minutes, then concluded with, "So, I'm not sure I should pursue this."

"Well, who am I to say whether the Lord is doing something here?" Don said. "Just go slowly. Did you tell Kiley what's going on?"

"Not yet."

"I think I would, sooner rather than later. She only knows the person we saw at church that morning. It might take her a minute to get used to the idea that Olivia's not a lunatic."

The word "lunatic" hurt, and Cole grimaced. "That's a little strong, but I see your point."

"Sorry. That was harsh," Don said, "but you get my drift."

Cole nodded.

"At the same time, God is God. If he has hold of Olivia, she'll change. Quickly or slowly, but she'll change."

"Yeah, no doubt."

"So, do you want to pray about this?" Don asked.

Cole nodded. Don led the prayer in muted tones.

20

THE COP MOTIONED HIM forward.

Another search. Just another day at the office.

I wonder if anyone has ever told this guy he looks like Abe Lincoln. Except that he looks perpetually angry.

If you worked here and looked like Abe, you'd probably look a little honked off, too.

Ah, a new wrinkle.

The dog looked like something from the Egyptian art exhibit Cole had seen a few years earlier. German Shepherd-like head. With black and brindle markings. Different body. Wrong body. Leaner, with longer legs. Light brown, almost gold, short-haired coat.

The dog sniffed Cole's shoes and trousers, then retreated to a dog bed on the left side of the search area.

"What breed is he?" Cole asked.

"Belgian Malinois," Abe said, his expression softening.

"He's beautiful," Cole said.

"He's a great worker, but stubborn," Abe said.

"He looks okay today."

"I told him he couldn't chase tennis balls tonight after work, if he acted up," Abe said, smiling.

"Well, you'd better behave," Cole said to the dog, eliciting a new smile from Abe.

When Cole took his spot on the stainless-steel stool, Kiley was already on her side of the glass. She looked better, as if she'd adjusted as much as could be expected to her new environment. The fear he'd seen in her eyes during their first visit had been replaced with an expression that exuded toughness and scrappiness.

I guess that's both good and bad.

He picked up his phone receiver, its shiny wire-encased cord more rigid than flexible.

I wish I could tell her about the new meeting spot, but there's no way.

Jail officials made it clear that all conversations are monitored and recorded. And they didn't need to know where New Hope planned to hang out.

Should he tell her about Olivia? Would she feel betrayed?

As he pondered what to say, Kiley moved the conversation beyond their greeting.

"Frank Hamilton wants me to take a plea deal," she said. Her voice was without emotion, as if she'd just said she'd gotten fries with her burger for lunch.

Okay, how do I react?

He raised an eyebrow.

"Involuntary manslaughter. Eight years. Out in a little less than seven with good behavior," Kiley said.

"Are you going to take it?"

"I'm seriously thinking about it. Frank Hamilton said the prosecution will seek the death penalty if I don't. And I have a feeling I know how that would turn out."

"Unfortunately, I think you're right. If this gets that far, the outcome's predictable. The guy Gonzalez appointed as attorney general is an absolute God hater."

Kiley nodded.

"At the same time, you've done nothing wrong," Cole said. "Saying you killed Johnson wouldn't be true. Anybody who honestly looks at the evidence can see you're innocent."

"Is anybody really going to do that?"

Kiley's indecision played on her face.

Her life, no doubt, would be a lot worse if she moved to a federal prison. County jail was preschool. The federal pen was a post-doc.

"I know it's a dumb question, but you've prayed about it, right?" Cole asked.

"Of course, but I still don't know what I'm supposed to do. Hamilton said you never know what a jury will do. This case may seem ridiculous to us, but the jury will be more immersed in the mainstream culture and apt to think I'm crazy."

Cole smiled sadly. He couldn't help her.

"Let's just both keep praying about this, okay, Sis?" he said.

Kiley nodded again.

"Before I go, there's something else I need you to pray about."

"What's that?"

"Do you remember the newswoman who came to the church the morning you were arrested?" He hesitated, then blurted it out. "I've been out with her a couple of times."

"You mean *out* out, as in on dates?" Kiley asked.

"Yeah, I think I might like her. I wanted you to know before things went any further."

Kiley's mouth fell open, and she was quiet for a beat.

"The woman who yelled and stomped out of the building that day? That woman?"

Cole nodded.

"How is that even possible?" Kiley asked.

"God," Cole said. "She's turned her life over to Jesus, and as far as I can tell, it's the real deal."

"Wow, I didn't see that coming."

"Yeah, I didn't, either. That disaster we saw at the church that morning was Olivia's life bottoming out. Her life was a mess, but a few weeks later, the Lord had her attention."

"Wow," Kiley repeated. "The whole thing is hard to fathom. I guess the Lord does change people. I'll definitely pray. Just be careful, Little Brother. I don't want to see you get hurt."

"I don't, either, Sis."

A deputy approached to lead Kiley back to her cell, and Cole reached up to touch the glass.

～

This is ridiculous. 4:09 a.m. Go to sleep, stupid.

Cole looked at his phone.

"Prez bans Bibles," the headline said.

Cole tapped. A half-dozen helmeted men stood on a darkened street and threw books into a fire.

How sad. History really does repeat itself.

The scene shifted. Gonzalez stood at a podium emblazoned with the presidential seal. The crisp contour of the White House gleamed from the middle of a blue-gray oval logo behind him. "Differences in religion are a source of tension among our men and women in the armed forces. Removing religious materials serves to unify our military and creates a more cohesive fighting force."

"Troops are not banned from studying religious materials during their off-duty time off base," a newswoman said. "They also are allowed to attend off-base religious services."

Yeah, but for how long?

Cole eyed two of his own Bibles on the coffee table.

Where am I going to hide them? Maybe in the crawlspace.

"President Gonzalez in July issued an executive order banning public religious gatherings," the newswoman said. "A federal judge in Alabama prevented that ban from going into effect, and the White House has since rescinded the order."

Well, that stuff will put you at peace and help you sleep.

Cole gulped a glass of water and clicked off his phone.

~

The line of giant porch swings hung from metal canopies along the arcing concrete walkway that ran beside the Ohio River. Cole didn't know how long the swings had been there, at least ten years. To his left, the early morning sun shone through the cables and around the sandstone towers of Cincinnati's historical Suspension Bridge. The span, an older sister of the Brooklyn Bridge, was more than a hundred years old.

He pushed himself gently in the swing, sipped his coffee, and looked across the river into Covington, Kentucky. The river was quiet this morning. A barge silently drifted his direction from beyond the city's sleek new interstate bridge to the northeast.

The Cincinnati skyline towered behind him, with the city's streets awakening and filling with traffic sounds.

I wish I could bottle this moment. In a half hour everything will be different. Noisier. Busier. Hotter.

He felt the hands over his eyes and the presence behind him before he could process the sound of the giggle. He lurched to his feet, his coffee cup flying and landing in the grass ten feet away.

"Jumpin' Jehosaphat, woman! You just about sent me to my grave!"

Olivia bent at the waist and clutched her chest, gales of laughter pouring from her.

"I'm sorry. Maybe," she said when she caught her breath.

The coffee Cole had bought her lay on its side on the swing, part of the drink dribbling through the hole in the cup's white plastic top.

"Do you see? Do you see what happens when you sneak up on people? God's vengeance," Cole said as he laughed and pointed at Olivia's toppled cup.

"I had that coming." she said as the last spasms of laughter began to ebb.

She wrapped her arms around him and pulled herself close. Cole breathed in the scent of her hair. Coconut. Her lips were gentle and delicate. Cole broke away, then returned for a second, more passionate kiss.

This is amazing. Life can't possibly get better than this.

They walked hand-in-hand toward the football stadium.

"Is Abby watching Stormy?" he asked.

Olivia nodded. "Yeah, they'll probably both still be in bed when I get home."

"Are you sure you have time to do this?" Cole asked.

"It'll be fine. It's early," she said. She squeezed his hand. "So, did you tell your sister about me?"

"Yeah, she was surprised but seemed okay with it."

"That's good. Surprised is a lot better than enraged. I'm sure I didn't make the best first impression."

"That you didn't, but I explained that you were going through some stuff and that the Lord used your circumstances to get your attention. Aren't you excited? You get to be a walking object lesson," Cole said, his voice mischievous.

Olivia smacked his shoulder.

"She's praying for us. So is Don Fisher."

"Good," Olivia leaned her head against his shoulder as they ambled along the riverbank.

The sun glinted off the olive-colored water, the buildings and dark green trees on the other side of the river.

"Perfect morning, isn't it?" Olivia said.

"Yeah." He looked at her and smiled, hoping she could see the love in his eyes.

They walked quietly.

"The government is offering a plea deal," Cole finally said.

"That's good. What's the deal?"

Cole explained.

"Is she going to take it?"

"She's still praying on it. So am I."

Just before reaching the football stadium, they turned and headed back the direction they'd come.

"Tough decision," Olivia said.

They strolled in comfortable silence for a few minutes.

"So, when are you looking at that farm, or whatever it is?" Olivia asked.

"This afternoon."

"I guess that's two things to add to the prayer list."

"There's always plenty of stuff on it, isn't there?" Cole said.

"Yeah, the more I pray, the more I feel like I need to pray."

Cole nodded.

They kissed good-bye, and Cole headed for the church.

21

EVERYTHING ABOUT THE OLD white cinderblock building looked bleached and faded. With its southwest exposure, the front of Jenkins Hardware bore the sun's punishment from late morning until sunset. The building rambled this way and that, an addition on this end, an expansion on that, and an addition to the addition.

Gas pumps at a hardware store? Okay, why not?

Cole pulled past the pumps and parked in the only open parking spot. The store's other five spots were occupied, four by pickup trucks and a Jeep.

His dashboard GPS showed only a gray rectangle with a straight gold line running through it. *Hmm, officially the middle of nowhere. So, where's St. Jonas?*

He zoomed out on the map.

Wait a minute, I passed it? Really? That wasn't even a town!

He recalled his conversation with Christie Collins.

"Where in the heck is St. Jonas? And who was he?"

"I have no idea who he was. Probably some settler who put a church and school on the main road between Grist Mill, Ohio, and Johnson Creek, Indiana."

Cole had passed a handful of buildings a mile or so back. They dotted a quarter-mile stretch of the two-lane roadway. Cole remembered the tiny redbrick church that looked abandoned and a neighboring one-room schoolhouse.

"That has to be it," he said aloud.

A pickup truck pulled out of the parking space next to his, and another truck immediately took its place. An array of excavators, front loaders and U-Haul trailers stood like prisoners in a cellblock behind an eight-foot-high chain-link fence.

"It must be rental equipment. I guess this place does quite the business," he said into the empty SUV. "It's probably been here forever."

A man in a dirty dark-blue T-shirt emblazoned with "Artic Monkeys," a Stihl ball cap, dusty jeans, and heavy well-worn boots came out of the store carrying a chain saw and something that looked like it went on an engine.

If the church gets this place down the road, I'm about to get an education.

Cole pulled out of the parking lot, turned left, and went back the way he came.

If there'd ever been commercial establishments in the hamlet, there was no sign of them now. With cornfields stretching to the horizon in every direction, St. Jonas was home to more barns, grain silos, and outbuildings than dwellings for human inhabitants.

Cole slowed to read the mailbox numbers. The church and the school stood off to his left a few seconds away. Chapel Road formed a *t* intersection there.

He glanced at the dashboard screen again.

Okay, it should be here on the right. There. That's Christie's car.

The sturdy redbrick farmhouse sat diagonally across from the church, a few hundred yards into a cornfield. It looked like it predated the church and school by several decades, maybe even a century.

Is that Colonial Revival or Georgian? One of these days I should take an architecture course. Bad idea, I've got better things to do.

Everything about the house was rectangular. Large symmetrical front windows stood on each side of the front door. Four windows ran across the top of the house, and two dormers emerged from the high-pitched hip roof. Stone chimneys pointed heavenward on each end of the building.

Wow, this place is beautiful.

Christie Collins, Jake Moore, and Tom Henderson stood in the gravel driveway.

"Did you pass it?" Christie called.

"Yeah, zoomed right by. I guess that's a good thing."

"This place is awesome," Jake said. "I'm not sure how many people we can get in here, but I love it."

"Just wait until you see what's in the back," Christie said. She moved in for a quick embrace.

Christie was a stocky fortyish woman with wavy strawberry blond hair that fell to her shoulders. She'd gone to New Hope for as long as Cole had been there. Her kids went there until they were in their twenties and moved out of town, and Cole had performed Christie's mom's funeral.

The house had been Christie's grandmother's, and it had been passed down to her mom.

"Come on in and look around."

Someone had restored the house to much of its original grandeur. Inside, the home was bedecked with rich, highly polished woodwork and hardwood floors as well as chandeliers in two of the rooms. Working fireplaces stood at each end of the building. Although the house was considered a mansion when it was built, its three bedrooms upstairs and a living room and dining room downstairs were small by twenty-first-century standards. Still, it could be a decent meeting spot.

"Did you say it has a barn?" Jake asked.

Large and open, with a dirt floor and high metal roof, the building looked like it had been used for equipment and hay storage at some point. Cole saw and smelled no evidence it had ever housed livestock. The barn's best feature was a stand of pine trees that cloaked the structure and made it all but invisible from the roadway. The hidden area could easily accommodate forty or fifty cars, and Cole could quietly refurbish and renovate the building to convert it into a church.

"I'm not sure we'll ever need it, but you say we can use this as long as we want?" Cole asked.

"Yeah. Nobody knows what to do with it," Christie said. "My grandparents contracted with K&O to farm the land, but no one has any use for the house or barn."

Cole recognized K&O. The company either owned or worked 20 percent of the farmland in the Midwest.

"K&O farms your dad's old place, don't they, Tom? Would the K&O people be a problem?" Cole asked.

"Probably not. Not if you stay out of their way. Maybe not meet here when they're planting or harvesting. But that would only be a few weeks a year."

"And, Christie, your dad or somebody deals with those guys, right? He and K&O take care of the whole farming operation," Cole said.

Christie nodded.

"So, do we rent the place, or what?" Jake asked.

"It's probably better to just do it on a handshake, with no paper trail," Christie said. "It gives me plausible deniability."

Cole laughed. "Sounds like you've been reading too many political novels."

"There's no such thing as too many," Christie said, smiling. "Anyway, all we ask is that you keep the place up and do routine maintenance and stuff around here."

Cole tried to imagine the barn buttoned up against the elements and filled with worshipers. The only drawback was the distance to anywhere. But that was actually a blessing. New Hope's endeavors were much less likely to be observed in St. Jonas than in the city, especially if Cole held services in the late evening or early morning.

"Do you think we could fix up the inside of the barn a little? Make it a little more comfortable for worship?" Cole asked.

"No problem. I think it would be great," Christie said.

"Can you give us a minute?" Cole asked.

Christie walked toward the front of the house.

"Are we jumping the gun?" Cole asked. "Do we really need this place? Gonzalez hasn't made any new noises about shutting down churches."

"Yeah, but look how quick he was to say he'd call up reserve units to enforce his crazy religion ban earlier this summer," Tom said. "He's not even halfway through his term in office."

"Tom's right. It's better to have it and not need it than to need it and not have it," Jake said.

Within minutes Cole, Jake, and Tom had each thanked Christie and sealed the deal with a hug. For the foreseeable future, New Hope had at least one place to hide.

~

Cole watched a vertical crease form between Frank Hamilton's eyes.

"You want to do *what?*" Hamilton sounded incredulous. "Absolutely not. A hundred years ago, you'd have been a sympathetic witness. Today, you're not, you're a crazy man who thinks a homeless guy died, got up out of his grave, and walked around. You'll only hurt her case. The prosecution will tear you up on cross-examination."

"Come on, Frank. You know Kiley's not taking the plea deal. She needs all the help she can get, and I influence people for a living," Cole said.

"No, the Holy Spirit influences them. You're just a mouthpiece."

"And how do you know the Holy Spirit won't influence the jury if I testify?"

"If he wants to move the jury one way or the other, he won't need your help."

Cole sighed. His irritation intensified. Why wouldn't Frank let him help his own sister?

The men stared at one another for several beats before Hamilton broke the silence.

"And just what do you think you're going to say?" he said. "The testimony of a Christian today is about as compelling as the testimony of an African American in Alabama in 1930. This jury is going to be prejudiced. It's not going to work, Cole."

"She's my sister, Frank. I got her into all this. I convinced her to go to church that morning, and I persuaded her to drive that truck. I have to do everything in my power to make this right. If I testify, Kiley might seem more human to the jury, not like some religious nut."

Hamilton sighed deeply and sat back in his chair. His eyes divulged his resignation.

≈

Cole drifted in the quiet. He'd probably always have his place in town, but he was glad he'd come to St. Jonas to finish his sermon. He found an inexplicable comfort in the old farmhouse and intensely felt the Spirit's presence. The refrigerator in the next room purred. Aside from that, he heard only his own breathing. The sun had just started to peek over the horizon. The crickets had gone to sleep, and the area's daytime creatures hadn't roused themselves, yet.

Thank you, Lord, for this moment.

He scanned the notes on the yellow legal pad.

Yeah, it'll preach.

He closed his eyes, laid his head back against the love seat, and drank in the hush.

Did Jesus savor the quiet when he went to secluded places to be alone with the Father? Probably.

The whistle from his phone announcing the incoming text shot through him.

Olivia: Thanks for yesterday morning. Got time for lunch? Need to tell you something.

Cole tapped the bank app on his phone.

Yeah, I still have a few bucks. I hate to admit it, but Gonzalez's monetary policies are working. For now. Disaster's probably right around the corner, but it'll be okay to spend a couple of bucks on a lunch.

~

College football teams ran back and forth on the sports bar's giant TVs. None of the games involved nearby or highly ranked teams. As a result, Cole and Olivia had a corner to themselves, and the restaurant was relatively quiet.

Olivia looked preoccupied, almost worried. What had happened in the last thirty hours?

"I want to tell you this before our relationship goes any further," she said.

Whoa, what could possibly be so bad?

Olivia quieted for a second. She seemed to carefully weigh her words.

"My childhood really wasn't . . . or really, my teen years really weren't that great," she resumed. "You know, I told you that my mom had died . . ."

"Yeah, I'm so sorry—"

"No, no, no, it's not that," she interjected. "It's just that . . . It was after my mom died." She again was quiet for a beat.

What was so difficult to say? Could she have done something *that* horrible?

She took a deep breath and resumed, "Okay, let me start again." She sounded more self-assured. "We both lost parents when we were fairly young, and I think that helped create a bond between us. At least on my part, it did."

"Mine, too," Cole said, nodding.

"It may be too early to tell you this, but Cole, I really like you, and I think we have potential to be . . . a lot more than friends," she said.

Uh-oh, where's this going? Is she already talking about a long-term relationship? Well, that's a little scary.

"Now believe me, I'm not rushing anything, but I think it's better that you find this out sooner rather than later."

Is she an ax murderer? Does she have bodies buried under her basement floor?

"So, my mom died when I was seventeen." Olivia began anew. "I could sit here and string together words all day, and they couldn't explain how much it hurt. What you clearly had with your dad, I had with my mom. It was a million little things. Girly things, I guess. Like doing our hair and makeup, getting mani-pedis, shopping for clothes, and talking.

"When she died, I was at that age when kids start to disengage from their parents, to form their own adult identities. Some kids get angry during that stage. But my mom, she seemed to know instinctively that my pulling away was a good, necessary thing. She knew she had to become less my . . . my . . . I don't know . . . boss, and a little more like a friend. I know there still would've been rules as I got older, and who's to say we wouldn't have fought later? But at that time, she was the most important person in my life."

Tears pooled in her eyes, probably simultaneously of joy and sadness. Cole had cried similar tears after his dad died.

He handed her a napkin from the stack between them.

Shouts from one corner of the bar told him one of the football teams had scored a touchdown. How annoying. He and Olivia needed to be somewhere else, in some quiet, cozy place where they could sit silently for a few minutes, and he could hold her and rock her in his arms.

He reached across the table and put his hand on hers.

Her lips curled into a weak smile.

"I'm so, so sorry," he said.

A single tear trickled down her right cheek.

"There was no one who could replace that. Intellectually, I tell myself that my dad tried," she said, her voice choked with emotion. "But he was dealing with his own grief. In a way, he just vanished after my mom died. He was so broken that even when he was there—right there in the room—he wasn't there. And he started working more and more. He just ran."

Cole nodded. He understood. His mom had done the same thing. After a month or two, she'd packed his dad's stuff into boxes and started donating things to charity. She couldn't bear to remember. But for Cole, it was almost like he *wasn't allowed* to remember. Bringing up any memories of Pops only caused his mom pain. But Cole wanted nothing more than to hang on to every possible memory as long as possible. Kiley had helped, and he hoped he had done the same for her.

"At first, I tried to be really good and tried to do special things to make him happy," Olivia said. "I tried to make him want to stay home. But he just didn't get it. How could he? He just wasn't a mom. He wasn't a teenage girl, either. He was a man who'd just lost the love of his life. And even though I can reason it all out logically, emotionally it still hurts. It's like I was abandoned twice, first by my mom and then by my dad."

Several comments went through Cole's mind, but he understood she needed him to listen, not to speak. They sat quietly for a minute.

The waitress headed their direction, and he shook his head. Catching a glimpse of Olivia's expression, she smiled sadly and turned away.

"So, what happened?" Cole asked.

"My friends at school tried to help, but I hurt so badly I couldn't let anyone in. Eventually, people quit trying. Except this one girl. Amber. I'd never hung around with her because I knew she was into drugs and sex. But she asked all the time how I was doing. One day, she asked me if I wanted some pills that would make everything go away. Of course, I said no at first, but eventually . . ." Olivia's voice trailed off.

Cole nodded.

"After a few weeks, she introduced me to her supplier, a guy named Ty."

"Red Chevy guy," Cole said.

Olivia nodded. "He was about twenty-two, and he knew just what to say. Within a month, it had turned into a sex-for-drugs thing."

Olivia stared at the table, where two tears had fallen.

Cole squeezed her hand.

"Obviously, you're not that girl anymore. You've moved forward and become a successful young woman."

She nodded.

Cole handed her another napkin. "And you can be certain Jesus loves you and has forgiven you if you've confessed all this to him. And, I'm certainly not one to judge. It's not as if my life has always been spotless."

Another nod followed by a raised eyebrow.

"After my dad died, I let a relationship go way too far. Then, when I came to my senses and wanted to stop having sex, it got ugly," Cole said.

Olivia smirked. "I know it must've been painful, but the idea of you running around with the chick from *Fatal Attraction* is almost funny to me. When I look at the way you are now, it seems so out of place."

"I didn't choose some of the coping mechanisms you did, but the pain was real, and the coping mechanisms I picked were just as sinful and ineffective."

Olivia nodded. Her body language had changed, her shoulders more relaxed, less tension in her neck.

"So, how'd you break free?" Cole asked.

"Eventually, I went with Ty to Kansas City. And pretty soon the sex wasn't enough for him. He was getting physically abusive and telling me I needed to pull my weight—financially, I mean—if I expected to keep getting drugs. That was when something clicked. I understood I was in real trouble."

"What happened?" Cole asked.

"Well, one night, we were at this bar, even though I was underage, and this guy, Ty's dealer, came in. So, after a minute, Ty and this guy went outside, and when they came back in, Ty said I had to go have sex with this dealer guy. Of course, I refused and screamed and tried to run, but Ty grabbed me by the arm and twisted it until I thought it would break. I begged him to stop, and he hit me. It felt like my head exploded. I thought he'd broken my cheekbone. I reeled backward and fell. A second later, he stood over me, and I had a clear shot. I kicked him as hard as I could. Where it counted. And he fell on the floor."

"Ouch." Cole couldn't restrain a chuckle. "So, did you run out of there then or what?"

"This woman, I found out later her name was Michelle, she grabbed me by the hand, and we ran to her car. I spent the night at her place."

"Wow. Brave. You're fortunate she was willing to get involved."

"She said she'd been in an abusive relationship once and didn't wish it on anyone."

"So, what happened after that?"

"I didn't know who to call. It was the middle of the night. But for some reason I called my Aunt Marilyn, actually my great aunt. She told me to stay put. She'd drive out from Cincy to get me, which was about a ten-hour drive. So, I tried to get some sleep. When she knocked on the door, and I opened it, she had this little smile on her face. And, all she said was, 'Would it be okay if I gave you a hug?' For a while we just sat on the bed, and she rocked me while I cried. Then we started talking, and we talked all day."

Cole nodded and squeezed Olivia's hand.

"I told her how sorry and ashamed I was," Olivia said. "And Aunt Marilyn said, 'It's appropriate that you feel sorry, but you need forgiveness from someone else a lot more than you need it from me and your dad.' So, we prayed, and Aunt Marilyn impressed upon me how much God loved me and wanted to forgive me. She pulled a little Bible out of her purse and read the story of the Prodigal Son. I'd heard it growing up, but this time it was different. Somehow, it sank in. Aunt Marilyn said she didn't think there was any other place in the Bible where God was pictured as running, except to welcome a child who wanted to come home."

"That's true. And so cool. God is so good," Cole said.

Another tear fell onto the table.

"I found out when I got back that I was pregnant."

"Stormy?" Cole asked.

Olivia nodded.

Cole felt the tears welling.

"I'm sure you'll choose better next time. Someone who sees how awesome and worthy you are in the Lord."

Olivia smiled and blushed.

"So, what about the drugs and alcohol? I don't know you that well, but I've never seen evidence of anything like that. And you're holding down a tough job."

"I had to go the hospital to get meds for the withdrawal symptoms, and after that, I went to a Christian twelve-step group. After I worked through some of the pain of losing my mom, I never had the desire to drink or do drugs again. I still go to meetings from time to time."

"So, Ty didn't come after you until a few months ago?" Cole asked.

"It'd been more than twelve years, but I knew it was him. I'll never forget that face. He was just sitting in his car down the street. Then, the morning of the protest, he was across the street from the TV station. That's why I was so crazy that morning we met. I was totally unhinged."

"Makes sense," Cole said. "Is he still around?"

"He was out there again the next day, and I asked my boss to scare him off. My boss is huge and pretty scary. I watched from the window while he walked up to the car. I don't know what he said, but Ty started the car and left."

Hopefully, he'd stay gone. Cole had no idea how to deal with psychopaths.

The waitress approached again, and Cole raised his glass.

"So, do you still want to go out with me?" Olivia asked after the waitress had left.

"Absolutely," Cole said. "You're not a seventeen-year-old runaway anymore. You're a new creation in Christ."

"What if Ty shows up again?" she asked.

"We'll cross that bridge when we come to it," Cole said. "One day at a time, right?" He squeezed Olivia's hand to punctuate the response.

They sat quietly for a few minutes, drained.

"So, would you like to come to church tomorrow?' Cole asked.

"Yeah," Olivia said. She nodded pensively. "I can't not go."

22

Frank Hamilton sat in a classic leather office chair at the head of the huge mahogany conference table. An oil portrait of Abraham Lincoln peered over his right shoulder.

Cole had never seen the man directly across the table. With light brown hair, a long face, and a high-priced haircut, Cole guessed the man to be in his late thirties. Cole immediately disliked the guy. He hadn't stood when Cole walked in, and something in his body language exuded hatred.

"Cole, this is Benjamin Fields from the Department of Justice. He's here to discuss a proposal with you," Hamilton said.

Fields offered no greeting or salutation but got straight to the point. "As you know, your sister's case is scheduled to be heard in about three weeks. I'm here to offer a proposal that would make the whole situation go away," Fields said. "The president is willing to grant Ms. Evans a pardon."

"The president? Seriously?" Cole said.

"That's who has the authority to pardon federal offenses," Hamilton said.

"Frank? You knew about this? Why didn't you tell me?"

"Sorry, Cole, a condition of the pardon was that you didn't know about it beforehand."

"All you need to do, Mr. Evans, is stop preaching," Fields said.

This guy can't be serious.

"And I need an answer immediately," Fields said.

No, no, no, no. Please, Lord, no. Neither decision is right.

Cole knew Fields's tactic. Salespeople used it all the time to get customers to make snap decisions. Bad decisions.

His chest hurt. *No, no, no, you can't start hyperventilating.*

Cole said nothing.

"Mr. Evans?" Fields said. "I need an answer." He pushed a document Cole's direction.

"If you want me to stop preaching, why not just arrest me?" Cole asked. "You guys can probably conjure up some hate crime or something to charge me with. The video outside the justice center that one day probably broke some crazy law or rule."

"That's just it, you're too popular. Millions of people have liked your videos on social media, and with midterm elections coming up, the president is concerned locking you up right now might result in another viral video that could cost the party too many votes. One thing you can count on, though, after the election, your days are numbered."

The videos have had that much impact? Cool. I can't believe this guy admitted that. Too bad it doesn't help Kiley.

"Give me just one minute," Cole said.

"Why, so you can *pray*?" Fields said mockingly.

Cole was in front of his third-grade class again, and Trevor Franklin was laughing.

He glared at Fields. The little pinhead.

I wonder what would happen if I reached across the table and grabbed the little twit by the silky blue necktie.

He heard his mother's voice, "*You don't have to defend a lion . . .*"

"Yeah, I need to pray. For your worthless soul," Cole said. He was surprised the words had come out of his mouth.

Both Fields and Hamilton winced.

"Take it easy, Cole. You might want to think about this," Hamilton said.

You called me to preach, Lord. Are you telling me something else here? For the millionth time, please save Kiley. Isn't there some way?

Cole heard nothing.

"C'mon, Evans, what's it gonna be? Preaching or your sister's life?" Fields said. "And you know, regardless of your decision, we'll inform Ms. Evans of the president's offer and the conditions of the pardon."

Cole had assumed that.

"You know what, Fields? You're seriously a useless lump of excrement. I don't see how God can even stand you, but by his grace, he can. He actually loves you, and he offers you the chance to avoid condemnation. Maybe that's the pardon we should be talking about."

"Cole, please," Hamilton pleaded.

Cole knew what Kiley would say. He could feel the tears welling. He didn't want to say what he knew he had to. "God told me to preach." His voice cracked, and the tears streamed down his cheeks.

"Okay, have it your way. Idiot," Fields said. He snatched up the document and pushed himself back from the table. "You know that at some point, your popularity will wane, and we'll come after you."

The sobs poured out as Hamilton showed Fields out of the office.

～

The coffee table sailed through the air and landed on its top, five feet from where it normally sat. Flipped upside down, it looked like roadkill with rigor mortis, its curved legs sticking up.

The crystal vase, a gift from someone at church, gleamed as it shot across the room and exploded against the wall above the sofa.

Pain burst through his knuckles as his hand went through the drywall next to the closet.

When he'd finished, Cole lay curled in the fetal position on the floor amid the debris. Sob after sob poured out.

Why, God? How could you be so cruel? What kind of God are you? I've been nothing but obedient, and Kiley has done nothing wrong.

Shards of glass poked into his hands and fell from his hair when he sat up.

What time is it? Wow, it's been an hour. Does that matter? Not really.

Yeah, it does. Come on. Pull yourself together. You can't give up. The battle is the Lord's. Get your butt up off the floor.

Tiny crystals from the vase glittered on the carpet and sofa in the light of the orange sunset.

"Well, Cole, you've made quite a mess," he said into the ransacked room.

He cursed as he went to get the vacuum cleaner.

～

Why was the hole in the wall so much bigger than his fist?

I guess they'll have something at the hardware store to fix that. I'll deal with it tomorrow.

Okay, now what? I don't want to dump on Olivia, but I sure could use a shoulder to lean on.

So, go lean on Don Fisher's.

Olivia's is a lot nicer shoulder.

He picked up a book near the TV and a metal coffee tumbler that had ricocheted into the hallway.

Everything in the living room was back in place.

I'll have to replace the picture frame from the foyer. But it was kind of cool how it arced and curved before it hit the lamp. Too bad the vase is history.

Okay, do I text her or not?

He unlocked his phone and texted.

Me: R U up for hanging out?

Olivia: Really exhausted, but ur welcome to come over.

Olivia: Maybe popcorn and a movie?

Me: Want me to pick up some Chinese?

Olivia: Moo goo gai pan. White rice. Egg roll. Fried wanton for Stormy. Let me know what it costs. Tnx.

⁓

Olivia wore jeans and a maroon Texas A&M sweatshirt, with her hair pulled into a ponytail. Even dressed down, she was gorgeous.

Before he'd even stepped inside the house, her arms wrapped around his neck, and he cradled her waist in his hands.

Olivia unwound herself, and Cole stepped inside. A small dining area lay to the left, with a tiny kitchen hidden in a nook beyond that. A TV took up the wall to the right, and straight ahead, two large windows looked into a wooded area and past a small stream.

Olivia's choice in furniture gave the place a sleek, modern feel.

Smooth jazz floated softly from speakers strategically stationed around the room, and a candle glowed in the middle of an arrangement on the dining table. She'd set out three plates, glasses and a pitcher of ice water.

"Great place. You have quite the eye for decorating. This makes my place look like a locker room."

Olivia chuckled. "Holly didn't fix the place up?"

"A little bit here and there, but she never lived there, of course, and we were saving for the wedding and hadn't bought any furniture. Besides, that's been a few years now."

"So, is it painted Cincinnati Bengals orange and black with velvet pictures of dogs playing pool, and the back end of a flatbed truck cut down for a dining table?"

Cole laughed.

"It's not *that* bad, although I *am* thinking about getting rid of those stadium seats in the living room."

"Good plan."

Olivia ushered him to the table.

"Stormy! Dinner!" she called.

The girl clomped down the stairs, her face stuck to her tablet.

"Put that away. It's time to eat. And have some manners. Say hello to Cole."

"Hey," Stormy said, not looking up from the device. She sounded indifferent.

What's going on? Why the cold shoulder? Is this normal twelve-year-old girl behavior? What should I say?

"Hey, Stormy. How was your day?"

"It sucked."

Whoa, I didn't expect that. So, do I ask why? Or would that be rewarding mopey behavior?

"Anything I can help with?" Cole said.

"No," Stormy said, her face still riveted to the screen.

"Stormy, I know you're upset, but you're being rude," Olivia said. "Put the tablet away, or I'll take it away. For a week."

"Mom!" She somehow turned it into a two-syllable word. Stormy huffed and put the device on the counter.

"Is it okay if I tell Cole why you're angry?"

"I don't care," Stormy said as she flopped herself into a spot at the dinner table and stared at her plate.

"Stormy introduced her friend Jenna to another friend at school a couple weeks ago, and now Jenna has stopped talking to Stormy."

Wow, I'm totally out of my depth here. What do I say? Do I try to fix it, or just listen?

"It stinks when that happens," Cole said. "Sometimes these things work out. Other times, they don't. Either way, the anger and sadness are real. I'm sorry you're going through that."

Stormy raised her eyes to meet his.

"I wish I could fix it for you," Cole said.

Stormy's expression softened. She still looked mad but was no longer aiming her anger his direction.

"C'mon, let's eat before this gets cold," Olivia said.

Stormy pushed the food around on her plate for five minutes and asked to be excused.

"Do you want to talk some more later?" Olivia asked as Stormy put her wonton back into its box.

"It's okay. We can talk about it in the morning," Stormy said. "Bye, Mr. Evans."

"Hey, I can clear out, if you guys need some time," Cole said.

"No, I really just want to be alone for a while," Stormy said.

He gave her a sympathetic smile. "It's 'Cole,' okay, not 'Mr. Evans.' Is it okay if I give you a hug?"

Stormy nodded, and Cole exchanged a glance with Olivia, who also nodded her approval.

He stood and offered a one-armed hug around the girl's shoulder. "Hang in there, cutie," he said.

"I wouldn't want to be twelve again for all the tea in China," he said as she clomped back up the stairs.

"Me, either," Olivia said.

"Did I handle that okay?"

"You were great," Olivia said.

Ten minutes later, he'd recounted all that had happened to him that day.

"That's horrible, and then you come over here, and Stormy's all snarky. Great end to a great day," Olivia said.

"I've definitely had better."

"I'd be lying if I said I couldn't believe what Gonzalez is doing."

The empathy flowed from her eyes.

"We really need to take this to the Lord," she said, moving her plate and half-empty food cartons aside.

Olivia reached across the table with both hands. Her touch was warm, her demeanor serious.

"Father God," she began, "thank you for Cole and for his faithfulness to you. Be near and help him to know that you're in control and that you'll protect Kiley. Help him understand he made the right decision and that you stand with him."

After Cole added his own petitions, and the prayer ended, Olivia gathered dinner's remnants. Cole added the dinnerware in front of him to the collection, and Olivia headed for the kitchen.

Cole followed.

"It's only a couple of things. I'll wash, you dry," he said.

A few minutes later, the chore complete, he shook the water from his hands.

"Do you want this?" Olivia asked, dangling the dish towel in front of him.

As he stretched a dripping hand her direction, she yanked the towel out of reach.

He reached for it again, and she yanked it away a second time, laughing.

"Oh, it is on!" Cole said.

Olivia squealed and bolted from the kitchen, dish towel in hand. She zoomed around the dining table and headed toward the far end of the couch.

They zigzagged at opposite ends of the sofa a few times, laughing, before Olivia made a break for the kitchen.

Cole cut her off, and she crashed into him, breathing harder than normal. He held her gently at the shoulders. The soft lights cast a gentle glow across her face.

"What are you going to do, now?" he asked.

Her eyes closed, and she melted into him.

Her kiss was intense but gentle, her body firm but soft.

When they broke away, his heart hammered. "You can have the towel if you want it," he said.

Olivia moved in for another kiss.

23

"No, LET'S KEEP GOING," Olivia said. "People think they're cute, but they're disgusting. They're poop throwers."

Cole laughed.

Chimpanzees screamed and swung from trees in an enclosure to the left.

Stormy pressed her face to the enclosure's bars, poked her elbows out to the sides, and scratched her ribs like a guerilla. "Just one more minute, Mom," she said. She copied the information from a plaque into her notebook.

Ahead, a giraffe reached for some leaves above a fence line.

"So, I have no idea what this story entails, but I want to find out," Olivia said.

"Good. Maybe it will be a nice byline," Cole said.

"Maybe. I hope so. Did you guys get much done at the building in St. Jonas?" Olivia asked.

"Yeah, we got most of the drywall up. It's almost starting to look like a church."

"Sounds like work."

"Yeah, I'm a little sore. Oh, wait, come to think of it, I think I may have hurt my lips," he said. "I think they really need to be kissed."

Olivia whacked him playfully and rolled her eyes.

"I'll take care of them later, not in front of the rhinos."

～

The barn was perfect, and Christie Collins had gotten permission from K&O to cut a maze into the field corn. With Christie's dad supervising, they'd stored the harvested ears in a silo, where the K&O folks would pick them up.

A hay wagon attached to a large green tractor waited between the house and the barn to take people on a hayride later that afternoon. Randomly arranged pumpkins, hay bales, and a table full of food completed the decor.

"Look, Mom! There's a pony! Can I ride him?" Stormy looked like she'd explode with excitement.

"The man who owns him should be here any minute," Cole said. "As soon as he gets here, you can get on."

The girl hugged him around the waist and ran toward the happy squeals and giggles that came from the bounce house.

"Looks like this turned out really well.," Olivia said.

"It did. God is good," Cole replied. "Want to get lost in the corn for a few minutes?"

Olivia smiled and pulled him toward the field.

~

Jake and Tom already sat at their usual table at The Pitchfork when Cole walked in.

Melody stood at the coffee machine next to the serving window. Her face contorted when she saw him. "Can you get these guys?" she called to Trina.

"Still hates me, huh?" Cole said as he pulled up a chair.

"She doesn't like us much better," Jake said.

"She'll pour our coffee but that's about it.She won't speak," Tom said.

"Who'd you say was lesbian?" Jake asked.

"Her daughter," Tom said.

"Well, clearly she doesn't want to hear what the Bible says about it," Jake said.

"I'm sorry. I wish she weren't taking this out on you guys," Cole said.

"You have to do what's right," Jake said. "Jesus said people would hate us."

"Well, he was right about that one," Cole said.

Trina arrived and took their order.

"Did you hear all this Christmas tree nonsense?" Cole asked.

"'Holiday trees,'" Tom said, making air quotes. "It's ridiculous. It'd be hilarious if it weren't so sad."

"What are you talking about?" Trina asked.

"Gonzalez signed an executive order banning Christmas trees, but a federal court, in Oklahoma I think, intervened and said Christmas had become a secular holiday 'essential to the nation's retail economy.'" This time Cole made air quotes.

"Yeah, we can still have them as long as we call them holiday trees," Tom said.

"You're making this up, right?" Trina asked.

"No, you couldn't make this stuff up," Cole said.

"I guess there are worse places to celebrate Christmas," Tom said.

He was right. A few days earlier, Cole had read about tiny groups of people who gathered to whisper their praises and songs in places like Saudi Arabia, and he'd read about one group of women in a North Korean labor camp who celebrated Christmas a few years earlier in an outhouse.

"I guess as long as we have Jesus, we have Christmas," Cole said. "We just celebrate it differently. And our celebration now may bless the Lord more than our traditional materialistic rituals did. We're more intentional and more focused on whom and why we're celebrating."

"I guess that's true," Tom said as Trina left. "So, did you invite Olivia to the Christmas party?"

"Yeah, but it's a little scary. It's kind of like taking your girlfriend to meet your parents."

Jake laughed. "C'mon, now, our church isn't that tough a crowd!"

"You've never stood in the pulpit, have you?" Cole said with a laugh.

"I guess a few of us have our moments," Tom said.

All three were silent for a beat, then Jake asked, "So, do you think this is serious? This thing with Olivia?"

"Probably. It's a little early to tell, but I think I may be twitterpated."

Jake raised an eyebrow. "Twitterpated?"

"Disney movie. *Bambi*, I think. Infatuated. In love," Tom said.

"I really think the Lord may be in this," Cole said.

"Well, good for you. I'll pray to bless whatever the Lord may be doing," Jake said.

"I appreciate it, Jake, and I appreciate you asking."

"Somebody has to keep an eye on you," Tom said, chuckling.

"Ron Kane's the one I'm most worried about," Cole said.

"Yeah, he can get his hackles up every now and then," Tom said.

"It's not like I need his approval, but with him being the head elder now, life might be simpler if I had it."

"I can see that," Jake said.

Tom raised his cup head high and Trina nodded.

~

Cole dipped the crystal ladle into the punch bowl.

I wonder what makes it so fizzy.

He dumped the ladle into his plastic cup, then took in the deco-rations—evergreens along the windowsills and around the doorframes, crimson- and Kelly-green napkins, and a crimson tablecloth with snowmen.

About thirty people had packed themselves into Don and Teresa Fisher's house. More than a dozen of them wore ugly Christmas sweaters. Tom's was particularly hideous. It depicted a reindeer with a curler in her hair, white fur-lined slippers, and a housecoat.

"Mr. Reindeer's sleeping on the couch," Tom said.

Tosha Moore laughed. "He probably deserved to be," she said.

At the other end of the dining room, Tom Henderson and Reed Bryant stood near the buffet, paper plates in hand, discussing Calvinism vs. Arminianism.

They haven't settled that in four hundred years, boys. I doubt you'll get it figured out tonight.

Songs about snow and Santa played in the background.

In the living room, Olivia chatted with Ron Kane and his wife.

I wonder what they're talking about.

All three smiled and nodded, then Ron's guffaw thundered through the house.

Thank you, Lord. Just thank you. I'm going to take that as confirmation that you're in all of this.

~

His Bible lay closed on the coffee table, and he leaned back on the couch. The words in the Google search box mocked him.

You're seriously asking Google if it's okay to tell Olivia you love her.

He shook his head. *You're off your rocker. Somebody needs to put you on meds.*

Really, what's going on here? Why is this even a decision?

Come on, you know why. Sex.

Cole leaned his head against the sofa and raked his hand through his hair. The sadness at the thought of disappointing God pressed into him like an x-ray room leaded vest.

You really probably need to talk to Don.

No, you don't. You need to talk to Jesus. Satan has twisted this whole thing around. Saying you love her doesn't automatically lead to premarital sex, despite your pasts, and despite what the culture says.

Will it be harder to be alone with her? Will the temptation be stronger? Maybe. But God's still God.

The flood of peace and 1 Corinthians 10:13 arrived at the same instant. *No temptation has overtaken you except what is common to mankind. And God is faithful; he will not let you be tempted beyond what you can bear. But when you are tempted, he will also provide a way out so that you can endure it.*

That poor verse gets misused all the time. God definitely does allow life circumstances *we can't bear. He wants us to realize that and turn to him. But he always gives us a way out of temptation.*

Okay, so whom are you going to believe?

He chuckled out loud. "I guess my utility bills will go down. My showers will be colder, and consequently quicker."

He opened his Bible and started his morning reading.

∽

Three weeks had passed since the Christmas party. Olivia wore a black scoop-necked top under a denim jacket, and white jeans. She moved around the room like a hummingbird, stopping to chat here, hugging someone there.

Most of the people who'd been at the Christmas party, plus a dozen more, stood in clusters or sat at folding tables strategically spaced around the barn. Some played board games, and bursts of chatter came from eight people embroiled in an intense euchre tournament in one corner.

"It didn't take her long to become part of the family, did it?" Don Fisher said.

"No, it's like she's known these people her entire life. I'm really blessed to have her."

"That you are, my friend," Don said, clapping a hand on Cole's shoulder.

Cole followed Don's gaze. Two members of New Hope's worship band played acoustic guitars and sang oldies.

"Looks like they're having a good time," Cole said.

"Yeah, it's good to see."

Olivia walked Cole's direction, smiled, and nodded toward a turned-down TV in the corner.

"Ah, it's time," Don said, and left to find Teresa.

Olivia took his hand as someone turned up the TV. People all over the room watched the ball on Times Square and joined in the countdown.

Should I say what I'm thinking? She already knows it, and I think she feels the same way. I think it's time to find out.

"Three . . . two . . . one."

Her lips were warm and tender, her arms around his neck gentle and graceful.

"I love you, Olivia Sandlin."

"I love you, too, Cole Evans."

They sealed the declaration with a deeper, more intense, kiss.

~

The early morning sun gently warmed his face and took some of the nip out of the air. The breeze stung his cheeks and the end of his nose.

The steady slap of a jogger's footfalls approached from behind. As Cole and Olivia moved to the edge of the asphalt path, a woman in cold-weather running gear trotted past and disappeared around a bend.

"He said either cover the trial or leave," Olivia said.

"Do you think he's still dishing out retribution because you rejected him? After the whole Ty thing, I mean."

"Maybe. But it might be more than that. He may actually hate the church, even though he won't admit it."

"What are you going to do?"

"The trial doesn't start for a few days. I still have time, but I'll have to let him know. Clearly, being involved with you creates a conflict of interest."

"You really don't think you could report objectively?"

A bicycle approached behind them, its gears clicking. Cole and Olivia again moved to the edge of the path.

"I think I could, but even the perception of a conflict is a problem. Besides, I don't think my boss and I have the same idea of what's objective, anymore."

They walked quietly for a minute.

"So, where would you work if you left?"

"No idea. Wherever I went, I'd take a pay cut."

A wind gust whipped across an open area, bringing with it an angry swirl of brown leaves. Cole wrapped an arm around Olivia's shoulder.

"Didn't you say you minored in prelaw?"

"Yeah, it helped with journalism, but I'm not sure what good it will do if I leave. It's like journalists know a little about a lot of things but not enough about anything to make a seamless career change."

"Yeah, I'd be in the same boat."

The jogger who'd passed earlier approached from in front of them, on her return trip.

"I'm open to whatever the Lord wants. I just wish he'd let me know. Send a text or post a tweet or something."

Cole chuckled. "Can you share that phone number with me?"

Olivia smiled.

"Hey, before I forget, my mom's coming in for the trial," Cole said.

"I expected she would. It will be weird to see her in person."

"Yeah, you can't tell when we FaceTime, but she's really tiny. She kind of reminds me of Yoda."

The playful slap landed on his upper arm.

"You're awful! I'm going to tell her you said that!"

"I'm serious! I even hinted at it once when I was a teenager. I asked her if she thought she had Yoda's forehead, and she asked me if I thought I might ever want to leave my room again."

"Well good for her."

"Just because she looks like Yoda doesn't mean I don't love her to death. Look at me. Look at this forehead. I look just like her. Backward syntax when I am old, I will start to use."

Another playful swat landed. "You're still awful. What sorts of things do you say about me when I'm not around?"

"That you're the prettiest girl I've ever seen, and I love you."

"Right," she said with mock sarcasm. "Now, shut up and kiss me so I can get out of here. I have an appointment."

Cole did as he was told.

24

FRANK HAMILTON HAD CALLED it exclusion and separation of witnesses.

"The court does it so you can't adapt your testimony based on what other witnesses have said," he'd explained.

The concept made sense in theory. It prevented witnesses from lying for one another. In his case, however, it served only as an annoyance.

Every night since the trial had started, he'd had to ask Olivia and Frank what they could tell him about the day's testimony. He wasn't sure what they were supposed to tell him, but he'd been able to pry a few details out of them.

The coroner had said that bruising and scrapes Trace had suffered could have come from being hit by a vehicle. Olivia had said Frank tried to get the jury to realize they also could have come from simply falling off the truck hood. "But I don't think the jury bought it," she'd said.

The accident reconstruction guy's testimony had been just as damaging. He said a crack in the truck's grill could have come from hitting Trace, even though Cole thought the grill had cracked when Trace put his foot on the bumper to hoist himself onto the hood. Frank had gotten the reconstruction guy to say a rock hitting the grill could have caused the crack, but again, the jury didn't seem impressed.

Now Cole waited.

A framed picture of George Washington crossing the Delaware hung on one wall in the witness waiting room. An old TV was mounted in one corner.

This place is almost as bad as the interrogation room. If I stretched out my arms, I could nearly touch the walls on each side.

The cubicle was only slightly longer than is was wide. An end table and a straight-backed chair like those at his doctor's office waiting room filled the space. On the TV, a woman in a nightgown had her hand on the bare chest of a tan, V-shaped man.

Cole grabbed the remote from the end table.

Great. Two other choices. A 1990s sitcom or a shopping channel.

"I feel like a prisoner in here," he said aloud.

Smooth move, stupid. There are probably cameras and mics somewhere.

He swung his gaze around the room but saw nothing suspicious.

Oh, well, does it really matter?

He muted the TV. Faces on two magazines on the end table peered up at him. A two-year-old men's fashion publication, and a six-month-old women's magazine.

That's no better than the TV.

I wish I could have brought my phone.

Cole learned on his first trip to the building no phones, cameras, or recording devices were allowed, and there was no place in the building to stow them. He'd had to go back to his car to put away his phone, and he'd almost been late to Kiley's initial appearance.

"What do they think I'm going to do, text someone in the court-room the answers to the test?" he'd quipped.

The court security guy hadn't been amused. "Do you want to come in here, or not?" he'd asked.

Cole closed his eyes and prayed. *Lord, it's been eight months, and I know your thoughts are higher than my thoughts, but I beg you, Lord. I've prayed this so many times, you're probably tired of hearing it.*

The noise startled him.

"They're ready for you." The bailiff, or whatever he was called in federal court, was older, thin, and with thinning gray hair.

"What time is it?" Cole asked.

"One-thirty."

"Well, here we go, I guess."

The bailiff didn't respond.

～

Kiley looked thinner but wore makeup and a business suit that Cole had given Hamilton a few days earlier. Her hair was pulled into a bun.

She's amazing. Despite everything she's endured, there's hope in her eyes.

The bailiff directed him to a spot next to the witness stand and told him to raise his right hand. Cole noticed the pew Bible from New Hope on a table with other stuff he assumed was evidence.

The oath ended with, "so help you." The government apparently didn't want the name of God uttered in the courtroom.

His mom sat along the gallery's center aisle. She looked older. Suddenly, she straddled the barrier between middle age and old age. This situation had clearly taken a toll. Olivia sat next to her. She nodded slightly when their eyes met. Did she feel strange sitting in the gallery while her former colleagues and competitors looked on? He couldn't read her expression. He was proud of her. She'd chosen her faith over her career and was looking for a job.

The Johnsons sat behind the prosecutor, while John Porter sat in the back-left corner of the room.

Okay, refocus. Watch your body language and facial expressions. Do everything Frank Hamilton said.

Hamilton's words ran through Cole's mind. "Make sure you pull the back of your shirt down as you sit, so your shirt's shoulders don't bunch up . . . Everything counts, Cole. Some members of the jury will be more impressed by your presence—your clothes, your hair, your facial expressions, your posture—than what comes out of your mouth."

Hamilton had gone on to talk about how people thought John F. Kennedy beat Richard Nixon in the nation's first televised presidential debate in 1960 because Kennedy simply looked better.

"People talked about Nixon's suit being bunched up in front, the legs of his slacks riding up, and his five-o'clock shadow," Hamilton said. "By contrast everything about Kennedy looked smooth and clean."

Hamilton had drilled Cole for a few hours the day before on questions he'd likely have to answer. He warned Cole to expect the worst during cross-examination.

"Remember, Cole, the prosecutor will try to get under your skin," Hamilton said. "He'll try to rattle you, to get you off balance. Don't let him. Make sure you control the script."

Okay, God's got this. Just do your best.

What's the jury thinking? Which side is winning?

Ten of the jurors followed Hamilton as he stood up and moved to the podium where he would ask questions. One juror, a thirtyish man with unkempt jet-black hair in the back row, picked his fingernails. A blond woman about the same age wearing jeans and a scoop-necked maroon blouse looked at someone in the gallery. The rest of the jurors looked like they were giving Hamilton's presentation fair consideration.

Okay, just let Hamilton lead you. Don't volunteer anything.

In response to Hamilton's questions, Cole recounted the June twenty-seventh events.

"And did the congregation participate in a worship service?" Hamilton asked at one point.

"Yes," Cole said. "But I asked them—no, pleaded with them—not to engage with any of the protesters."

In wrapping up his questioning, Hamilton gestured toward Kiley and asked, "Did Kiley express anger or ill will toward anyone that morning?"

Cole pushed back a wave of sadness. "No, sir. She was concerned for my safety and didn't want to drive my truck to pick me up. She simply tried to protect herself as she left the church. She was in the wrong place when someone who was trying to hurt me injured Mr. Johnson, instead."

Cole paused. Kimi and Mark Johnson sat expressionless. If only they could see his compassion. Neither Kimi nor Mark had spoken as Cole passed them in the hallway that morning.

Others in the gallery watched him intently. Olivia had bowed her head slightly and closed her eyes.

"That's all I have, Your Honor," Hamilton said.

When Hamilton sat down, Peters came around the prosecution table like he was on roller skates.

Whoa, what's happening? Did I give him ammo?

Something about the energy in the room shifted, as if the opposing team was about to score a last-second touchdown. The air somehow felt tighter.

Everyone in the jury box was riveted on the prosecutor.

What did they see and hear that I missed?

Peters leaned forward behind the podium.

"You're a pastor, are you not, Mr. Evans?" Peters began.

"Objection! Irrelevant," Hamilton called from his spot next to Kiley.

"Overruled, you can answer the question," the judge said.

"Yes," Cole said.

Keep the answer short. Don't volunteer anything that Peters can twist.

"And as a pastor, you've studied the Bible," Peters said.

"Objection! Your Honor, I fail to see—" Hamilton was animated, but the judge cut him off.

"Overruled, Mr. Hamilton. I'm allowing this line of questioning," the judge said.

"I have studied the Bible," Cole said.

"And, so you have at least some familiarity with the book of Leviticus. Would that be fair to say, Pastor Evans?"

Where's he going with this?

"Yes."

"Does this appear to be one of the Bibles from your church?" Peters said, holding up the pew Bible.

"It does."

"And do you teach from this Bible?"

"One like it or others that are similar. Some may be different translations, but I teach from the Bible," Cole said.

Peters looked at his yellow legal pad, then flipped through the Bible. "Correct me if I'm wrong. Doesn't it say here in Leviticus, 'Do not have sexual relations with a man as one does with a woman; that is detestable'? I believe that's Leviticus 18:22."

There's no way I can deny that. What do I say?

"It does," Cole said.

"It says it's 'detestable,' doesn't it, Pastor Evans? 'Detestable,' that's the word they used, right?"

"Yes."

"How would you define the word 'detestable,' Pastor Evans?"

"I guess I'd say it's something outrageously bad," Cole said.

This is not good. I see where he's going. How do I steer him somewhere else? Why didn't Hamilton see this coming?

Peters flipped a couple of pages and went on. "Doesn't it also say in Leviticus 20:13, 'If a man has sexual relations with a man as one does with a woman, both of them have done what is detestable; they are to be put to death; their blood will be on their own heads'?"

Cole's stomach dropped.

"It does, but that was in the Old Testament. Jesus tells us—"

"Fine. We'll look at the New Testament. Doesn't it say in the book of Romans . . ." Peters looked back at his legal pad, then flipped through the Bible. "Doesn't it say in Romans 1:26–27, 'Because of this, God gave them over to shameful lusts. Even their women exchanged natural sexual relations for unnatural ones. In the same way, the men also abandoned natural relations with women and were inflamed with lust for one another. Men committed shameful acts with other men and received in

themselves the due penalty for their error'? They're talking about homosexuality there, aren't they, Pastor Evans?"

"Yes. And idol worship. But the overall message of the Gospel—"

"Just 'yes' or 'no,' Pastor Evans." Peters was onto his next question
before Cole could complete his answer. "In the Gospels, are there not
stories about Jesus performing a so-called cleansing of the temple?"

"There are," Cole said.

"And what does Jesus do in those stories?"

"He turns over tables of moneychangers and scatters the sacrificial
animals that were being sold."

"I think you'd agree that Jesus, assuming he actually existed, was
quite passionate at times." Peters didn't wait for a response. "Doesn't the
book of Revelation quote Jesus as saying he will spit out lukewarm Christians?" Peters asked, making quotation marks with his fingers around the
words "spit out."

Oh, this is bad. This is really bad. Think, think, think, think, think.

"What do you take that passage to mean?" Peters asked.

"Objection, Your Honor! This is ridiculous." Hamilton shot out of
his chair, his face crimson.

"Did you not hear me the first few times, counselor? Now sit down,
Mr. Hamilton, and let Mr. Peters finish," the judge said.

Hamilton sat but looked defiant.

Peters repeated his question.

"I take it to mean we're to be passionate about our faith," Cole said.

"So, Christians believe homosexuality is wrong," Peters said. "Are
Christians supposed to be passionate about that?"

"It says homosexuality's a sin, but we can't take Scripture out of
con—"

"Would Ms. Evans ever deny that she is a Christian?" Peters asked.

"Calls for conjecture, Your Honor," Hamilton said, but Cole answered before the judge ruled.

"I don't know, ask her," he said.

Kiley bit at the nail of her right index finger. Her jaw had tightened,
and the worry flickered in her eyes.

"He's asking you, Mr. Evans. Answer the question," the judge said.

Hamilton bounded from his chair again.

"Objection, Your Honor! Conjecture! The witness can't possibly
know what another person is thinking!"

"The witness may answer," the judge said.

Hamilton mumbled something about any conviction being overturned on judicial error.

Cole flinched at the crack of the gavel.

"One more comment, Mr. Hamilton, and I'll hold you in contempt," the judge said, his face now red. "Answer the question, Mr. Evans."

"I don't believe she would ever deny her Christianity," Cole said.

Peters leaned forward even further behind the podium. His eyes blazed.

Cole tried to control his posture and facial expressions but felt as imposing as an ice cream cone.

"And she's supposed to be passionate about that, isn't she, Pastor Evans? Maybe even passionate enough to hit a man with her car?"

The legs of Hamilton's chair squealed across the floor as he stood up. "Your Honor, this is a mockery!"

"Overruled. For the last time! Sit down and shut up, Mr. Hamilton!"

"Nothing further, Your Honor," Peters said.

Peters returned to the prosecution table with a smirk. Hamilton stared blankly at his yellow legal pad. Kiley looked stunned, fear and astonishment in her eyes.

Oh, Lord, please, please help. I think I've just helped convict her.

Cole hoped Peters could see the hatred in his eyes. He ached to leap from the witness stand and pummel the man. As he imagined slamming Peters into the courtroom wall, Cole realized Frank Hamilton had repeated himself.

"I'm sorry, Mr. Hamilton, could you repeat the question?" Cole said.

"We're not to judge others, especially those in the church, are we, Mr. Evans?"

"No. Jesus says in Matthew 7:4 a person can't look at the speck of sawdust in someone else's eye until he gets the plank out of his own eye."

"And were you looking at the speck of sawdust in Mr. Porter's or Mr. Johnson's eye?"

"I certainly hope not, at least not without taking the plank out of mine," Cole said.

"Do you hate gay people?" Hamilton asked.

Whoa, I didn't see that coming.

"Of course not!" Cole said. "Jesus didn't just die for straight people, he died for gay people, too! His grace extends to everyone who will accept it. And I'm no more deserving of his grace than a gay person. So, I need to get to know the whole person, not just his or her sexuality, and I need to love that person regardless of his or her sexual preference."

"Then why wouldn't you marry Mr. Porter and Mr. Johnson?"

Okay, think. Make this good. This may be your only chance to help Kiley.

"The Bible and common sense make it clear we weren't designed for homosexuality. If I believe God is our creator—and I do—and if I believe the Bible is his instruction book, then I would be doing these men a great disservice by encouraging them to live in a way they weren't designed to live. God has something much better for them, and I want them to have that."

Two jurors nodded. He'd gotten through.

"So, you believe your decision not to marry them was loving," Hamilton said.

"I do," Cole said.

Peters again approached the podium like he was headed to a fire.

"You're at least somewhat familiar with church history, aren't you Pastor Evans?"

Oh, boy, now what?

"Sure. Somewhat."

"The church hasn't always gotten it right, has it, Pastor Evans? Didn't the Roman Catholic Church condemn Galileo for saying the earth moves around the sun?"

"Objection, Your Honor!" Hamilton was again animated.

"Never mind. I'll withdraw the question."

"The jury will disregard," the judge instructed.

Yeah, right. I'm sure they will.

∾

At the bottom of the courthouse steps, a twenty-something man with a scruffy goatee and a reporter's notebook stopped him. "Do you think your sister can beat this?"

If you don't get out of my face, you'll need to get that notebook surgically removed.

He brushed past without making eye contact.

He prayed as he walked toward the parking lot. *I don't even know what to pray, Lord. Please just help us.*

The passage from Psalm 3:1–4 came to mind:

Lord, how many are my foes!
How many rise up against me!
Many are saying of me,
"God will not deliver him."
But you, Lord, are a shield around me,
my glory, the One who lifts my head high.
I call out to the Lord,
and he answers me from his holy mountain.

Cole had never been passionate about poetry and, for that reason, didn't especially like the book of Psalms before Kiley's arrest. He hadn't disliked the book, the way he disliked the book of Lamentations, he just didn't love the psalms.

That had changed, however. Time and again in recent months, he'd dipped into the book to read how David poured out his heart to the Lord and asked for deliverance from his enemies.

He plopped himself into the SUV's driver's seat. Even though autumn had arrived a few weeks earlier, remnants of summer were determined to hang on, and the sun coming through the car window created a greenhouse effect.

Seeing no media in sight, he rolled down the window and let the crisp air slap the side of his face. He laid his head on the seat's headrest and prayed, *Lord, please don't make Kiley pay for my mistakes.*

The opening car door startled him.

"I thought you could use some company," Olivia said.

"I feel like such an idiot. I don't know what to say," Cole said.

"Sometimes, there are no words," Olivia said. She squeezed his hand. "I know I'm not in your shoes but try to hang in and trust."

Compassion filled her eyes, and she leaned her head on his shoulder. Cole stared at the dashboard.

"I wish I could take this pain from you," Olivia said.

"I'm glad you can't," Cole replied.

～

Cole felt as if he'd been run through a meat grinder. His body ached. Breathing caused a dull pain in his torso, particularly in the muscles in the sides of his chest, those he'd overused weeping the previous night.

The judge hadn't yet emerged from chambers when marshals led Kiley into the courtroom. She stared at the floor. Her posture was stiff, almost rigid. From what little he could make out, her lips looked tightly pressed together. Those who didn't know her might not notice, but Cole could see the anger radiating out of her.

"She thinks it's my fault. She doesn't want to look at me. I can't blame her. I don't even want to see myself," Cole whispered to Olivia.

"I'll admit none of this looks good, but God is still sovereign. This will all work out the way he wants it to."

Cole tried to take comfort in her words but found little.

The arrogance oozed out of Peters. His chin jutted too far, and he looked down his nose.

Cole crossed his arms and leaned back in his seat as he listened to closing arguments.

"We heard from Pastor Evans, who told us that Christians are expected to have a zeal for their faith," the prosecutor said. He walked back and forth in front of the jury box as he spoke, his tone moving between wooing and self-righteous. "We have shown that the defendant took that zeal to hate-fueled criminal extremes."

Lord, this battle is yours. Please, let the truth come out.

Olivia looked into her lap with hands folded. Cole felt her prayers.

Hamilton got up and spoke. The momentum swung his direction. Juror's eyes followed him, and heads nodded.

But court procedures gave the prosecution the final shot.

"They have the burden of proof. They get two turns," Hamilton had said over the phone a few days earlier.

As he had during his first pass at the jury, Peters charmed the panel one minute and dripped contempt for Kiley the next.

"I want you to look at that woman," he said angrily, pointing at Kiley. "Now, I want you to look at these people," he said, gently gesturing toward Mark and Kimi Johnson. "Their son Trace is gone, and they deserve justice."

The righteousness again rose in Peters's voice. "For the sake of Mark and Kimi Johnson, and for the sake of all that is lawful and just, you can do nothing less than bring back a verdict of guilty."

25

JIMMY'S MOUSE-BROWN HAIR FELL across his face, long and scraggly, and the flannel shirt he wore unbuttoned over his T-shirt hung like a robe from his sinewy frame. Jimmy's brother was in on a criminal trespass conviction. The woman at the head of the line, Sierra, dark-haired, round and portly, had a son doing six months on a drug charge. Cole couldn't say he and his fellow visitors to the jail every week were friends, but they talked. They shared a sadness most people couldn't understand.

His heart went out to Sierra.

"At what point does helping become enabling?" she'd asked once. Cole wasn't sure he'd given her a good answer.

He hadn't realized it, but before things went sideways for Kiley, he'd felt superior to incarcerated people. His pride smacked him in the middle of the forehead the first time he saw Kiley behind the glass partition. He'd often uttered the John Bradford quote, "There but for the grace of God go I," but he hadn't understood it. Not truly.

This would be his last visit before the jury got the case.

Garcia motioned him forward. Cole didn't know the deputy's first name. Swarthy, slightly shorter than average, and stocky, Cole was sure Garcia could hold his own in a brawl. Unlike some deputies who processed in visitors, Garcia was always pleasant. The man had never confessed it, but something told Cole that Garcia was a believer.

"Hey pastor, sorry to hear how things went in court this week," he said. He sounded sincere.

Cole was sure everyone in the building knew. The story had led the local news. For all he knew, it had gone national.

"Thanks, Garcia," Cole said.

The deputy's eyes roamed his computer screen, and he punched a few keys. He punched a few more.

This isn't right. It's taking way too long.

"Sorry, pastor, she's taken you off her visitors list."

What? He has to be kidding!

"Are you sure? Can you check again?"

Garcia typed, then shook his head. "Sorry, man, maybe next week."

Cole felt his chest tighten. He squeezed his eyes shut to fight back the tears.

She blames me, and she's right.

He avoided eye contact as he made his way out of the jail.

∾

Cole stared at the dust on the steering column. He was glad to have his truck back, but it needed a good cleaning.

Clearly, the folks at the police impound lot don't provide a car detailing service.

Should he call Don Fisher?

What can he do? He can't help. Nobody can.

If one of his church members came to him feeling the way he did now, Cole knew he'd find a way to help that person understand everything would be okay, even if Jesus called someone home. But he couldn't conjure up the words to bring himself that assurance.

Two hours later, he studied the white speckled laminate countertop at The Pitchfork. The place was empty and quiet, save for tinny oldies music that bopped through an ancient box speaker in the corner. Behind him, Chandra swept around the empty tables.

An oily sheen floated on the black liquid in his mug. The stuff tasted like rubber. Cole felt himself scowl as the fluid hit the back of his tongue.

"You want me to make you a new pot?" Trina asked.

"No, you guys close in ten minutes. It would be a waste."

"It'd be no trouble."

"No, really. Thanks, Trina."

"You look like you could use something stronger," Trina said with a chuckle.

"Kiley took me off her visitors list. I testified at her trial the other day, and the prosecutor pretty much ripped me to shreds and made Kiley look like a murderous religious zealot. After that, closing arguments didn't go well. When I went to visit her this morning, she'd taken me off her list of visitors."

"Oh, Cole, I'm so sorry," Trina said, her hand touching his.

"I can't blame her. I may have cost her her life."

"You can't do that to yourself, Cole. I'm sure you did everything you could. And I know you didn't plan for things to turn out this way." She gently squeezed his hand.

"I appreciate what you're saying, Trina, but I'm not sure my good intent carries much weight right now. What's worse, her lawyer warned me not to testify. He said I'd be a liability, and he was right."

"You didn't put her in that cell, Cole." Trina's voice took on a knowing, almost authoritative tone. "Crooked politicians put her in there. I have a feeling, have had it all along, that the government would do anything to make an example of her."

"Well, let's just hope the jury sees what's happening. Deliberations start Monday."

"You're a good man, Cole. As hard as it may be, try not to blame yourself."

"Sorry, Trina. I don't know why I'm unloading this on you. Forgive me."

"Oh, stop it, you big goofball! How many years have we known each other?"

"Probably about twenty, I guess," Cole said.

"You should know by now I love you like a brother." She wrote her number on her order pad and ripped off the top sheet. "You call me if you need to talk. Day or night. I mean it."

I don't know what to say. It sounds like she does mean it. I had no idea she felt that way.

He managed a weak smile as Chandra began sweeping around his stool.

"Why don't you take a break, even if it's just a temporary diversion?" Trina said. "Why don't you and your girlfriend come to The Whistle Stop tonight? Jerry and I are going over with Chandra. Right?" she asked Chandra.

"Yup. Best wings and daiquiris in town."

"I probably shouldn't."

"C'mon! You look like you've been run over by a freight train," Trina said.

"Olivia's out of town at a job interview."

"All the more reason. You don't want to just sit around and mope. That'll just make things worse. Besides, Jerry will be there, and he'd probably appreciate some male company."

"It'd be nice, but it just doesn't feel right. Maybe we can do it when Olivia gets back."

"Okay. You always were a Goody two-shoes," Trina said.

"Comes with the job description, I guess," Cole said, laying a few bills on the counter, including enough for a generous tip.

"You call me if you need to, you hear?" Trina said.

"Yes, ma'am," Cole said.

He knew he shouldn't and probably wouldn't. As a pastor, he had to limit his number of confessors to a very tight handful of trustworthy men. First of all, talking to a woman whom he wasn't close to could give the wrong impression. And secondly, he had to know what he said would be held in confidence. Pastors had to live a clean life, but some people thought that meant a perfect life, and people sometimes got mad at pastors for things that seemed unreasonable. Steve Collins, a pastor across town, had told him a few months back that he lost a church member because the man thought the car Steve had purchased was too new, even though it was three years old. "You just never know what will set people off," Steve had said.

Cole folded the order pad page and put it in his shirt pocket.

That night, he called Olivia, then Don Fisher, and spent the evening watching college football.

∾

Cole paced back and forth across his office in the old church building as he listened to *Uncle Tom's Cabin* on his tablet. His mom had taken up residence on the sofa across the room. Simon Legree had just threatened to kill Tom.

Cole glanced at the clock. Three-thirty Friday afternoon.

"You don't think we'll be here next week, do you?" Cole said.

"If it means Kiley is found innocent, I don't care if we're here two weeks from now. They can deliberate as long as they want."

"Good point."

Cole and his mom had gone to the church every day during the deliberations because it was closer to the courthouse than his house was. Frank Hamilton had said he was sure he could get the judge to wait at least thirty minutes before reconvening, once the jury had a verdict. A half hour was plenty of time to get from the church to court.

"I wonder how Kiley's holding up. The waiting is driving me crazy, it must be killing her," Cole said.

"Bad choice of words, but I can't imagine," his mom said.

~

Most of the jurors wore stoic expressions as they shuffled in. One woman, Juror Number Four, a middle-aged pudgy woman with dull gray hair, scowled. She either didn't like the verdict or didn't like the law she was called to uphold. Either way, it looked like bad news.

As had been her practice in recent days, Kiley didn't look at him. She still blamed him. Cole could feel it.

His heart pounded. He closed his eyes and tried to pray.

The judge prattled and finally asked, "Madam forewoman, do you have a verdict?"

The forewoman, middle-aged with unruly auburn hair and large bags under her eyes, looked at the piece of paper she held, apparently unable to meet Kiley's eyes.

"As to Count One of the indictment, murder in the first degree, we, the jury, find Defendant Kiley S. Evans guilty."

Cole's breath caught in his throat.

Kiley looked stunned.

"As to Count Two of the indictment, engaging in hate crimes resulting in the death of another, we, the jury, find Defendant Kiley S. Evans guilty."

Cole put his head in his hands. Olivia's arm draped across his shoulder. His silent tears burned, then dripped onto his trousers.

"As to Count Three of the indictment, inducing panic, we, the jury, find Defendant Kiley S. Evans guilty."

Cole couldn't look at her. He was sure she hadn't looked at him, either.

"As to Count Four of the indictment, obstruction of justice, we, the jury, find Defendant Kiley S. Evans guilty."

26

THE COURTROOM LOOKED NO different than it had three weeks earlier, although more media had crammed themselves into the room than during earlier proceedings. Reporters spilled from the corner set aside for them and into a section of the main gallery. People sat shoulder to shoulder. The eagle on the Great Seal behind the judge's bench glared into the room.

Kiley had essentially been through two trials, one in which she was convicted, and a second in which the same jury that found her guilty recommended the death penalty. Cole didn't know how things had worked in times past, but the court now had the power to override the jury's recommendation.

Kiley shuffled into the room gaunt and expressionless, swimming in her orange jumpsuit. Her shoulders rolled forward, and the chains on her ankles clinked as she made her way to her seat.

Her eyes shot daggers as she glanced Cole's direction.

She looked drugged. Had the jail medical staff given her something? Did the jail even have a medical staff?

Cole had written her several times, apologizing and pouring out his heart. The letters had had no effect. Had she even read them?

Cole, his mom, and Olivia sat directly behind the defense table. Hamilton had moved into Cole's line of sight, and he could no longer see Kiley's face. He could only observe her body language.

Cole heard the words "presentence report" and watched a man climb onto the witness stand.

Okay, who's this guy? Charlie Brown's teacher. Wah-wah wah, wah-wah-wah wah-wah.

Even if the worst happens, this can't be over fast enough.

Trace Johnson's dad spoke. "This young lady stole something we can never get back." He turned to Kiley. "You robbed us, and you're totally without remorse."

Wow, he's in such deep denial about Trace's part in all of this, and Kiley has absolutely shown appropriate sorrow, especially considering she's done nothing wrong.

Olivia shook her head and mouthed, "I can't believe this."

Horror filled his mom's eyes.

Kiley's chains jingled as she moved to behind the podium. Her body language changed when she faced the judge. She held her shoulders back and her head high. Her voice rang out clear and strong.

"Your Honor, I'm truly sorry for the Johnson family's loss. But, as God is my witness, I did not cause Trace Johnson's death. Had all the evidence been admitted in this trial, namely the video evidence that you wouldn't allow, the jury could have come to no decision but acquittal."

Wow, I've never heard her speak so eloquently or confidently. Obviously, she practiced.

"Even though I'm certain my next statement will engender only negative regard from you, I'm compelled to go on record to say that this trial has not been fair and impartial. Indeed, Lady Justice has set down her scales and covered her eyes. I'm sure you've heard countless defendants say they're innocent. But I believe, in my case, you know that to be true. Your actions in the next few minutes will demonstrate what kind of human being you are. If you hand down the sentence I expect, may God have mercy on your soul."

The silence in the courtroom shrieked, and the color drained from the judge's face.

As Kiley sat, the judge glanced out the window, then at his bench. He took a deep breath and began. "The facts of this case are fairly simple, as is the reason for these proceedings today. The jury has recommended the death penalty in this matter and, after weighing the evidence and the jury's guilty verdict, and applying the law, this court has no choice but to impose capital punishment."

The words slammed into Cole. His guts twisted. He felt dizzy.

He couldn't see Kiley's face. Her shoulders, however, drooped.

The courtroom erupted. Johnson's family cheered and cried. A low groan escaped Olivia, and she put her hand across her mouth. From his spot in the back-left corner, John Porter smiled and appeared to be restraining the urge to pump his fist.

When Kiley finally looked Cole's way, she looked bewildered. Her eyes pleaded as a deputy marshal led her from the courtroom.

Cole slumped back against the pew, pinned by a tidal wave of sadness and guilt.

He struggled to make his legs work. Finally, he stood as Hamilton reached across the bar and grabbed him by the elbow.

"Hey, this is far from over," Hamilton said.

Cole knew Hamilton was right. Still, the lawyer's words didn't help. If anything, they made things worse. He numbly shook Hamilton's hand and thanked him before Hamilton left.

~

Cole stared at the Bible and saw nothing. Just a sea of gray ink.

I may have to call Tom Henderson to see if he can preach on Thursday. I've got nothing.

He tried to pray.

Lord, I don't even know what to ask you. Do you want me to preach anymore? Is there anything you want me to say to New Hope? New Hope, right. What a joke. No Hope's more like it.

He studied the swirls in ceiling's drywall, or whatever the ceiling was made of. *Yep, that's where the prayers have been going.*

His phone vibrated on the desk. It vibrated a few more seconds before the number on the screen registered in his brain. He seized the gadget and swiped.

"This is a collect call from the Hamilton County, Ohio Jail," the automated voice said. "Do you accept?"

"Yes!" He spat out the word.

The phone clicked, and he heard background noise.

"Hi! Thank you for calling." It sounded lame, but he didn't know what else to say.

"Hey, there. I'm sorry I blamed you. I was pretty much mad at everybody." Kiley sounded worn out.

"It's understandable. If I were in your place, I'd probably still be mad. My own pride played a part in this, and I hope you can somehow forgive me."

"There's no time for blame and hanging onto anger right now. I can't expend the energy. I'm sorry, Cole, and I love you."

"I love you too, Sis, more than you'll ever know."

"Please come and see me," she said. "I get transferred to the federal prison in Terre Haute on Monday."

"Indiana. It could be worse. You could be headed across the country."

"Mm-hmm."

"This call will end in ten seconds," the robotic voice interjected.

"I'll definitely see you tomorrow. Love you, Sis."

"Love y—"

~

Getting in to see Kiley took forever. The list, the searches, the waiting. Deputies seemed determined to stretch the process out as long as possible.

Finally, he was in the visitors' room. Kiley was already on her side of the glass. She'd pulled her hair back into a ponytail, exposing new furrows on her brow. New crow's feet had developed around her eyes, as well.

She offered a weak smile. "Hi, I'm so happy and so sad," she said.

"You know I'd take your place if I could, right? I'd do anything to spare you from having to go through this." Cole meant it, and he sensed Kiley believed him.

"I know, but I'm okay right now. I've prayed a lot and read the Bible a lot over the last few weeks. For some reason, they didn't take it away from me at the jail after the president's executive order. Maybe because it's not a federal facility. Anyway, Jesus has got this. He'll either get me out of this, or I'll get to walk with him sooner than I might have otherwise."

"Well, from my perspective, I hope he gets you the heck out of there."

"One day at a time. It's a cliché, but clichés become clichés because they're true," Kiley said.

"So, I guess we'll have to figure out how visits work at Terre Haute." Cole said.

"If I even get them. Who knows what they do with people on death row?"

"No idea."

"Just remember, I love you, Little Brother," Kiley said.

The sadness in her eyes at the end of the visit tore at him.

I'll never be able to erase this image. I am so, so sorry.

Tears burned his eyes and he gulped down the lump in his throat. He gazed at the ground as he walked through the jailhouse and across the parking lot.

His rearview mirror reflected the jailhouse.

You can't look back there. You have to go.

His vision blurred, and he dug his knuckles into his eyes, then stuck the key in the ignition.

All right, now what do I do with myself? I can't sit around and mope, but I still need to be someplace alone so I can feel some of these emotions.

He turned left on Walnut and headed toward the car parts store.

~

Cole worked in circles about two- to three-feet in diameter. Under the partly cloudy sky, and with temperatures in the low eighties, the swirls of car polish quickly dried to a haze on the truck's crimson fender.

He'd cried twice and was pretty sure there were more tears where those had come from.

He squatted, buffing towel in hand, as he removed the dry polish from around the wheel well.

His phone vibrated in his pocket.

"Hey, there? You up for a little celebration tonight?" Olivia sounded ecstatic.

Does she not realize I just came from seeing my sister for what might be the last time?

Sure, she does. But just because my life sucks right now doesn't mean hers can't continue. "I could use some happy news. What's going on?"

"I ran into Frank Hamilton at the grocery store today, and we got to talking. He offered me a job!"

"You're kidding! That's awesome! Doing what?"

"Legal record searches and a little bit of other investigative stuff. He said he'd send me to paralegal school if I was interested."

"That's fantastic!"

"Yeah, his other girl is moving to Tennessee. I start Monday, and she'll help train me."

"Well, at least *some* good has come out of all this," Cole said.

"Yeah, I guess Romans 8:28 is still true."

"No doubt. What time are we celebrating and where?"

"My place. Seven."

"Is Stormy celebrating with us?"

"I could see if Abby could take her somewhere."

"No, don't. She should celebrate, too. I'll bring that mint chocolate chip ice cream she likes."

"I love you, Cole Evans."

"I love you, too, Miss Legal Assistant."

He buffed the polish a little faster.

27

A FEW LANES WIDE on each side and lined with restaurants and various other retail establishments, one main drag, Route Forty-One, ran north-south through Terre Haute.

As Cole turned off the thoroughfare, the business district soon gave way to farmland, and as he passed a Dollar General, the city of red brick, stone slab and barbed wire came into view. A pistachio-colored water tower rose over the prison complex like a map pin.

Kiley was in the new women's prison. Two prisons had existed at Terre Haute before the women's prison was built. One was a medium-security men's facility, the other the penitentiary for men, where federal death row and the federal death house were located.

As he pulled into his parking space, the women's prison stretched out in front of him, a maze of massive gray concrete blocks. Everything was gray. The buildings were gray, the sidewalks were gray, the lookout towers were gray, and even the sky was gray. Had it been cost-effective, even the grass would've been gray.

Did they do that on purpose just to depress everybody, or is gray concrete the only choice when you hire the lowest bidder?

Cole stowed his cell phone and got out of the car. He saw no one, yet he felt eyes on him as he crossed the parking lot.

He stood at the door for a beat. Tinted brown glass. Did he really want to do this? He had to. There was no other way to see Kiley.

Inside the visitor's entrance, fake bamboo trees stood in planters in the corners, and huge wood beams stretched across the ceiling.

Home, sweet home.

Cole flinched when a voice came from behind a saucer-sized window to his left.

"Prisoner's name."

He'd heard a deep baritone like that once, an actor named James Earl Jones. "No, I am your father." The movie line typically was misquoted as, "Luke, I am your father," which irked Cole for some reason, but whatever. He had more important things to worry about than Star Wars.

"Uh, Kiley Evans."

The dark-haired stone-faced man was barely visible through the tiny circular window. A keyboard clacked, and a door opened behind him.

"In here."

Is that a man or woman? Woman. I think. Maybe.

Tiny menacing black eyes impaled him. The woman's mouse-brown hair had been styled with a jig saw, and her lips disappeared somewhere between the heavy jowls.

The thick hand thrust an old-fashioned digital signature pad his direction. The woman's forearm was thicker than his leg.

"It's consent for the retinal scan, blood test and cavity search."

His jaw clenched.

"Do I do that every time I come in?" he asked.

"Yup. You'll get used to it. Or stay home."

Ten minutes later, the buzzer pierced the side of his skull.

Beyond the door, another woman in uniform led him along a wide corridor with concrete floors waxed and buffed to a gleam. Off-white paint covered the concrete slab walls, grooved steel roof and steel girders. Only the occasional blue-gray steel door broke the monotony. Huge globes that hung from the girders lit the passageway.

Although he was not yet in the prison proper, the noise buffeted him. Yelled conversations, curses, screams, and wails bounced from the building's hard surfaces like balls in a pin ball machine. Radios attempted to out-blare one another, toilets flushed, and women created sound simply by milling about.

An odor akin to sweat and urine mixed with pine-scented floor cleanser assailed him.

Finally, a single cubby, about four feet across with a single wood chair and a phone mounted to one wall greeted him.

Kiley wore leg irons. Her handcuffs were linked to a chain around her waist. She looked tired, but otherwise well-groomed. Her so-called work uniform, a khaki button-down shirt with navy work pants, looked crisp, a sure signal to veteran inmates that Kiley was new.

Kiley tried to smile as she approached, but her facial expression and body language told Cole she was confused and stunned.

"Hi, Sis, how are you adjusting?"

"I don't know. Overwhelmed. There are tons of rules and piles of jargon and acronyms that we're supposed to know by osmosis or something, and we get screamed at or worse if we don't. We're up every day at six, and we have to make our beds and clean our areas, which I guess is actually bearable. The isolation is hard," Kiley said. "We're not in the general prison population. We spend twenty-three hours a day in our cells."

"Don't you go to a mess hall or something?"

"Not in our pod," Kiley said. "Our trays are passed through a slot in our doors."

"So, it's almost like solitary confinement," Cole said.

Cole had read the Supreme Court at some point had ruled it unconstitutional to put someone in solitary without an explicit disciplinary reason. The court had agreed with a group of psychologists that prolonged solitary confinement drove prisoners insane and unnecessarily endangered prison staff.

"We're not technically in solitary because we can talk through the walls to the people on either side of us, and we can see onto the catwalk. And if we haven't been in trouble, we can go to the yard, one at a time, for a half hour a day. Some women on other pods get out of their cells to do jobs on the unit. I haven't figured out how that works yet or if it's even possible for people on The Row."

Cole nodded.

"I got to go to the prison library once," she said. "It seemed like a long walk. It's three steps from one end of my cell to the other. I've only been out that one time, expect to go to the yard. This is my second time out."

Wow, what happened to her? She sounds like a first grader. Did someone drug her? Is she in shock? Lord, please help her.

"You can hear stuff from all over the pod. I heard a huge argument yesterday because one woman looked at another woman's candy bar. A guard had to break it up. A candy bar is a big deal in here," she said.

"In a place like this, it's easy to see how just about anything can result in a fight," Cole said.

Kiley became more coherent after a few minutes and said a lot of the violence occurred along racial lines and was carried out by gangs.

"Gangs charge rent on some of the pods. If people don't pay—things like cigarettes or stuff from the commissary—they get beaten up. Other times, gangs force prisoners to carry drugs."

"I can't imagine," Cole said.

"I can't, either, and I'm living it," Kiley said. "Nothing in life could have prepared me for this. It may sound like a cliché, but it really is like I've died and gone to hell. You constantly have to look over your shoulder. And if you look weak or scared, bad things happen."

Cole didn't want to think about those things. He didn't know how to respond. Nothing seemed appropriate. He nodded.

"You can hear the noise, right?" Kiley asked.

Cole nodded again.

She'd already talked about that, twice, but he couldn't bring himself to interrupt.

Voices came from every direction.

"People yell all night long and bang on pipes and stuff at all hours. It makes it impossible to sleep. Maybe I'll get used to it."

Cole couldn't fathom how dehumanized Kiley felt.

"As hard as I try, I can't imagine," he said.

"One of the things I miss most is just normal human contact. I miss being affirmed or valued in small ways. Not in some sick narcissistic way, but just in the casual ways people living normal lives show small acts of kindness. I'd give anything to wave to the guy next door as he's pulling into his driveway or to hear the lady at the bank say, 'Have a good day.' God really didn't design us to be alone, but in here, that's exactly what we are, we're loners at best. We're treated more like animals than humans."

"I'm so, so sorry, Sis. I don't know what else to say," Cole said.

"Do you want to know the worst part? Not being able to read the Bible," Kiley said.

"What do you mean?" Cole asked.

"Do you remember that executive order banning Bibles on military installations?" Kiley asked. "It applied to all federal property. Including federal prisons." Kiley sighed deeply. "I feel like I can't even take refuge in the Lord. They've taken my last vestige of hope."

"What! That's awful. I'd like to wring someone's neck!"

Kiley nodded. "Well, what are you going to do?"

The idea flashed into his brain like a lightning bolt. "Hey, wait a minute. I have an idea. Whatever you do, don't lose hope." The edge in his voice surprised him. "Trust me, I'll take care of this. I know exactly who to talk to."

28

BRUCE UPTON LOOKED OLDER. His hair had turned to salt and pepper, and he'd put on a few pounds. Cole did the math. Bruce had to be pushing fifty. He'd been in the Army nearly twenty years when they'd served together in the Middle East.

"Thanks for meeting me," Cole said.

The coffee shop, about a half-hour drive for both men, was nearly empty, and Cole and Bruce found a spot in the corner, as far as possible from everyone else. Still, Cole worried about mics and cameras.

The men caught up with each other's lives for a few minutes before Bruce moved the conversation along.

"You said you need a hand with something," he said.

"I need you to think about where we met for a minute," Cole said.

They'd been attached to an intelligence unit. While Cole worked at one end of the hall on psychological operations to mess with the enemy's mind, Bruce holed up at the opposite end of the building breaking codes.

"Okay?" Bruce said. It was a question.

"When the court struck down the executive order banning church services, I thought we might be okay, but the courts *haven't* struck down the order banning Bibles in federal facilities, yet."

Bruce nodded but still didn't look like he understood.

"The court has basically said, 'Sure, you have the right to worship, you just can't have religious materials on federal installations.' That includes prisons," Cole said.

The light bulb went on. Understanding lit Bruce's face. "And the people at the prison have taken away Kiley's Bible," Bruce said.

"Yeah. I'm wondering if you can put something simple together for me. Something easy enough for Kiley to learn."

"Okay! Yeah, gotcha! Great idea," Bruce said. "We can do something right now," he said. Then, almost at a whisper, "It's called a key number code."

On his napkin, he wrote the number thirty-one. Then he wrote, "hi." Next, he wrote, "kj".

Cole stared at the cipher for a moment, unable to grasp what Bruce had done. Bruce ran his finger from the *h* to the 3 to the *k*. And the tumblers fell into place. Cole nodded. The *k* was three letters from the *h*, and the *j* was one letter higher than the *i*.

"She'll get this," Cole said. "She's always had a knack for spotting patterns. She won't even need an explanation. Besides, decrypting passages will keep her occupied and help pass the time."

"No doubt," Bruce said.

Cole laughed at the code's simple brilliance.

"I know if someone looks at it for more than a few minutes, they'll figure it out," Bruce said. "But you should be able to at least get some Scripture into her hands before somebody gets wise."

"Absolutely," Cole said.

He thanked Bruce several times, but Bruce waved him off.

"Nothing to it, man. Glad I could help."

Bruce nodded toward something and then, almost imperceptibly, shook his head.

What was he saying? Cars? Buildings? Flagpole! That was it! Bruce was motioning toward a flag waving from a poll across the street. He wasn't pleased with what the government was up to.

Cole nodded.

They sipped their coffees and talked another ten minutes before Bruce said, "Call me if you need something a little more sophisticated."

❧

They sat next to each other at Cole's dining room table, the jigsaw puzzle's border in place. Cole examined a piece, then put it in a pile of similar-looking tree-line fragments.

"With what Bruce gave me, I can encode the Scriptures, I just don't know how I'll get them into Kiley's hands. I'm not allowed to carry anything into the prison. Besides, we're on opposite sides of a window."

Olivia inserted a piece into the puzzle. Dark green leaves and pale blue sky.

"Well, she can receive mail, including magazines, right?" Olivia asked. "Maybe replace magazine pages with encrypted Scripture?"

"Where do I get glossy paper?"

"Yeah, you'd probably need a new printer, too."

"It's doable, I guess, but there has to be a better way," Cole said.

He inserted a piece of lakeshore into the picture.

"We could break your arm. Then you could smuggle Bible pages in your cast and get a guard to give them to her."

"Thanks. I can tell you really love me," Cole said.

"Hey, it's an idea," Olivia said.

"Not a good one."

"That's because your girlfriend is starving. Feed me, Preacher Man."

Olivia's phone dinged, and she read an incoming text. "Frank. What's he want at this hour? Hey, wait a minute! Frank represents a guy who used to publish Bibles!"

~

Cole stood when Olivia and the stranger walked in.

"Thanks for agreeing to meet here," Cole said. He stuck out a hand.

Ben Singleton was shorter than average, midfifties, and balding. What hair he still possessed was chestnut colored. He sported a dark blue suit and a silk tie. Cole didn't know what brand of shoes Singleton wore, but they looked expensive.

Singleton's handshake was neither firm nor mushy.

"Honestly, I'm not sure I'm interested in what you're trying to do, but I trust Olivia," Singleton said. He nodded her direction.

"I appreciate you coming, too," Olivia said. "At this point, however, I should leave. Since our firm represents you, Ben, ethically, I can't be party to anything you decide that might be illegal."

She offered her hand and Singleton shook it.

Five minutes later, the small thin handmade books lay fanned out in front of Singleton. He held a single sheet of paper with what looked like a word-search puzzle.

Cole pointed out the small "hi 31 kj" in the upper left corner, then explained the code.

Singleton's finger ran along the rows of letters. He slowly wrote on a separate sheet of paper the opening words of the book of John. "In the beginning was the Word, and the Word was with God . . ."

Some words broke in the middle and continued on the next line of the puzzle, but Singleton kept writing. He smiled as he wrote.

Cole had him.

". . . He was . . ."

"What do you think?" Cole asked.

"Do you think people would understand it?" Singleton asked.

"You understood it immediately. I think others would get it. Even if they didn't pick it up as quickly as you did, they'd be the type of people who like looking for patterns, and they'd be motivated to learn."

"Did you encrypt this?" Singleton asked, then backpedaled. "Never mind, I don't want to know."

Singleton examined the puzzle. "It's fun, but how do I sell it? It's not like we can say, 'Come check out our cool new coded Bible texts.'"

"That's for sure," Cole said. "Truthfully, I have no clue how you market it. The money thing really isn't my gig, I just want to get the message out."

"I can appreciate that, but I can't go broke publishing these," Singleton said.

"I hear you, but I know people buy and sell street drugs every day, and somehow people who want them know how to find them. I also know the Bible was the world's all-time best seller. How many people who live on federal facilities do you think got scared and got rid of their Bibles when the president banned religious material? And who's to say the Bible won't be banned in other places? I know there's a demand out there, and once people hear about these encrypted texts, they'll find you, you won't have to go looking for them."

"I wish you'd compared the Bible to something besides street drugs, but point taken," Singleton said.

Both men fell silent.

Cole sized him up. Should he say anything else, or had he made the sale?

"Okay, let's forget about the money thing for a minute," Singleton said.

Cole smiled inwardly. Did the statement mean this deal was done? Had Singleton moved on to figuring out *how* to make it work rather than *if* he could make it work?

"How do we get the explanation of the code into people's hands?" Singleton asked.

"I thought maybe you do an invoice. With a fake return address, of course. Maybe for zero dollars or something, or saying, 'paid in full'—in red, of course—and sent separately from the puzzles. You put the key at the bottom of the invoice."

"Do you think people would go through all that effort?" Singleton asked.

"Maybe you put the code in tiny print on the corner of the page, or somewhere," Cole said.

Singleton looked at what he'd written and sighed. "I don't know."

"Look, Ben, people need and want the Bible. You know they do," Cole said. "People in some countries risk their lives to get their hands on the Bible."

As the words spilled out, Cole wished he could reel them back in.

Doubt flashed in Singleton's eyes. "What happens when I get caught?" he asked.

If there were ever a time Cole wanted to lie, this was it. But he couldn't.

"Let me just be straight with you," Cole said. "This all started because my sister Kiley is in prison falsely charged with a hate crime because she's a Christian."

"Yeah, I followed the story," Ben said.

"Well, she desperately wants to read the Word but can't, of course, because the Bible is banned in federal facilities. I thought the encrypted texts would at least get some Scriptures into her hands.

Ben nodded.

"I thought about replacing pages in a regular word-search puzzle, but you probably know that all books and magazines that go into prisons have to come directly from a bookstore or publisher."

"Mm-hmm."

Cole pulled out his phone and thumbed through photos as he continued talking. "The more I thought about this, the more I realized this is so much bigger than Kiley. I'm sure there are people everywhere who regret having trashed or destroyed their Bibles. And they're real people. Just like my sister."

He set the phone in front of Singleton. The photo showed Kiley lying in the grass, with a puppy licking her face. It was over-the-top, but hopefully, it would work.

Singleton sighed deeply and sat back.

Cole received the letter six weeks later.

"Thanks for ordering the word-search books," Kiley had written. "They're a great way to pass the time," she said. "I've also been praying a lot. For some reason I keep thinking of John chapter 31."

Cole restrained the urge to leap for joy. She'd broken the code. The Gospel of John has only twenty-one chapters.

29

YOU CAN'T LET ANGER *get the best of you. It's unproductive.*

Still, he felt the blood rising into his face.

"I drive three hours one way to get here. Isn't there some way I could be notified?"

"Sorry, sir. That's not within our protocol." The guard's face was impassive. He gestured and looked over Cole's shoulder toward the next visitor.

"Can you tell me why she's in the hole?" Cole asked. He didn't expect an answer.

The guard's expression softened, and he looked back at is computer screen.

"Says here contraband," the guard said. "I heard she was writing some kind of religious junk. Now, would you mind?" The guard nodded toward the woman behind Cole.

Contraband. Writing religious junk. It doesn't sound like they found the puzzles, or they didn't figure out what they were. Sounds like they only found the decrypted Scriptures. Kiley, I'm so sorry. I wonder how long she's in solitary. Lord, please help her.

∽

A week had passed, and Kiley and Cole were ten minutes into their visit. As he'd suspected, guards had found her decryption. No one had figured out the puzzles contained Bible text.

"I lost track of time, but one of the guards told me I was in for two days," she said.

"Is it as awful as people say it is?"

"Worse. I had moments when I thought I was losing it. After a while, I started seeing things out of the corner of my eye," she said. "At first, I thought I saw bugs, and then I kept thinking I saw someone else in the cell. It was terrifying. When I got out, I was totally stiff. My back and neck ached, and I had a migraine. Probably just from being so anxious. I stayed on my bunk as much as I could for the next couple of days until the soreness went away."

"I'm really sorry, Sis."

"I've been thinking a lot lately about what the Lord wants from me while I'm in here."

"And?"

"I think I'm supposed to tell them to put their money where their mouth is. If they think they can stop Christianity by killing me, hurry up and do it."

Cole heard himself gasp. Was she still delusional? What was he supposed to say to that? He knew he couldn't meet her gaze until he composed himself. He studied the cinderblocks on the other side of the glass partition. Glossy eggshell white paint with off-white tile floors. He shifted his eyes. Kiley looked thin and pasty, but nothing in her expression or demeanor suggested she'd left reality.

"No, Kiley. It's ridiculous."

"You're not listening," Kiley said. "I've prayed a lot since I got out of solitary, and I get a sense I believe is from the Lord, and I think I'm supposed to face death and possibly die in order to achieve his purposes."

"Do you really want to give up? I don't think so. You're just rattled because they threw you in solitary," Cole said.

"No, I'm not. I've never been less rattled."

She did look calm. Almost eerily calm.

"I know he still has a purpose for me," Kiley continued.

"And what purpose is that, Kiley? To roll over and let the government do whatever it wants?" Cole heard the anger in his voice and wished he could rein it in, but the words gushed out of their own accord. "You've done nothing wrong!"

"I think God wants to use me," Kiley reiterated.

The quiet in Kiley's voice unnerved him.

"How's God going to use you if you're *dead*?" Cole demanded. "This is so selfish of you, Kiley."

"Is it?" Kiley asked. "Do you think I really want to be here? Don't you think I want to be with you? And the rest of our friends and family?

Don't you think I want to fall in love with someone and get married? And have kids? Do you think I want to let them jab that needle into my arm and shoot me full of poison, Cole? No, I don't. But the Word says, whoever doesn't take up their cross and follow is unworthy. If this is my cross, then this is my cross. I have to let this death sentence go forward."

"But you don't have to *push* it forward. You don't have to waive your appeals. When did you develop such a Messiah complex?"

The anger radiated from her now, although her voice remained calm. "I won't do anyone any good sitting on death row for ten or fifteen years, just waiting to die. At least this way, I'll make a statement. A declaration that the government may be able to persecute us, even to kill us, but they won't stop the Gospel. And if I die, I go to be with Jesus. And maybe a remnant of Christians in America will realize how far the nation has wandered. Maybe people will turn back to the Lord."

Something deep inside told Cole that Kiley was probably right. But he didn't want her to be. He wanted to push back as hard as he could. He didn't want to entertain the thought that he'd be without her. Still, he knew trying to persuade her right now was no use. He'd seen that expression before. She was resolute.

A Bible passage crossed his mind, Isaiah 50:7:
Because the Sovereign LORD *helps me,*
I will not be disgraced.
Therefore have I set my face like flint,
and I know I will not be put to shame.

Commentators have said the prophet is simultaneously talking about his own attitude toward carrying out his work, and about the future Messiah's resolve to fulfill God's purposes.

Maybe this is a God thing. Maybe Kiley has set her face like flint to accomplish something that God wants to achieve.

No, that was a prophet and the Messiah working to save the world. This is Kiley, someone who's anxious and depressed because she's on death row and doesn't have the faith to believe she'll eventually be set free.

He didn't know how the legal process had worked in times past, but these days, one appeal was automatic in a federal death-penalty case. A panel of judges made sure the lawyers and judge used proper procedures during the case, and that the condemned was afforded all his or her rights. Kiley had lost that appeal, despite Hamilton's assertion that the judge had erred in demanding that Cole testify about what Kiley might be thinking, and in not allowing the news footage and church security videos as evidence. The appeals panel said Hamilton's arguments were irrelevant. Kiley could seek an appeal to reexamine the evidence or to introduce new evidence. That was the appeal she wanted to forego, even though new videos had surfaced that showed what had happened the morning she was arrested.

"Kiley. Please," Cole said.

"Sorry, Cole. If the Lord wants to spare me, he will."

He felt like he'd been hit in the gut with a bowling ball. He wanted to say something else. To plead his case. He opened his mouth to speak but knew it was pointless.

Kiley raised her hand to touch the glass. "Cole, I love you, but I know this is what I have to do. And I think you know it, too."

Cole raised his hand to meet hers.

"I love you, too, Sis. I wish you'd think and pray about this some more," Cole said.

"I will. I hope you will, too."

~

The flat terrain stretched in every direction. It was probably still a little more than two hours back to Cincinnati. What a mess. Why was Kiley doing this? Had anger set in? Or hopelessness? It had been two years since her arrest, and she hadn't really gone through any prolonged angry phases. If the phases of grief were real, some angry periods seemed reasonable. But, based on how Kiley looked, that didn't fit. Had she really heard from the Lord?

Cole knew he had once, on the night after he told his class he wanted to be a preacher.

As they'd gathered the red-and-white-striped boxes and wrappers from the take-out chicken his dad had brought home, Cole had told his parents what had happened at school.

"I felt like I wanted to punch Trevor, but I knew that wasn't good," Cole had said. "It made me feel . . . I don't know the word."

"Maybe a little embarrassed?" his mom had asked.

"Yeah, and mad because it was like they were making fun of Jesus."

"You know, Cole, I know it hurt," his mom said. "It was mean, no doubt about it. It's embarrassing to get laughed at that way. But as for Jesus, don't worry about him. He can take care of himself. A very wise man, a great preacher named Charles Spurgeon, once said, 'You don't have to defend a lion. All you have to do is let the lion loose, and the lion will defend itself. Do you understand what I mean?"

"You mean Jesus is a *lion*?"

"He isn't *really* a lion. He's not an animal that runs through the jungle eating other animals. He's *like* a lion. He's strong and able to take care of himself, like a lion can. He won't be hurt just because somebody said something mean about him. Understand?" his mom had asked.

Cole went to bed knowing it was all right to want to preach, even though following God wouldn't always be easy.

As if to confirm everything his mom had said, he dreamed that night. He was in a beautiful old house, with exposed brick walls and exquisite woodwork and hardwood floors. The house was empty, without furniture, because the family who lived there was moving. The mom, dad, and son walked toward the front door, away from Cole. An open treasure chest, filled to the top with diamonds and gold, stood at Cole's feet, and he called to them, "Hey, you forgot your treasure!" When he woke up the next morning, he knew that when people walked away from Jesus, they walked away from life's greatest treasure. He knew he had to tell people about him.

A passing truck roused Cole from his reverie. *So . . . what's up with Kiley? Lord, help her. No, all of us. If this is of you, please confirm it. If she's angry or afraid, help her get through it. Help her not lose hope. And me, too, Lord. I can't take much more.*

Cole felt as if his prayers went no further than the car roof. God seemed distant, silent.

So, how would the case move forward if Kiley waived her appeal? Certainly, the government would say it needed to decide if Kiley was competent to waive her rights. Which almost certainly meant psych exams and court hearings.

He'd read of some cases where death-row inmates were denied permission to waive appeals because judges thought granting the waiver amounted to state-assisted suicide. The state had a duty to punish the condemned, not allow them a way out through suicide. The state even went to great lengths to keep them healthy. They wiped the spot where they injected the death drugs with an alcohol pad, for crying out loud.

Is that what Kiley is really trying to do, commit suicide? No, no way. She didn't seem depressed to me, she seemed almost joyful.

Okay, come on, you need to pray.

The thoughts tumbled around in his mind like clothes in a dryer. If he'd heard from the Lord in the past, he wasn't hearing from him now. At least he didn't think he was. He felt abandoned.

By the time he reached Cincinnati almost three hours later, he was exhausted. And his anger had rekindled. He was mad at both Kiley and God. None of this was fair. He tried to be obedient, and what did it get him?

As he exited the highway toward White Pine, he called Tom Henderson.

"Tom, it's Cole. Hey, do you think you'd be able to handle tomorrow's service? Do you have a sermon you could tweak or recycle?"

"No problem. Are you okay?" Tom asked.

"Yeah. Well, not really. I went out to Terre Haute today to see Kiley, and she said she wants to drop the rest of her appeals. It's like I got kicked in the gut, and I know I don't have a sermon or a lesson in me right now."

"I'm really sorry, Cole. I'll take care of it, and I'll definitely keep you in my prayers. Is there anything else I can do?"

"I don't think so, Tom. Thanks."

The dashboard clock and Cole's stomach told him it was past lunchtime. The Pitchfork was a half mile up the road.

When he walked in, the place was nearly empty.

Trina emerged from the kitchen as Cole pulled up a stool at the counter.

"You look like something the cat dragged in," she said as she set a glass of water in front of him.

"Thanks, I love you, too."

"Sorry. Something bad happen?"

Cole told her.

"I'm really sorry, Cole. You deserve better."

"I said essentially the same thing just a few minutes ago."

She reached across the counter and put her hand on his. Her touch was light and delicate.

"How long has she been in now?" Trina asked.

"It'll be three years on June twenty-seventh," Cole said.

Trina shook her head. "You're a good man, Cole. Most people would have given up by now."

"I can't, Trina. She's a victim here. She didn't do anything wrong. I saw the videos. I know exactly what happened. The government has totally twisted the facts."

"Hey, Jerry and I are going to The Whistle Stop again tonight. Are you sure you and Olivia don't want to join?" Trina asked.

"It's funny. Every time you ask, Olivia is out of town. She's working on something for her boss and won't be back until midday tomorrow."

"Well, text her and tell her you're going out with the two of us. She won't mind."

Do I do this? I could use a diversion, and Trina's right, Olivia probably won't mind.

"What time?" he asked.

30

COLE HAD DRIVEN PAST The Whistle Stop dozens of times. The historic building, with its old redbrick facade, huge arched windows, and remnants of a railway platform, sat across the street from Bangkok Terrace, a Thai restaurant that was one of Olivia's favorites. He'd never gone to The Whistle Stop, but he'd heard the place served good food.

Wow, it's dark enough in here. It's like stepping into a black hole.

Thick window shades blocked most of the light from outside and created an almost theatre-like atmosphere. Huge TVs hung in various spots around the room.

He counted.

Ten.

High-top tables sat at random spots in the center of the room, and a row of booths lined one wall. A bar ran parallel to another wall. Near the bar, the old train station ticket window functioned as a serving window between the dining area and kitchen. A rounded archway farther down the wall led to a room with pool tables and old-fashioned video games.

TV announcers, video games, and patrons all competed to be heard, and a mild scent of stale beer tempered the aroma of roasting barbecue.

This isn't right. You shouldn't be here. No matter how lousy life is, you need to take this disaster to Jesus. You need to get into the Bible, pray, and surround yourself with other Christians.

Yeah, right. Fat lot of good that's done.

His eyes adjusted to the low light. Trina and Jerry sat at a high-top near the center of the room. A pitcher with a frozen pink concoction sat between them. Probably strawberry daiquiris.

You need to turn around and leave. It's not too late.

Trina waved him over.

Crap. Do I just turn and bolt or walk over and say I can't stay?
Fascinating. This floor feels really hard. And slick.

You have to say you can't stay. It wouldn't look good if people at church knew you were here. And Olivia was probably just being nice when she said she was okay with this. Most importantly, what would Kiley think?

Look, you need to stop wondering what Kiley thinks. She's not coming back. She's a dead woman.

It was the first time he'd ever thought those words. Sure, he'd thought at times her sentence might be carried out. But now, with Kiley not fighting execution, something felt different. He no longer believed she *might* die. He knew she *would* die. Somehow, walking into the bar had caused his denial and false hope to crumble. The weight of reality landed on him like an anvil. Almost overwhelmed by the sudden wave of fear, sadness, and anger, he stood at the bar stool. Cocktail napkins, damp from sweaty glasses, stuck to the table, and a water ring glistened. Images from a TV flickered on the tabletop's glossy surface.

Turn around. Before you burst into tears. You can explain the next time you're at The Pitchfork. Trina will understand. And if she doesn't, so what?

"You okay?" Trina asked. "Hop on up here and have one of these. You'll feel better."

He climbed the stool. *Just a little relief, even if it's just for a while.*

"I can only stay for a minute."

"It's all good. Relax," Jerry said.

Before Cole could say another word, Trina motioned the waitress to bring another pitcher and a glass for Cole.

The glass felt cool and damp, and the smell of strawberries wafted to his nostrils.

Cole sipped. *Mm. Nice. What else is in here? Something smells citrussy.*

He'd tasted a strawberry daiquiri once. As he recalled, he liked it.

Probably not a very manly drink. Real men probably drink bourbon. Or at least beer. What does it matter? Kiley is going to die.

Cole stared at the glass for a beat and then took a sip. The frozen liquid felt cold on his tongue, and then the flavors exploded. Strawberry. Something sweet. Something like vanilla or butterscotch, or maybe molasses. And then he felt the burn. A warm scratchiness at the back of his mouth and in the top of his throat.

This is nice. And since I don't drink, this should do its job in no time.

From the corner of his eye, he saw Trina wave. He followed her gaze. A short buxom woman with coppery red hair and eyeglasses stood at the door. She was about his age.

Trina jumped from her stool and stretched out her arms as the woman drew near.

"Oh my gosh, Barbara! You look great! This single life is good for you!" Trina held the woman at arm's length and admired her.

"I'm meeting Denise. After dinner, we'll probably do some bar hopping. Do you and Jerry want to come along?" Barbara said.

"No, I'm getting too old for that stuff. I'll be in bed by ten!" Trina said with a laugh. "But sit down and tell me what you've been up to. I haven't seen you in what? Six months?"

When Trina made introductions, Cole learned Trina had known Barbara and the yet-to-arrive Denise from a yoga class. The women had met a decade earlier.

He didn't know why, but he immediately disliked Barbara. Her first words to him confirmed his instincts.

"Oh, you're that religious dude. On that video. Your sister's the one who ran over that poor guy outside the church. Do you really believe all that Jesus stuff? And why are you people so homophobic?"

A string of four-letter words crossed his mind. And he wanted to dump the pitcher on her head, or use it to smash in her teeth.

"Cole's taking a little break tonight," Trina said. "Jerry and I thought we'd take him out and loosen him up a little."

"Well, good. You guys need to chill out a little," Barbara said to Cole.

Before he could respond, Trina asked Barbara about her love life.

Thank you, Trina. I don't know if that was by design to intervene, or if it was just happenstance. Either way, I'll take it.

He took another pull on his drink and felt the tension begin to melt. A slight lightheadedness began to set in.

He tuned Barbara out. As he swished the stuff around in his glass, a loud groan erupted around the restaurant, followed by laughter.

The spectacle replayed itself on three TVs. A New York Yankee ran in slow motion and looked into the sky. A second player entered the picture from the top of the frame. Almost immediately they collided, their faces masks of confusion and pain. As each fell backward, the ball lit on the very top of the first player's head. The image froze, and people in the restaurant erupted into new laughter. The image was funny, as long as no one was hurt.

Barbara and Jerry giggled while Trina doubled over and convulsed. When she straightened up and caught her breath, she announced she'd laughed so hard, she'd nearly peed.

She headed toward the restroom.

"I'm tired of waiting on our server. I think I'll grab another pitcher of these," Jerry said, and he got up and walked toward the bar.

As Jerry walked away, Cole felt Barbara's bare toes touch his ankle.

Keep your toes to yourself, witch.

The gentle stroking returned a second later, and Barbara had pasted a wanton smile on her puss.

What the heck? Get your stinkin' toes away from me.

I need to leave.

No, quit it. Stop being such a puritan. She's just playing. It'll be okay. If you really don't like it, just move out of range. Just have another drink.

Her hand came across the table and rested on his forearm.

"I need to loosen you up a little more, Jesus-man," she said with a squeeze.

Okay, she was pretty. Glowing red hair and a nice shape.

No, no, no, no, no. What is wrong *with you? Has the alcohol annihilated every last brain cell? Don't even entertain the idea. You absolutely cannot go there. You're in love with another woman!*

His legs sprang to life, and he met Jerry halfway across the room.

"Hey buddy, I need to leave," he said.

"It's early. Your food hasn't even come, yet. Are you sure you can't stay?"

Should I rat Barbara out or just make an excuse? Whoa, the room has started to slant.

"I think Barbara may be a little more interested in me than I'm comfortable with."

"Yeah, sorry. She divorced about eight or ten months ago, and you're a breathing male," Jerry said.

"That's gotta be tough," Cole said. "But I really can't be anywhere near her."

His body swayed. He was in no shape to drive. *Should I order an Uber and wait outside?*

"Come on back and have another drink and at least wait till your food arrives. I'll run interference for you," Jerry said.

"All right. But make sure she keeps her toes and any other body parts away from mine."

Jerry laughed. "Will do, buddy."

When they returned to the table, Jerry asked Barbara if she was still teaching Zumba.

The toes tickled Cole's ankle again. He stared into his drink and tried to determine if his body really was moving, or if the rocking sensation was all in his head.

~

Do I really need to open my eyes? His head hurt. It was a weird tingly pain, like hitting your funny bone, but it was in the back of his head, and it made him woozy.

I guess I never made it past the couch.

He rolled onto his phone, and the plastic stuck to the side of his face. As he peeled the gadget away, the room tipped and churned. His stomach reeled. Its contents surged upward, and he fought to prevent making a mess.

His biceps burned as he pushed himself into a sitting position. More intense dizziness and nausea rolled over him. His legs ached as he swung them over the side of the sofa.

Why do my limbs hurt? Oh, dehydration. I need fluids. Sports drink with electrolytes. Those fizzy immune system boosters might help, too.

He rubbed his eyes.

How'd I get home?

The last thing he clearly remembered was steadying himself as he wobbled to the restroom at The Whistle Stop.

He walked to the living room window to look for his truck. The light jabbed his brain like a fire poker. The truck wasn't there.

Is it at The Whistle Stop? Did I take an Uber?

The phone whistled as a text arrived. The high-pitched tweet registered somewhere in the center of his skull.

Barbara: Hey, Sweetie, how ya feelin?

Barbara? Who in the heck is Barbara? Ohhh! Barbra. Crap. Did something happen? Apparently, you at least exchanged numbers.

The memory assembled itself.

He'd climbed down from his bar stool, and she stood in front of him, as drunken as he was. She leaned heavily into him wrapped her wrists around the back of his neck and said, "You sure I can't take you home and take care of you?"

"I have to go, or the Uber will leave."

"Well, at least let me give you my number."

He remembered thinking if she took it, she'd stop pestering him, and he could catch his ride.

Another shrill assault from the phone.

Barbara: Wanna pick up where we left off last night?

A part of him, the part he hated, wanted to respond.

If I ignore her, hopefully she'll just go away.

Well, at least nothing happened. On my part. I think. I hope.

His brain sloshed to the right side of his head as he flopped himself onto the couch.

You're a fool. You're an utter failure. I can't imagine anyone less deserving of God's grace.

I should pray. A prayer. Yeah, right. After last night's escapades, you don't have one.

31

COLE CLOSED THE BLINDS while he waited for the pain reliever to silence the jackhammer in his brain.

Maybe coffee would help. The cup felt warm and comforting, but Cole froze as the drink approached his lips. The aroma caused the tidal wave in his stomach to rush toward his throat. His muscles clenched as he forced things back down.

"Does this ever end?" he said, setting down the cup.

Barbara's text glared at him from the phone's screen. "Wanna pick up where we left off last night?"

A groan escaped him, and he jabbed the button to go back to the phone's home screen.

The knock at the door connected with the side of his head like a mallet. The person hadn't pounded, but the rapping was loud enough to make him want to bury his head under the sofa's throw pillow, not that that would accomplish anything.

Cole wobbled to the door and looked out the peephole.

Olivia! Fantastic! Oh, wait, is it? What's she doing here?

He glanced at his clothes. The same dark blue polo shirt and khakis he'd worn the day before. A sea of wrinkles.

Oh well, they'll have to do.

Don't let her knock again. Your head can't take it.

Intense light stabbed his eyes as the door swung open. Immediately, new pain detonated in his left cheekbone and eye socket. His head whipped to the right.

Wait a minute. She just slapped me in the face! What the—?

"What was *that* for?"

He blinked, and Olivia's features swam back into focus. Her hand remained poised for another swing. "You know what it was for. Do you need me to do it again?"

"No, what are you talking about?"

"I got home a little early last night and grabbed takeout at Bangkok Terrace."

Oh, got it. The restaurant across the street from The Whistle Stop. Did she see me going in or coming out?

Guilt washed over him. Every verse he'd ever read about adultery in the book of Proverbs thundered through his mind.

Proverbs 23:27. For an adulterous woman is a deep pit, and a wayward wife is a narrow well.

Proverbs 5:3 and 4. For the lips of the adulterous woman drip honey, and her speech is smoother than oil; but in the end she is bitter as gall, sharp as a double-edged sword.

Proverbs 7:21 and 22: With persuasive words she led him astray; she seduced him with her smooth talk. All at once he followed her like an ox going to the slaughter.

"You were staggering like a drunken sailor," Olivia said, answering Cole's unvoiced question. "You toppled into the Uber right as I drove over. I peeked into the bar and saw that waitress from The Pitchfork, some guy and, a second woman. You were there with a *woman*!"

Cole pressed his fingers over his cheek. His face burned.

"No. She was one of Trina's friends who just happened to show up."

"I can't tell you how disgusted I am with you right now. I thought I *meant* something to you!"

Her volume and pitch climbed, sending a sabre through his brain.

"You do mean something to me. You mean *everything* to me!"

His lip started to throb, and he noticed the blood droplet on the floor.

Must have bit it when she whacked me.

He wet a paper towel, wrung it, and applied it to his mouth. The dampness felt cool and comforting.

Guilt and self-pity grappled in his mind. Sure, he'd screwed up, but who wouldn't? His sister had just said she wanted to *die*, for heaven's sake.

Olivia stood on the other side of the kitchen island, hands on her hips.

"I can't trust you, Cole. How are we supposed to move forward?" Her eyes glistened with betrayal.

"I promise you, it's not what you think." Cole said. He sounded weak even to himself. "You have no idea what you're talking about."

"I know what I saw, Cole."

"You only know what you *think* you saw. Kiley is dropping all her appeals. She's going to die, Olivia. And it's all my fault. I just needed a break from the pain for a while."

"That makes absolutely no sense to me, Cole. You're sad because you might lose Kiley, so you go drinking with another woman."

Put that way, the situation did seem absurd.

"I told you, I didn't go drinking with another woman. I went drinking with Trina and Jerry, and she showed up."

"Oh, that makes it a lot better, now doesn't it?"

Cole fixed his gaze on Olivia. She glared back.

"You're so weak, Cole. What happened to all your sermons? Persevere under trial. Never give up. Blah, blah, blah. You're nothing but a weak, cheating hypocrite. I can't do this anymore." In four strides, she was out of the house, and the door thundered shut behind her.

Cole dropped onto the couch and pressed his palm into his forehead.

Was he really a hypocrite? He hated hypocrisy, especially if he found it in himself. It was bad enough when others were hypocritical. It was a hundred times worse if pastors were. That caused Christians to be a stench to people outside the church. It drove them away from God and was one of the reasons Jesus was so hard on the Pharisees.

"You're such a waste, Cole," he said aloud. He groaned and flopped sideways on the sofa, his feet still on the floor.

32

I WONDER WHAT RON Kane's going to say. Sure, his heart's in the right place. Usually. But I've seen him overreact. Am I being a realist or a pessimist? Who knows?

"Are you okay?" Don said, breaking the silence in the car.

"Ron's going to ask for my resignation."

They'd prayed for fifteen minutes before Don offered to drive Cole to the church.

Don slowed to a stop at the traffic light a couple of blocks from the building.

The traffic signal's yellow housing had faded to flax.

"He won't, and if he does, I'll talk him off the ledge. I'll be right beside you. Besides, none of the other elders will side with him. Everybody knows what you've gone through. If anybody deserves a little grace, you do."

Cole's eye socket felt the size of a softball. He reached up and tenderly touched the swollen lump. "I wish Olivia had felt that way a couple of hours ago."

"Well, you weren't totally repentant then. You were still struggling with whether you enjoyed Barbara's attention." Don looked at Cole, then broke into a smile. "You look like a disaster. I guess, I'm sorry she slugged you. I'm glad for the result, though."

Up and down Washington Street, nothing moved. Even though it was early afternoon, White Pine was quiet.

The light changed, and Don eased down Main Street.

∼

Ron Kane mopped the upper portion of his forehead with a white handkerchief. Cole noted the man's hairline had receded further since New Hope went underground, and his remaining salt-and-pepper hair had turned mostly to salt.

The heat hung dense and damp in the room. As if on cue, the air conditioner rumbled to life, a sound like four quick beats on a kettle drum.

"I know what I did was wrong and, as painful as it was both physically and emotionally, I'm glad Olivia confronted me," Cole said.

"I should've seen something like this coming," Ron said. His voice was compassionate. "I can only speak for myself, but I should've been more attuned to our spiritual battle and should've more consistently prayed for your protection."

Cole read gentle concern in the man's eyes.

"My guess is we all should have," Jeff Sanders said.

Heads around the table nodded, then Ron suggested the group pray.

The room was silent for a couple of beats after the prayer ended. The Spirit seemed to hover in the place, both heavy and peaceful.

Thank you, Lord. Thank you for being in control. Thank you for watching over us.

"Here's what I'd like to propose," Ron said. "If you think it will help, take a little time off to really soak in the Lord. Do whatever you need to do to prepare yourself spiritually, emotionally, and physically to get back behind the pulpit. Then come back with recharged batteries."

"So, you're proposing a sort of sabbatical," Jeff said. "Are we rewarding bad behavior?"

"I've talked to Cole," Tom Henderson said. "He sounds pretty contrite and repentant to me."

"I get the same impression. At the same time, I don't think he's ready to get back behind the pulpit," Ron said. "The Bible says we're to restore one another. That's what I think we need to do for Cole. He needs our support, right now, not our condemnation. I, for one, want to make myself available for anything Cole needs, day or night."

"Well, sabbatical has traditionally been a month, and we can pay that. What if Cole needs a little more time than that?" Tom Henderson asked.

"It'll be okay. We'll trust the Lord, and he'll provide," Ron said.

Thank you, Lord. For what you've done for me, and what you've done in Ron's heart. Help me make the best of this opportunity.

"There's only one condition, something I'm sure you'll agree to," Ron said. "You need to cut off all contact with the woman."

"Absolutely," Cole said. "There'd been none before last night, and I'll make sure she understands there's to be none in the future."

~

Barbara had her back to the door when Cole walked into The Pitchfork. Her eyes lit up when she saw him.

Wow, I thought I'd only seen her through beer goggles. She's actually kind of pretty.

Olivia's never coming back, and it's not like God's done me any favors lately.

No, you can't go there, fathead. Were you not in that room with the elders yesterday? Did you not feel the Spirit's presence?

Get behind me, Satan! You have no authority here!

Barbara's long slender fingers were on his forearm, warm and soft. Her electric blue eyes sparkled.

"Thanks for asking to meet," she said.

Lord, you know what I need to do, and you know I need your help.

He looked at the white paper napkin and fork on the speckled counter.

Trina came out of the kitchen carrying a tray of food. Her nod reassured him.

Okay, here we go. This will be brutal. It has to be, or it won't work.

He locked his eyes on hers. "Barbara, look, I owe you an apology. I don't know what I said or did the other night, but I'm not interested in you. At all."

The surprise and hurt registered on her face.

"I'm in love with someone else, and I'm a pastor, and what I did a couple of nights ago was wrong on many levels. I'm sorry you got swept up in my craziness."

"But Cole, I thought—"

He cut her off. "The texts need to stop, and I need you to stay away from me."

He'd tried to keep his voice gentle and compassionate.

She'd crossed her arms, the bewilderment etched across her face. "Well, I can't *make* you want me."

Ooh, a guilt trip.

With the comment, something in Cole changed. He still felt empathy, but the remark obliterated any attraction. Someone had thrown a switch in his spirit. He couldn't wait to leave.

"Please just leave me alone and stop texting me. Otherwise, I'll get a restraining order." The sentence had come out louder and angrier than Cole had intended.

Diners turned and stared. Trina's nod from across the room told him he'd said what he'd needed to say.

Barbara's eyes flashed with anger.

Cole didn't want to hear her response. Whatever it was going to be, it would be irrelevant. He turned and walked toward the door.

Barbara's pronouncement that he was a piece of male anatomy followed him out of the building.

33

COLE STUDIED THE CABIN'S rough-hewn timbers and the stone fireplace. The place had electricity and running water, but that was about it. No internet, and he was sure he couldn't get cell service out here.

A cool late-spring breeze swept through the open unscreened windows. Cole looked out at the various shades of green.

He felt physically different. He couldn't quite find the right word. His back and shoulders felt looser somehow.

"I guess that's where you've been carrying your stress," he said. His voice sounded loud in the empty room.

Was it un-Christian to be stressed over Kiley? Maybe. Maybe not. He had to constantly remind himself he couldn't control what happened around him. He reminded himself a hundred times a day God still ran things and knew what he was doing. And that he'd said time and again in the Bible to have no fear. Still, weren't there times when even Jesus was stressed out? Didn't Luke say that Jesus was in such anguish in the Garden of Gethsemane that his sweat became like drops of blood? Some Bible commentators even claim his sweat was mixed with blood. Doctors have said it's possible for tiny blood vessels around sweat glands to constrict and cause blood to ooze out with sweat.

Hema-something-or-other-rosis.

"You're seriously comparing himself with Jesus? You're a dolt," he said aloud. "On top of that, you're talking to yourself."

He looked around, glad no one had witnessed his conversation.

"You need to get yourself a volleyball or something." Cole smiled at his own joke. He couldn't remember the name of the old movie, but a guy marooned alone on an island after a plane crash spent a lot of time talking to a Wilson-brand volleyball. He even called the ball Wilson.

Cole glanced around the cabin and spotted the cooler.

"Coleman. It just doesn't have the same ring. Besides, a ball looks more like a human."

He shook his head. He was contemplating talking to a cooler.

"I guess it shows that God created people to live in community," he said. "We get a little weird if we're alone too long. Now, about Kiley's letter. What do I say, Lord?"

Cole prayed a few more minutes and decided the seemingly random stream of thoughts was from the Lord.

He kept the letter to Kiley as innocuous as possible.

"Hey, there, you were right. You need to go where the Lord leads, and I need to get back to a place where I can hear his voice. The elders have given me some time off, and I'm spending a week or two in the cabin at Lake Chambers. I'll be here longer if it seems like the Lord is leading me to. Just me, the Bible, and God's creation."

Kiley knew about the cabin. They'd spent weekends there when they were kids.

"Remember Pops burning the bacon over the campfire?" Cole smiled as he wrote. He'd laughed until his sides hurt over how horrible the stuff tasted. Tears had streamed down Kiley's face as she guffawed.

"It looks like charcoal," Kiley had said, giggling as the chunklets clinked onto her metal plate. They'd thrown away the frying pan after the trip.

Now, the words flowed easily from his pen. Cole told her he missed her and was proud she was his sister.

"I'm glad you're being obedient to the Lord," he wrote.

He hoped the letter wouldn't earn Kiley another stretch in the hole. When he finished writing, Cole lay back on the cabin's bunk and stared into the rafters. He thought about the book of Judges in the Old Testament and how it showed the Lord's desire to reconcile his people to himself. The book records how the Lord appointed men and women over the centuries to lead Israel back to God after the nation wandered away.

The next thought seemed to come from nowhere. Cole felt compelled to read the book of Amos.

"Amos? Seriously, Lord? Who reads Amos?"

He opened the Bible and searched. "It's somewhere here in the middle."

He read, captivated as the prophet poured out warning after warning, first against surrounding nations, then against Israel because the nation had become too self-dependent and had stopped paying attention to the needs of the less fortunate.

Cole didn't see how all that applied to him. Until he got to Amos 9:11.

"In that day I will restore David's fallen shelter—I will repair its broken walls and restore its ruins—and will rebuild it as it used to be."

He understood. Despite his recent foibles, the Lord wasn't finished using him.

He couldn't name what he felt. Relief. Thankfulness. Humility. Unworthiness and, at the same time, worthiness through Christ. And overwhelming gratitude.

"Thank you, Lord. I don't know what else to say. No words seem adequate to express my joy and thanksgiving."

As if in confirmation, part of Isaiah 40:31 floated into Cole's mind. "They will soar on wings like eagles; they will run and not grow weary."

～

Kiley's letter was in the mailbox when Cole got back from the cabin. She talked about life in her cell block. "I pray every day for a way to read more of the Word in here," she said.

The answer to her prayers arrived via UPS two days later. In a box from Ben's publishing house.

Cole's hand dipped slightly when the driver handed him the box.

"What'd he send me, a brick?" Cole asked the driver, laughing.

"Doesn't feel like light reading," the driver said.

"Ooh, dude, you better keep that day job."

The driver laughed as he climbed back into the truck.

Cole opened the box. *War and Peace.* He flipped it open and scanned the first couple of pages. The seventh paragraph said, "In the beginning, God created the heavens and the earth."

The fourteenth paragraph said, "Now the earth was formless and empty, darkness was over the surface of the deep, and the Spirit of God was hovering over the waters."

Cole smiled. Ben had hidden the Word in plain sight. No need for encryption. At least not for now. He pulled out his phone and texted.

"Thanks, Ben! This is awesome! Can you send one to Kiley?"

"Already on its way."

～

Cole's dining room chair swayed slightly when he shifted his weight. *You need to tighten those legs, man.*

He'd thought about buying a new dining room set, as he and Holly had planned, but he couldn't bring himself to do it. Buying new furniture without Holly seemed too painful. But the dining room set was pretty decrepit at this point. And he'd moved on. Maybe it was time for the furniture to move on, too.

The snow fell fast and thick, A white veil obscured his view of the trees behind the house. An inch had already accumulated on the deck railing.

"It's way too quiet in here. I need a dog or something," he said into the silence. "Nah, it'd be too hard on him on days when I drive to Terre Haute. Maybe a cat. They're easier. Except that you don't like cats. Coleman, you could always bring Coleman back."

Cole spent several nights a week out of the house, but he was free on Tuesdays.

"I hate Tuesdays. All I do is sit around missing Olivia, remembering Holly, and worrying about Kiley."

He shuffled the puzzle pieces in the box in front of him, looking for a piece of sky. He'd worked the puzzle three times since Kiley went to prison.

"Kiley could probably do this thing in half the time it takes me," he said. "I should start timing myself."

A snowplow rumbled in the distance, drawing his gaze toward the kitchen window. He couldn't see the houses across the street.

"Man, it's really coming down."

He swished the pieces in the puzzle box again.

"Well, guess this is as good as it gets. For now, at least."

He connected two pieces of the puzzle's perimeter.

"Not a dog, or Coleman. A goldfish. We could hang out and stare at each other."

∾

Road crews had done a good job, and the trip had taken no longer than usual.

The prison guard was huge, the embodiment of John Steinbeck's Lennie Small character in *Of Mice and Men*. Cole was sure the man, like Lennie, had no concept of his own size and strength. His gleaming shaven head was the size of a watermelon.

He probably possesses a greater mental capacity than Lennie, or at least I hope he does.

He motioned Cole forward.

"Over here . . . Spread . . . Arms out . . . Turn." The directions were explosive grunts.

The wand passed over Cole and squealed only slightly at his belt buckle, but the guard crowded toward him, swallowing up Cole's personal space.

The man's hands forcefully pressed into Cole's arms and torso as he searched, nearly pushing Cole off balance. A moment later, the man pressed even more of his weight into him, and the giant paw was part way into Cole's front pants pocket.

Crap! What's happening? Is this goon going to grope me? If he is, there's nothing I can do about it.

"Really guy, you've already x-rayed me, wanded me, and patted me down. Do you really need to shove your hands into my pockets?"

"I'll give you a full body cavity search in a minute if you don't shut up. Now get in there before I refuse you access," the guard said, gesturing toward a door.

As he crossed the threshold, Cole felt something in his pocket.

What the heck? Did he shove drugs into my pocket? Or something else that will get me tossed out of here? Or worse? Guess I'll find out. Later rather than sooner, I hope.

Cole's breath caught when he saw Kiley. A lump under her left eye gleamed green, yellow, and black.

"A guard was taking me to the yard, and another guard was bringing another prisoner back. As we passed one another, I made the mistake of telling her I liked her shoes. I can only guess she assumed I wanted to steal them."

"How would you even have access to them?" Cole asked.

"Nobody said the people in here are sane and logical," Kiley said. "A lot of them are probably mentally ill."

"Point taken."

Cole considered telling her about what had happened with Olivia but thought better of it. Instead, he told her about the severity of the morning's search.

"That's probably Rodney," she said. "He said he'd be looking for you."

"That can't be good. Why would a prison guard be looking for me?"

"It's nothing to worry about," Kiley said, shifting her gaze toward her hands.

At the base of the window, Kiley had slightly unfurled three fingers on one hand and one on the other.

Awesome! John thirty-one.

"Believer?" Cole mouthed. He knew the visit was being recorded and hoped if anyone noticed, they couldn't lipread.

"Yeah. New one. I just kept talking, and he just kept listening."

"How awesome is that?" Cole said.

"Yeah, four or five guards now. It's really going around."

"Really? That's amazing!"

"Not for our Poppa."

"Well, that's true. Before you know it, there's going to be an outbreak of peace and love in here."

Kiley chuckled.

The sadness tore at him, when his visiting time was up. The glass partition felt cold and thick.

"I'm so proud of you, Kiley," he said, "and so sorry all this is happening."

"Me, too, Little Brother. I love you."

∾

When he got to his truck, he smoothed the crumpled scrap of yellow paper. "Bailey Park 5:30."

That's it? Guess it's all I need to know. And I guess I won't be heading straight back to Cincinnati. That's all right. I didn't have any plans tonight, anyway.

So where in the world is Baily Park?

He typed the name into his GPS and studied the map.

I have an hour to kill. Any bookstores around there?

∾

The park stretched about the length of two football fields and twice the width behind a boxy cinderblock community center. Clumps of green and blotches of brown peeked from what remained of the snow. Mature trees towered around three sides of the park opposite a gravel parking area. Although they were now barren, Cole imagined the trees provided leafy cool shade in the summer.

A half-dozen kids played football in the muddy open space at the park's center. Eight picnic tables strategically positioned around the field's perimeter remained unoccupied.

"Pass it, Tanner, pass it!" One kid's prepubescent voice rang out above the others as the cluster of boys drifted left to right across the field.

Which way was west?

Cole looked at the sun and looked at his watch. 4:48. He then selected a table at the far end of the park, where the sun had the best opportunity to warm him. Spring was a few weeks away, and the shadows remained chilly.

The boys' voices faded into the background. He immersed himself in *Of Mice and Men*, which he'd picked up at the bookstore in honor of Rodney. In the tale, Curley's wife told Lennie she was lonely.

Tires crunched in the gravel lot, bringing Cole back into the twenty-first century. He glanced at his watch. 5:29.

The guard Cole had seen earlier unfolded himself and straightened up as he climbed out of a black sedan. A second shaven-headed man, slim and of average height, maybe a smidge shorter, spilled from the passenger side, and the back passenger-side door opened to deposit an older, taller man, with an average build, silver hair parted to the side, and black-rimmed glasses. Cole had seen the passengers on previous prison visits.

Rodney stuck out an enormous paw as he approached. "Pastor Evans? I'm Rodney Baines. Sorry about that search today. I guess you figured out why is had to be so . . . well, intense."

"No worries," Cole said. "Kiley told me what's happening. Call me Cole."

Rodney introduced his younger companion as Joe and the middle-aged man as Dennis.

With introductions and small talk out of the way, Rodney got to the point.

"All three of us are babies," he said, "born within the past couple of weeks, thanks to your sister and the Holy Spirit."

"Amazing. It sounds like real revival is happening over there," Cole said.

"It is. Your sister is awesome. She explains things in ways that just make sense. After I talked to her two or three times, I just knew what I needed to do," Rodney said.

Cole loved it. Rodney's zeal and excitement were contagious. There was nothing like being around baby Christians.

"Word is spreading, and people all over the facility are making the same decision we have," Rodney said, gesturing to Dennis and Joe. "But Kiley said she shouldn't really be the person who takes things from here. She said she'd be more comfortable, and it would probably be more proper, if we worked with a guy."

"She's right."

"You're the only guy I know of who teaches this stuff. Do you think you could work with us?"

Okay, Lord, are these guys for real? Well, if they're not, I guess I'll get the cell next to Kiley's.

The four men talked for a few more minutes, stared at their phones, and agreed on a schedule.

"Kiley said you'd have stuff to read," Rodney said.

"Are you looking for word-search puzzles or something else?" Cole asked.

"Something I can read at my house," Rodney said. His buddies agreed.

"I have some material. If I bring extra, do you think you could get any to Kiley?" Cole asked.

All three said they could.

"Awesome, I'll see you in a couple weeks then," Cole said. "In the meantime, read the Gospel of John, if you can get your hands on it."

Cole climbed into his truck a minute later.

～

As he shifted into park in his driveway, heels clicked across the concrete next door. Olivia.

Great. What could she want? To kick me in the shin? Or somewhere higher?

The dashboard clock read 9:18. Late.

Cole extricated himself from the truck and turned in the direction of the scurrying feet.

Whoa, what's going on?

Olivia's face was etched with sorrow.

"I'm sorry to just pop over like this," she said, halfway up the driveway. "I had to see you. This couldn't wait."

Whatever's going on, Lord, please be in the middle of it.

"I am so, so sorry," she said. "I was just at the store and ran into Trina from The Pitchfork. She told me what happened between you and that girl. Barbara, or whatever her name was. I am so, so sorry," Olivia repeated.

The happiness surged through him.

"I'm sorry I put myself in that situation to begin with," he said. "If I hadn't been someplace I didn't belong, none of it would have happened."

"That may be true," Olivia said. "But in hindsight, I can see how it happened. Trina said that Barbara woman threw herself all over you, and you kept trying to get away. She said any girl would've been proud of how you handled her at the bar and at the restaurant a couple of days later."

"It's nice to know she feels that way," Cole said.

"I feel so badly about jumping to conclusions."

"I tried to convince you I was just witless, and not a cheating liar," he joked.

"Can you forgive me, and could we maybe start over?"

The emotions churned in her eyes, and his own feelings swung wildly between wariness and euphoria.

"Can we make different mistakes as we go forward?" Cole asked.

Her arms wrapped around his neck, and she pressed her body against his. Her kisses were warm, soft and lingering.

34

COLE PULLED UP A chair at Joe's kitchen table. The country-themed décor gave the room a comfortable, rustic feel. Cartoonish pictures of veggies canned in Mason jars adorned the curtains, while the dish towels, floor mats and coffee cups bore likenesses of chickens, barns, and tractors. A small ceramic crock on the counter held several ladles and wooden spoons, and an antique stoneware butter churn stood in one scorner.

"Red or white?" Rodney asked Dennis as held up two coffee mugs.

"Do you really need to ask?" Joe said.

"What can I say, I'm a creature of habit," Dennis said.

"He's a creature all right," Rodney said, eliciting a round of laughter as he handed Dennis the red mug.

Thank you, Lord. It's been such a blessing to help these guys get to know you. Thank you for letting me be a part of this. Thank you for these friendships.

Cole opened his Bible and pulled out a yellow legal pad full of notes.

"Okay, so why is there pain and suffering in the world?" he began. "Let's pray about this before we get started."

When Cole had finished his lesson, he pulled a novel from his brief-case. Cole had pasted encoded Scriptures over several pages near the center of the murder mystery.

"Could one of you guys get this to Kiley?" he asked Rodney and Dennis.

"No sweat," Dennis said. "I'll get it to her today."

"You won't get in trouble, will you?" Cole asked.

"Nope," said Dennis, "because I'm not going to get caught."

"What'd you encode?" Rodney asked.

"Daniel. Great stories about keeping the faith, even when the government wants to kill you for it."

"Good choice," Joe said.

"I'll see if I can get you some copies of *War and Peace*," Cole said. "We were able to hide half the Bible in it."

"I'm not surprised," Dennis said. "And I bet no one even noticed."

The men chatted another ten minutes, then hugged heartily.

"Have a good visit, and safe travels home, my brother," Joe said.

"You guys be careful, too," Cole said.

"We may be locked up in a building with criminals all day, but sometimes, I'd rather take my chances with them than the drivers on I-74," Rodney said.

"Yeah, the bad guys are more predictable," Dennis said.

～

Kiley beamed as she climbed onto the stool on her side of the glass.

"So, I hear you're a regular Billy Graham," Cole said.

"Rodney told you?"

"Yeah, I talked to him today. How exciting!" Cole said.

"I didn't do anything but flap my gums. The Holy Spirit's the one who did the work."

"True, but it's still pretty cool," Cole said. "And you did make yourself available and follow his prompting."

"I guess that's true," Kiley said.

"Who was the woman?"

"The girl in the next cell over."

"Awesome!" Cole said. "What happened?"

"We were talking about how crazy and corrupt the system is when she said she was in for killing her neighbor and the neighbor's husband. I was surprised she volunteered that."

"Why?"

"People just don't want to talk about it. They feel like the system shafted them, or they feel like crap about themselves because they know they're such horrible specimens of humanity they can't even be around normal people."

"That makes sense, I guess," Cole said.

"So, you don't ask, and people don't tell, unless they feel close to you or something."

"What a crazy world," he said.

"It is. Anyway, after she told me what she was in for, I just told her I'm here for serving Jesus. I was kind of afraid to say that because, in here, you don't want to do *anything* that can be perceived as weak. Still, something told me I needed to say it, so I did."

"Wow, way to go, Sis," Cole said.

"At first, she said, 'You don't actually believe that stuff, do you?' But then she kept asking questions. Since our cells are right next to each other, we're within earshot of one another twenty-two or twenty-three hours a day. She'd ask a question that I'd answer, and thirty minutes or an hour later, she'd ask another. That went on for three days. On the last day, she cried a lot, and finally asked if it was possible to turn your life over to the Lord, even on death row. I told her there was no better place."

"Wow, who'da thunk?" Cole said.

"I gave her all of my John thirty-one stuff. Do you think you can get me some more?"

Cole almost laughed but he knew what she was asking. He'd already encrypted more of the Scriptures and had been offering them to people at church services. Ben Singleton also was working on several texts.

"You know I'm not allowed to bring religious stuff in here," he said with a wink that he hoped a camera somewhere didn't capture. "If I get caught, our visiting privileges could be suspended, or worse." Cole set his hands on the frame of the glass partition with three fingers slightly uncurled on one hand and one finger slightly uncurled on the other.

Kiley nodded. She'd seen it. "You're right," she said. "I guess I just thought it might be worth a try." Kiley unfurled her fingers along the bottom of the pane to match Cole's.

Before Cole left, he and Kiley touched through the glass. The surface's slick coolness still caused a lump in his throat, but he was beginning to understand he needed to get used to not getting what he wanted.

35

EVEN THOUGH HE NEVER changed the recipe, the coffee tasted better some mornings than others. This was a good morning. With a dab of cream, the light brown liquid glided across his tongue, not sweet but not too bitter.

The snow fell steadily, thickening the blanket that softened the edges of everything it covered.

"So why don't you go ahead and do it?" Don Fisher asked. "You've prayed about it, right?"

Cole set down his piece of buttered toast and slid the phone closer.

"I don't know. Fear? Maybe I'm afraid of rejection. Maybe I'm afraid I'll lose her like I lost Holly."

"I've never known you to be afraid of anything, Cole," Don said.

"Yeah, but this is important."

"I know it is, so no 'yeah-buts,'" Don said. "What's the Bible say about fear?"

"It's usually unwarranted."

"Right, and do you think it's helpful to worry about whether someone is going to get sick and die?"

Cole sighed. Don was right. "No."

"It seems to me Olivia might be the real deal, Cole. She understands why you can't have physical intimacy, she helps you encrypt Bible texts, and she eats your lousy cooking. What more could you want?"

"Yeah, you're right," Cole said. "I'm going to do it. Today. This snow is the perfect opportunity."

$\sim$

He drummed his fingers on the steering wheel as the woman got out of her car, gathered her coat around herself against the biting wind, and scurried toward the building.

The gray blanket of low-hanging snow clouds hadn't given way to the sun yet, but the forecast said the worst of the weather was over. The heater in his old truck blew noisily.

Small tufts of blond hair peeked from under a pink toboggan cap as the woman lifted the small cover on a scanner next to the front door, used her teeth to yank off her right glove, and held her thumb to the scanner.

Should he call Olivia? Would it be suspicious? No, it would be fine. She was probably expecting his call.

"Hey there, are you working from home today?"

"Yep. At least until it gets a little warmer, and the roads get better. I'll probably go in this afternoon."

Awesome. His first assumption was correct. Now, he needed to see how the rest of this played out. If she had tons to do, it wouldn't work.

"Wanna do a long lunch? Maybe an hour? Maybe grab takeout and go for a ride?"

"What are you up to?" Her voice was suspicious.

Was I really that suspicious-sounding, or does she have some sort of sixth sense?

"Nothing! I promise!"

"Did you buy that stupid Jeep you were looking at?"

"No, I promise, I didn't buy a Jeep. Can't a guy want to hang out with a gorgeous woman on a beautiful snowy day?"

"You're incorrigible."

"Well, that may be true, but I promise, you'll like this."

"It won't be too cold, will it?"

"No, we'll get you back inside if you get cold."

Olivia was silent for a beat.

Okay, what's she thinking? At least she's considering it. Say "yes," Olivia, Say "yes."

"Okay. Pick me up at noon, but I have to be at the office by one thirty."

"Wear boots," he said. "Love you. Bye!"

Cole pumped his fist and whooped, then looked around the parking lot to determine if anyone had seen him.

～

He studied the glass display cases filled with shiny stones.

"Well, honestly," he told the clerk, "I'm not made of money. A lot of these rings are beautiful, but way out of my price range."

"How about this?" The woman placed a white gold solitaire with a round diamond on the black velvet display pad.

The tiny stone gleamed and twinkled under bright counter lamp.

"I wish it could be bigger," Cole said.

"Does she love you?" the saleswoman asked.

"Of course," Cole said.

"Then it won't matter. You can get a bigger diamond later."

His next stop was at a thrift store, where he found a woman's hat, gloves, scarf, large hoop earrings, and a costume necklace.

~

The shin-high spheres lay scattered across the barnyard like Goliath-sized lawn ornaments. Cole had cleared a path through the eight-inch mantle of snow from the driveway to the barn.

"You're such a goofball," Olivia said.

Her honey-colored hair flowed from under a fuchsia toboggan cap, and a matching scarf encircled her to the chin.

"I take it those are snowman parts," she said.

"Snow *couple* parts," Cole said.

Olivia opened the thrift store bag and peered in.

"Nice. Mine even gets jewelry. Okay, for you I'll stand out here in the cold and build a snowwoman, but just this once. Don't expect me to do this every time it snows."

"Deal," Cole said. "I know you're not that kind of girl." He dodged the incoming snowball.

Cole's boots squeaked as he led Olivia toward the assembly area. The cold scratched the insides of his nostrils and the back of his throat.

This would have to be quick. No more than five or ten minutes.

He stacked three snowballs and set Olivia to work selecting parts from a pile of branches, buttons, stones and pieces of fruits and veggies.

As quickly as he could, he stacked two snowballs for his own snowman, then removed a chunk out of the third sphere and placed it behind the others, then shaped it to try to give the impression the snowman was on one knee.

He glanced over his shoulder.

Good, she's focused on hers.

His fingers ached, even gloved. He rammed the second tree-branch arm into the snowman's side so that it stretched toward the snowwoman.

Olivia had dressed her snowwoman and was putting on the jewelry.

Crud. I need to hurry. Work fingers, work!

He wedged the navy-blue velvet box between a couple of large twigs that formed the snowman's "hand," then shoved in his snowman's rock eyes and a smile.

Olivia stood a couple of feet from her snowwoman, looking her up and down.

He inserted a piece of broccoli for the nose just as Olivia turned.

"Why's yours so short? Did he topple over?"

Her eyes scanned the snowman. "I didn't—"

Her eyes widened and her breath caught.

Cole sank to his left knee and retrieved the velvet box.

Please say, "yes," Olivia. Please say, "yes."

"Olivia Sandlin, will you marry me?"

Her gray-green eyes sparkled as she squealed and yanked the glove off her left hand.

They rolled around in the snow, kissing and laughing.

36

THE MORNING RAIN AND slate gray clouds had given way to a perfect afternoon. The sun shone bright yellow against a cloudless azure sky.

Two platoons of white folding chairs stood in perfect formation facing the gazebo.

Tom Henderson stood on the structure's second step wearing a black tux. He craned his neck and tugged at his stiff white shirt collar.

"You guys clean up pretty well," he said. "Who's this guy, and what'd he do with Cole?" he said to Don Fisher.

"I know, right? I never thought I'd see the day someone stuffed him into a tux," Don said.

The sweat ran down Cole's back, and the shiny black shoes crushed his toes.

"If you guys are around for my funeral, make sure I get to wear jeans and a T-shirt, will you?" Cole said. "And sneakers. Don't forget the sneakers."

"This, too, shall pass," Don said, laying a hand on Cole's shoulder. "Tonight, you'll be on your honeymoon."

The honeymoon wouldn't be fancy or extravagant, a few days in the Adirondacks.

Olivia's Aunt Marilyn had paid for most of the wedding and had helped Olivia plan. "You've always been the daughter I never had," she'd told Olivia.

Four women who looked to be in their thirties and forties made up a string quartet who sat at the back of the gazebo. Bach's "Jesu, Joy of Man's Desiring" danced across the field. The cellist's head and upper torso dipped and bobbed. The three other musicians remained less animated, with their eyes riveted on their sheet music.

The white chairs continued to fill. Joe and his wife, Dennis and his wife, Trina and Jerry, and Don Fisher's wife occupied the second row. Others from New Hope filled the rest of the chairs.

Rodney Baines led Olivia's Aunt Marilyn down the center aisle. In her late seventies, her chestnut-colored hair was piled into an updo and she wore a charcoal tea-length dress with a textured applique.

The quartet played Pachelbel's "Cannon in D."

Cole knew the tune's name, as well as the others being played, only because he'd heard the names many times over the years while helping other couples plan weddings.

He'd wondered if the Supreme Court would eventually put a crimp in America's wedding industry. Would all music that at one time was Christian be banned? So far, it hadn't been. And it might not be. The media and marketers had pretty much taken God out of most weddings. The ceremonies had turned into a chance for people to worship *themselves* rather than God.

Cole was proud of Olivia. Sure, there were flowers and music, and there'd be cake and food. But all in all, the wedding was modest. All by Olivia's choice.

"Well, this is it, fellas," Tom Henderson said.

Cole's mom sat in the front row next to Rodney. She looked better than she had in months. Olivia's Aunt Marilyn sat across the aisle.

Cole glanced down at his shoes and slacks one last time.

I guess this is as good as it gets.

His collar rubbed his neck. Was his hair still okay?

Olivia's sisters smiled from across the aisle. Their coral-colored dresses swept to the floor and highlighted a bouquet of white roses and hydrangeas. Stormy fidgeted and fiddled with the strap on her gown. *She's turned into a beautiful young woman. Her resemblance to Olivia was uncanny.*

"The Bridal Chorus" began.

His breath caught. The veil cascaded to Olivia's bare shoulders, its crisp whiteness accenting her tan and the gray-green of her eyes.

Thank you, Lord. She's gorgeous.

She floated down the aisle, her eyes sparkling.

Cole hadn't met her dad in person until this morning. He'd flown in from D.C. Olivia had his nose and cheekbones.

The older man kissed her on the cheek, nodded toward Cole, and moved to his seat next to Aunt Marilyn.

Tom Henderson began. "In most traditional Christian wedding ceremonies, there's a lot of talk about First Corinthians thirteen, about love being patient and kind, not being envious, not boasting, and not proud," he said. "I want to talk about the last few attributes in that list. In addition to those first few qualities, the passage says love always protects, always trusts, always hopes, always perseveres. As Cole and Olivia begin their life together, those latter attributes are especially important. Because as Cole and Olivia lead New Hope, there's little question they'll face many ups and downs. Probably more than a married couple who isn't in church leadership. The more successful a ministry, the more flaming darts the enemy seems to shoot at its leaders."

Great, Tom, I've got it. Let's move along.

She is so beautiful. Look at how that veil softens her features.

Wait a minute. Did he just say, 'toughness and tenacity'? I get it, Tom. Someday soon, it'll be illegal to follow our faith. Let's just exchange the vows. Let's do this.

". . . serving God and others," Tom said.

Just marry us already, Tom.

"Can I have you guys join hands for the exchange of the vows?" Tom said.

Her touch was a feather. He was lost in her smile.

I can't believe I actually get to do this.

Cole swallowed the lump in his throat. ". . . to have and to hold, from this day forward, for better, for worse, for richer, for poorer, in sickness and in health, to love and to cherish, till death do us part."

Olivia's eyes pooled, but her voice was clear and strong.

Tom beamed. "I now pronounce you . . ."

Her kiss was gentle, yet insistent.

37

THE HOTEL ROOM WAS comfortable enough, slightly glitzier than necessary, and more expensive than Cole had imagined. But it was the only room he could find. Every hotel in and around Terre Haute was fully booked.

Cole stood outside the steam-filled bathroom and dried his face. He silently prayed Psalm 23.

The LORD is my shepherd, I lack nothing.
He makes me lie down in green pastures,
he leads me beside quiet waters,
he refreshes my soul.
He guides me along the right paths
for his name's sake.

The white towel scratched across his skin.

At a place this expensive, you'd think they could afford fabric softener.

Olivia sat on the edge of the bed with her head bowed, hands folded. The room was quiet, save for the air conditioner's low whine.

She didn't look up as he crossed to the window. He parted the drapes slightly, allowing the gray morning light to sidle in.

Rivers of headlights flowed in both directions on I-70. Signs glared outside hotels, gas stations, and fast food places.

The fatigue weighed five hundred pounds, and he struggled to keep his eyes open.

Lord, for the millionth time, please save Kiley, and if that's not in your plan, please help us get through the grief.

They needed to leave. Aunt Marilyn had already gone. They had to be at the prison in twenty minutes. And there'd be crowds and security check-ins.

The shiny silver deadbolt protruded across the edge of the door frame, propping his mom's door open. He tapped gently and looked in.

She sat fully dressed on the unused queen-size bed and wept quietly. Tiny, somewhat hunched over, and with her gray hair pulled into a tight bun, she looked older than she had the night before.

You did this, Cole. What kind of lousy human being are you? You set off the chain of events that, in an hour or so, will have killed Kiley. You had to be proud and tough, didn't you? You had to preach that morning instead of sending people home.

Get out, Accuser, you have no authority here! You're a liar and the father of lies!

"Ready?" It was all he knew to say.

He went to the bed, offered his mom his arm, and led the old lady out of the room.

She leaned into him, as if she couldn't expend the energy to walk.

With Olivia following, they trudged the long corridor. No one spoke. Cole's feet sank into the well-padded carpet. Uniform white doors broke up the earth tones in the hall, a little like the blue-gray doors had broken up the gray in the prison.

They rode the elevator in silence. The machine hummed. Fingerprints dotted the grain in the stainless-steel door.

The cacophony crashed into him when the door opened. People talked too loudly, their tones and gestures too animated. Cole had experienced an ambiance like this once, when he went to a World Series game in Boston with his dad when he was twelve. The hotel lobby there on the afternoon before the game had the same vibe. Now, the energy was too intense, like a song played in the wrong key and at a breakneck tempo.

Lord, please help Kiley, and forgive me for what I've done to our mom. I didn't intend to sin. I didn't know how else to lead New Hope. Please help us through this sadness.

His mom clung to him as they walked through the expansive atrium.

At another time, the room would've impressed him. A lush Asian-style area rug accented polished mahogany floors. A grouping of several trees, either ficus or some variety of bamboo, rose from a large planter in the center of the cavernous room. People occupied the half-dozen plush coffee-colored chairs that sat around the planter. Men sipped coffee from large disposable cups, and women talked on cell phones or used them to check schedules or for myriad other reasons.

What was Kiley doing? Had she slept? No, there was no way she'd slept.

A TV crew with several bags of equipment and a camera that was not in use, checked out. A lean dark-haired man, probably in his forties, wore a dark blue windbreaker with the station's call letters emblazoned in yellow across the back.

Why hadn't they left their camera equipment in their van overnight? On second thought, it was probably prudent to bring it in.

The crew almost certainly was headed to the prison. Everyone was. Reporters from around the globe had converged on Terre Haute.

His mom still leaned against him as they walked.

"Do you want any breakfast, Mom?" Cole asked.

"No, let's just go." It was almost a whisper.

The glass doors hummed and separated, and a wave of hot, humid air engulfed them. Heat already radiated from the parking lot's fresh, newly striped blacktop.

What kind of circus would they find at the prison?

Olivia squeezed his hand. "Here, Mom, why don't you sit up front?"

The car's air conditioner dried the perspiration that had already sprung up under Cole's shirt. With the town in the rearview mirror, a sea of gently undulating waist high corn stretched in all directions.

They didn't speak. Cole prayed Psalm 28.

> To you, Lord, I call; you are my Rock,
> do not turn a deaf ear to me.
> For if you remain silent,
> I will be like those who go down to the pit.
> Hear my cry for mercy
> as I call to you for help,
> as I lift up my hands
> toward your Most Holy Place.

Cole was sure his mom and Olivia prayed as well.

Cole's breath caught as they passed a Dollar General store on the right, and the prison grounds came into view. Dozens of busses and what looked like thousands of cars sat in neat rows in a field.

"Wow, it looks like we're going into a theme park," he said.

"Quite a spectacle isn't it?" his mom said.

Plastic orange net barricades, like those along marathon routes, corralled a group of silent demonstrators. Troops in black riot gear with automatic weapons kept watch both inside and outside the enclosure. Some demonstrators held candles. Others had signs. One said, "Sad day for the USA." Another sign proclaimed, "You might kill her," and in smaller print "but you can't kill him." Was the word "him" legal in that context? If it wasn't, the protesters were getting away with it, for now.

Cole stopped at a barricade. A man in black riot gear and carrying an assault rifle spoke. "IDs please."

The man swiped a tablet a few times, handed back the IDs, and motioned Cole forward.

A quarter mile down the road the noise from the second demonstration area announced the protesters' presence before the corral-like enclosure came into view. Loud music with obscene lyrics thumped through the air as the scene grew into focus. Like the first location, mesh fencing surrounded the site, and troops in riot gear stood vigil. In contrast to the first site, people danced and jumped up and down. Topless women sat on shirtless men's shoulders.

One man carried a burning effigy of Kiley. A few news people videoed the scene.

Cole sniffed. His eyes burned.

"She doesn't deserve this," Cole's mom said, her voice choked with emotion.

"I wish I could say it's unbelievable," Olivia said. "But I can't. These are unsaved people acting like unsaved people."

They stopped at a second checkpoint, where their IDs again were checked.

Ahead, a city of white tents spread across an area the size of a supercenter parking lot. Scores of media trucks idled in a field nearby, and people drove back and forth in golf carts.

Beyond the tents, the sun gleamed off the tangles of razor wire. The wire didn't merely run along the top of the fence but curled and snaked its way around the prison's perimeter from ground level to the top of the fifteen-foot-high electrified chin-link barrier.

Two helmeted National Guardsmen with machine guns waited at the gatehouse where Cole had been instructed to enter. Other men with machine guns stood silhouetted in lookout towers.

"IDs please." The guard's tone was neither pleasant nor unpleasant, but instead, almost robotic.

The man thumbed a tablet. "Please step out of the vehicle."

Even though a prison liaison had outlined the procedure a week earlier during a video chat, the guard's glare bore through Cole's chest.

He'd just as soon shoot us as let us pass.

"You, too, ma'am," the guard said to Cole's mom.

"Please step over here," the second guard said, pointing to a spot between the car and the gatehouse.

Another car pulled up behind Cole's.

"Do we have permission to search your vehicle?" the first guard said.

I already signed a consent via email, and I really don't have a choice, now, do I?

"Yes, go ahead," he said.

One of the guards poked his torso into the car and craned his neck left and right. He looked under the seats and in the trunk. A second guard used a camera on a flexible fiberglass pole to look under the car.

"Max, come!" It was the second guard.

A German Shepard with classic black and tan markings, trotted out of the gatehouse.

Crud, I didn't see him. That thing's huge. He must weigh over a hundred pounds.

"Find the bomb," the dog handler said.

"Find the bomb?" He can't think of a more creative command than that? Cole stifled a smile but froze as the beast neared. *Look at the size of that head! It's the size of a basketball.*

He stiffened further as the black snout and leathery nose neared an area Cole would need if he planned to have children.

This animal will rip a chunk out of me, maybe even an important chunk, if I make the wrong move.

His palms felt damp.

The dog turned away, then back. One last sniff of Cole's left shoe.

Olivia's eyes widened as the dog turned toward her. Max circled her and gave a cursory sniff, again in an area that's not discussed in polite company.

The dog looked at Cole's mom, licked her once on the hand, and moved to the car's perimeter.

Max circled the car slowly, sniffing every section, then stopped at the right rear wheel.

Uh-oh, what's he doing? Seriously? He thinks there's a bomb?

He moved away, then sniffed the wheel again. Then, as if to proclaim his satisfaction, lifted a leg and peed on the tire.

Cole let out a breath and felt the tension ease from his chest and shoulders.

"No explosives, they're good," the dog handler said.

The other guard wordlessly handed Cole the IDs, motioned him back into the car, and pointed toward a parking area inside the wall of razor wire. Two other gun-toting men in camouflage directed people to parking spots closer to the building.

As he turned off the car, Cole lay his head back against the seat, sighed and closed his eyes. *Can't I just sit here for a few minutes and weep?*

A silhouetted guard on top of the building looked left and right.

We need to move. If we wait too long, one of the goons will show up. He'll either move us along, or worse, toss us out of here.

"Well, here we go," he said.

Olivia tilted her eyes skyward and prayed. "Lord, you're an awesome God. You spoke the universe into existence. You made a way to save us from death, itself. We know you're able to spare Kiley's life. We just pray that you will."

～

A guard pressed a chubby thumb against a lock pad until the windowless metal door in front of them buzzed and popped open.

Inside, a guard with football-sized veiny biceps gestured to a small, windowless room, with bare off-white walls and white floor tiles.

The guard in that room was smaller than the first two men had been, but his demeanor said he'd dealt with his share of tough guys. And won. He held out a cotton swab on steroids.

"Open," he said, holding the swab to Cole's mouth.

The procedure was old hat, something Cole endured each time he visited Kiley.

Cole winced as the swab jammed into the inside his left cheek, raked across the roof of his mouth, and assaulted the inside of his other cheek.

"DNA?" Olivia asked as the guard jammed the swab into a small vial.

"Drug screen," the officer said. "It'll change colors if you have anything like heroin or cocaine in your system."

"Amazing," Olivia said.

"If you say so," the officer said. Satisfied, he set the vial aside and motioned Cole through the cylindrical body scanner.

All morning, Cole's emotions had come in waves. He was okay at the moment, reconciled to the fact there was nothing he could do. Everything was in God's hands.

"Step into the next room and step behind the curtain," the guard said.

"You're kidding me, right?"

"No, sir. Standard procedure for any civilians going to the death house. Believe me, it's no picnic for us, either."

As much as he didn't want it to, it made sense. There was no telling what weapons someone might want to smuggle in, and where they might hide them.

The stone-faced man in the next room said nothing, only pointed. The turquoise curtain hung from a track in the ceiling, like those that wrap around a hospital bed.

Okay, let the games begin.

The guard pulled the drape shut, and Cole balanced himself with a hand against the wall to remove his shoes and socks.

The tiles felt cool on his soles.

Next, he dumped his pants and shirt.

"Underwear, too?"

"All of it."

Cole did as he was told.

He averted his eyes from his wiry, pale frame and away from the guard's eyes.

"Do a deep knee bend and cough," the guard said.

Could this possibly get any more humiliating? Unfortunately, I'm sure it could.

"What was that for?" Cole asked after he'd complied.

"If you had any weapons inside your body, coughing in that position would've been very uncomfortable."

"That was uncomfortable enough, thank you."

"It made my day, too," the guard said, stepping to the other side of the curtain.

Cole pulled on his underwear and pants.

Well, at least Olivia and Mom didn't have to witness it. Too bad they'll have to endure it.

A stocky barrel-shaped woman who looked like she'd just chewed a handful of coffee grounds came into the room as Cole pulled the curtain open.

Lord, please be with the women.

The male guard pointed to a door to Cole's right.

~

Frank Hamilton and Jennifer Michaels already waited in the van when Cole climbed in.

"Do lawyers have to go through that lovely search process?" Cole asked.

"They wouldn't want to let family members have all the fun," Frank said.

The van's air conditioner cooled him, and Cole's eyelids began to droop.

Seriously? You're going to let yourself fall asleep when your sister is due to be executed in half an hour?

"*Then Jesus went with his disciples to a place called Gethsemane . . . Stay here and keep watch with me . . . Couldn't you men keep watch with me for one hour?*"

Where is that? Matthew 25? No, 26.

Cole shook himself awake.

The driver touched his earpiece. "Ten-four." He put the van in gear.

"What about my fiancé and my mom?" Cole asked.

"They'll be in the next van," the driver said.

Guards walked on either side of the van as the vehicle crept toward the death house.

Cole's head bobbed, and he snapped himself awake. *What kind of human being are you?*

One who hasn't slept in days and has earned the right to feel emotionally and physically exhausted.

Really? You can't stay awake on a quarter-mile van ride?

Leave me alone, Satan. You have no authority here. Lord, please help me. Please help Kiley.

"I don't want you to get your hopes up, but Kiley let me file a last-minute appeal last night," Hamilton said.

A bolt of adrenaline surged through him. "What? How'd you get her to agree to it?"

"I got her to believe the Lord might want to use a last-minute stay to achieve his purposes."

"Watch the religious references, sir," the driver said.

"My apologies," Hamilton said.

"What'd you base the appeal on?"

"Some of the new video evidence."

Yes! Yes! Cole fought back the urge to pump his fist. *Lord, please let this work!*

The van rounded a corner, and the death house came into view.

$$\sim$$

One last chain-link fence topped with curls of razor wire separated the van from the squatty, windowless death house.

A guard opened a gate, and the van crept through.

6:52. Will Kiley already be on the gurney? What is she thinking about? Is she scared?

Cole's legs felt weak.

I'm not sure I can get out. Okay, dude, pull it together. For Kiley and Mom.

The van door opened, and a wave of humidity swam in.

A baby-faced guard waited, pity filling his eyes. "You okay, sir?"

"Yeah, thanks."

The menacing rust-colored door loomed straight ahead.

I can't go in there. I can't see this.

You have to. For Kiley.

Baby-Face and three others surrounded him.

He trudged as if he were climbing a sand dune. *Six strides. You can do it. Four strides.*

But I don't want to. Lord, you created the universe. Why don't you do something?

Crickets.

Three more strides.

Cole had seen pictures and diagrams of the building on the internet. He knew Johnson's family and the media would use identical doors near other corners of the building.

Is the family already in there?

He remembered the ten media witnesses entered and exited last.

"One reason for keeping everyone separate is to help protect the families from unwanted questions and harassment," Hamilton had said.

From the corner of his eye, Cole spotted the van carrying his mom and Olivia, its attachment of guards surrounding the vehicle.

The rust-colored door swung open.

Lord, be with Mom. Comfort her as much as possible.

He strained to see in the dim lighting as he moved toward the last of five metal folding chairs.

He stopped before he got to the last chair and turned toward Jennifer Michaels and Frank Hamilton. "Do you mind if I sit between Olivia and my mom?"

"To preserve the dignity of the condemned, there's no talking in the facility, sir." The guard's words were quiet, yet intense.

Dignity. Right.

The lawyers squeezed past.

Drawn dark gray curtains on the other side of a large window hid the death chamber.

A surge of light and heat behind him accompanied Olivia and his mom into the room.

His mom wobbled, rubber-legged. Olivia's features were drawn tight, her lips stretched to a thin line.

She must really love me to be willing to do this.

Olivia moved past, and his mom fell trembling into the seat closest to the door.

The familiar rope in his stomach knotted and re-knotted, and he forced the lump down in his throat.

"It will be at least another ten minutes," the corrections officer outside the observation room said. "Remember, out of respect for the condemned, no talking is permitted."

Condemned. I can't stand that word.

Frank Hamilton and Jennifer Michaels stared straight forward. Olivia sat with her head bowed, eyes closed. His mom wept quietly.

He silently prayed through Psalm 82:

> *Defend the weak and the fatherless;*
> *uphold the cause of the poor and the oppressed.*
> *Rescue the weak and the needy;*
> *deliver them from the hand of the wicked.*

The unmistakable thump of a metal door came from somewhere to his left. Probably the media.

Several media outlets had sued to televise Kiley's entire execution process, from the time she was moved to the death house, to the time her body was taken away in the hearse.

"Americans have a right to know exactly what their government does when it kills someone," one reporter had said on a news show. Cole had experienced mixed emotions. He agreed that people should see what happens immediately before the execution; he didn't think televising an actual execution served any purpose other than to satisfy the public's morbid curiosity and media company stockholders' thirst for advertising dollars.

A small motor whined, and the curtain moved slightly.

The curtain in the temple was torn in two, from top to bottom.

Slowly, the curtain crept to his left, revealing the execution chamber. Neat rows and columns of gray-green tile covered the walls.

Rodney, Joe, and Dennis followed two other men out of the execution chamber. The door closed behind Dennis.

What? No, no, no, no!

The meager contents of Cole's stomach rushed upward.

No, do not hurl in here.

The wave passed. Cole inhaled deeply and breathed slowly.

How could they? They actually tied her down, so she could be executed!

Cole's body shook.

They pretended to be my friends! How could they do that?

Was this how Jesus felt when Judas walked up to him and kissed him? If it were possible, was this worse, since Jesus already understood Judas was about to betray him?

His eyes swept across the tiles and came to rest on the gurney. A white sheet covered Kiley almost to her chin. Three tubes ran from the ceiling and disappeared under the sheet in the area of her right calf.

Kiley's eyes were closed, and Cole saw no tension in her face or neck. She breathed easily. She looked at peace.

Does she see anything? Angels? Light? He pondered the passage in the book of Acts when Stephen was stoned to death. *"Look," he said, "I see heaven open and the Son of Man standing at the right hand of God."*

In its own weird way, even the gurney looked biblical. The leather contraption's movable armrests held Kiley's arms almost straight out at shoulder height, as if she was on a cross.

A man Cole assumed was the warden stood near an old-fashioned red landline mounted to the wall. The vintage gadget looked out of place in their hi-tech world, but Cole assumed it was used because it was still reliable. If people *had* to reach one another in a hurry, a landline always got the job done. The chamber's bright ceiling lights gleamed off the phone's receiver.

Come on! Ring. Ring! Let one of the motions Hamilton filed be granted. Lord, let a judge somewhere stop the execution.

What is she thinking? Is she scared? Is she in the arms of Jesus?

Cole felt numb. Kiley would be gone in a few minutes, and his three friends helped make it happen.

The warden moved toward the landline, slightly to Kiley's right. Balding, stocky, and middle-aged, he stood within arm's reach of the phone. He wore a cheap dark-brown suit and a crimson necktie. A shirt that had once been white strained to stretch over his beach-ball-shaped belly. Large jowls worked silently, and huge circles hung under his eyes.

Come on, phone! Ring!

I guess, this is probably tough for the warden, too. Unless he's totally heartless, putting someone to death must be hard. Does he know Kiley's innocent? Is he being asked to do something he doesn't agree with? Or is he a Christian-hater?

The warden picked up a remote and pushed a button. Sounds from the execution chamber came through speakers in the ceiling. He picked up the land line, punched two numbers and said, "Anything? No? Roger that. Thanks." He then turned to Kiley and asked, "Ms. Evans, would you like to make a final brief statement?"

Kiley raised her head slightly from the table and looked at the windows to the observation rooms.

Does she know which observers are in each room? Can she see in here?

Wow, look how placid she looks.

Olivia's face remained taut. His mom clamped cold bony fingers into his hand. Cole couldn't see Aunt Marilyn, who was in the row of chairs behind him.

Lord, help poor Mom. No woman should have to go through this.

Kiley looked pale under the execution room's lights. Part of her unhealthy pallor undoubtedly was a result of not being exposed to daylight in years. Kiley had told him that even when she was out of her cell, she was indoors and rarely allowed to go out.

Her forehead, cheeks, and lips still revealed no tension. Cole read only serenity. Had they drugged her?

She must have done nothing but pray the last several days.

"Yes, warden. Thank you," Kiley said. Her voice sounded clear, calm, and strong. "I'd like to begin by expressing my condolences to the Johnson family."

She looked toward the room to Cole's left. She knew who was in each room.

"Many years have passed since Trace Johnson's death, and I'm sure neither the years nor my sympathies will fully assuage your pain. Still, I want to tell you how sorry I am for the grief you are feeling."

A whimper came from the adjoining observation room, an older woman's voice.

Kimi Johnson? Probably.

"That being said, I want to reiterate that Mr. Johnson's death was unintentional . . . and at the hand of someone who has never been brought to account for what happened. As Mr. Johnson stood on the hood of my brother's truck, a brick thrown by someone in that crowd struck Mr. Johnson. Several videos have come to light that show what happened. But the court didn't see fit to allow those videos to be shown. The court wasn't interested in the truth, only in persecuting Christians."

A wail came from the next room.

"I know that brings Mr. Johnson's family no comfort. Again, I am sorry for their pain. Nonetheless, what I've said today is truth. I affirm it as I prepare to meet my maker, a God this nation has rejected. Whether the government or the people of the United States want it to be so or not, Jesus Christ is the Lord. He was born of a virgin, crucified for our sins, and rose from the dead. Through him, anyone who believes can have forgiveness of sins, peace with God, and the hope of living eternally with him in heaven. That is the truth. And if I have to die to proclaim it, so be it."

She now looked directly at him.

"Cole, Mom, I love you more than words could ever say. When I'm gone, always hold on to Jesus. That's all I have to say, warden."

Tears streamed down Cole's face now.

His mom shook and sobbed beside him.

Olivia tightened her grip on his hand. She looked silently straight ahead.

The warden looked to his right, to someone behind a wall, someone Cole couldn't see. A small window gave the executioner visual access into the death room. Cole couldn't remember if the prison liaison had told him about the window or if he'd read about it. At the warden's command, the person behind the glass would open the valves to allow the chemicals to flow into the IV and into Kiley.

A marshal in the death room and the warden both nodded toward the executioner's window. "Begin the execution," the warden said, his voice scripted.

The men glanced from the window to the tubes, to Kiley, and back again.

Seconds passed. Then more seconds.

It must have been close to a minute. Why isn't anything happening? Shouldn't we see liquid in the tubes or something?

Still nothing.

What's happening? What's Kiley thinking? Is she scared? This must be killing Mom.

"Everything okay back there?" the warden asked.

Cole knew all the systems in the room had been tested and retested in the days before the execution. Or so he'd read.

The warden moved away from the phone and disappeared through a door.

Muffled words came through the speaker, followed by a male voice. "No, I'm not going to do it, Brice."

"We have an order from a judge! Push the button, Wendall! Right now!"

"No! This woman is innocent! In the name of Jesus, I refuse. I won't do it!"

What happens if the guy doesn't open the valve? How long will they argue about it? Will they bring in someone else to do the job? If so, how long will that take? Will we wait here? Will Kiley just lie there strapped to the table?

Rustling and scuffling came from behind the wall.

Crack!!!

Wait, what just happened? Gunshot! Do I need to run? Get on the floor?

His ears rang. His mom's eyes bulged. Olivia's nails dug into his thumb.

No. No need to run. Whatever happened is over. Did the warden shoot the guy behind the wall, or was the warden shot? Is Kiley okay?

Two guards in the death room drew weapons and jerked their gaze left and right.

The silence carried an energy, as if everyone and everything, and even the building, itself, worked to piece together what had just happened. Cole realized he was standing but wasn't sure why. The others in the observation room had followed his lead.

"Everyone out! Now! Exit the building and move to your left!" It was one of the guards who'd led Cole in from the van.

Kiley opened her eyes, and her chest rose higher and more quickly than it had.

The warden emerged from the room where the shooting had happened. Blood soaked his white shirt and splattered his suit and face.

"This execution is postponed. Close that curtain, marshal," the warden snarled. Then, picking up the landline, he barked, "Get me a bus over here . . . No, stupid, not that kind of bus, an ambulance."

The curtain began to creep across the window.

Cole followed Olivia into the bright sunlight. A guard, tall with a blond buzzcut, waved his pistol around.

Guards in other areas shouted orders.

Cole's mom clung to him. Olivia's hand felt sweaty, and the color had drained from her face. Jennifer Michaels repeatedly looked side to side. Hamilton wore a stoic expression and looked straight ahead.

"You, Family Member Witness . . ."

Is he talking to me? I guess so.

"Get against the wall and face the wall! Spread out. Farther!"

Cole stared at the bricks. Shards of brown and red. Vehicle noise grabbed his attention, and he turned his eyes toward the sound.

A gleaming black Hummer screamed toward the death house. A second identical vehicle appeared around the corner a couple of hundred yards away. An ambulance with lights flashing brought up the rear.

"Eyes straight ahead." It was the guard behind Cole.

He again stared at the brick wall, studying its texture. Male voices snapped commands, and other men ran.

Cole stared at the grout. From the corner of his eye he saw that his mom trembled. A glance the other direction showed that Olivia stared blankly forward.

More vehicles roared toward the death house. Probably vans.

Are they loading us up? Where are they taking us?

"Okay, Family Member Witnesses, you can turn around." The guard sounded less intense.

A line of gun-carrying guards formed a picket just inside the chain-link fence. Three vans pulled up in tandem behind the guards.

A guard escorted Frank Hamilton to the lead van. When Hamilton's door closed, a second guard took Jenifer Michaels to a second van.

Where are they going? Are we going to be allowed out of here? Trapped in a prison. Not a great feeling. Lord, what's going on? Please help us.

~

As he climbed out of the van, Cole let out the breath he hadn't realized he'd been holding. He'd been on the verge of terror when they put him in the vehicle ten minutes earlier. His thoughts had run to the police interrogation room, and he'd been certain this would be worse. The feds had interrogators whose sole job was to squeeze information out of people. He'd envisioned huge men, and smaller men with twisted faces, dragging power tools and car batteries into a concrete-walled room lit by a single incandescent bulb hanging from the ceiling. He hadn't known how he would avoid giving them information about who was in his church and where it met, and where people in the congregation lived.

Now, a man in an expensive gray suit, white shirt, and necktie led him through one of the prison's executive wings, past a reception area and two cubicles where women sat behind desks. Brass name plates gleamed beside each door as they moved along a carpeted hallway. Cole noted one of the job titles. Assistant Deputy Chief of Staff. He caught himself smiling. An assistant to the assistant to the chief assistant.

Maybe Tom Henderson and I should get a couple of those.

The suit ushered Cole into a conference room. Large windows with half-open blinds looked onto a section of the parking lot. The sun, higher in the sky now and bright yellow, glinted from windshields. A long conference table and chairs left just enough space to move around comfortably. Photos of law enforcement equipment and machinery adorned the walls. A gleaming black helicopter. A black armored personnel carrier. A shoulder-fired multi-round Taser that mildly resembled a 1930s Tommy Gun.

"We just need you to give us a written statement about what you saw and heard at the execution facility this morning," the man said as he slid a blank piece of paper and a pen to a spot at the table, then gestured toward a chair.

"It can be as long or short as you want, but anything you're able to tell us could be helpful, even if it may not seem important. When you're done, just signal us. As you can see, there's a camera in here." The man gestured to a small dark globe that protruded from the ceiling in the corner.

Cole wasn't surprised.

"You'll be free to go when you're done. If you came with someone, a staff member will stay with you in the front reception area until everyone in your party is ready to leave."

Cole's sigh filled the room as soon as the man left.

Well, at least I'm not in some torture chamber. They seem to have moved into cover-your-rear-end mode. Now, where do I start? How about with a prayer?

He couldn't remember where in the Psalms he'd read it, but it fit. *Deliver me, my God, from the hand of the wicked, from the grasp of those who are evil and cruel.*

What was happening with Kiley? Or to her? Where was she? Was she back in the cell in the death house, or was she back on her pod? Would they attempt the execution again? How soon? Surely, the witnesses would have to be invited again. Had an execution ever been botched so badly the government had to set a new execution date? Cole had never heard anything like that. He'd read of the needle coming out and needing to be reinserted and about guys needing additional jolts of electricity when states used the electric chair. He'd even heard of people's body parts catching on fire when executioners used synthetic sponges instead of natural ones with the electric chair. But he'd never heard of an execution being stopped because someone refused to finish the job.

Where did Rodney, Joe, and Dennis fit in? Were they working to execute Kiley or save her?

The white page yawned in front of him. Interesting. Why did they want this written on physical paper? Why not just park him at a computer? Probably so they could destroy the evidence and not leave a digital trail if they didn't like what he said.

I wish this paper had lines on it. Dude, if you had a brain, you'd be dangerous. Why do you constantly get caught up in minutia? You have to write something.

Okay, okay, I know. Where do I start?

"My sister was already strapped to the gurney when the curtain opened . . . The last thing I saw as the guy with the gun led us out was the warden coming back into the room. His clothes were bloody, and blood had spattered across his face. He was yelling into the landline as the guards moved me out."

The small, uneven printing ran slightly up and down across the page. Blue ink against the stark white paper. Could he read it? Yeah, pretty easily. Not bad. He'd written an entire page in just a few minutes.

~

His mom's face sagged in exhaustion, and she walked toward the exit in small, slow steps. Not a shuffle, merely a slow, steady gait. Cole supported her on one side, Olivia the other. She'd aged twenty years since breakfast.

Cole looked around as soon as they were outside. Media trucks lined the roadway. Prison officials most likely had asked them to leave the grounds as soon as the media witnesses came out of the building. That was good. Cole didn't want to talk to reporters, and Mom was in no shape to deal with them.

She said nothing as they inched across the parking lot. Was she okay? Had something happened physically, or was she just tired?

She breathed heavily as she plopped herself into the passenger seat. Was this ordeal going to kill her?

"Do you need anything? Water or anything?"

Please, Lord. Don't let her die.

"No. Thank you, Cole. I just need to catch my breath. I don't know if I'm happy or sad."

"I know what you mean," Olivia said. "I wonder what happens next?"

"I don't know. I tried to ask that Mr. Hamilton, but a guard told us to stop talking," Cole's mom said.

Her breathing had slowed but still sounded somewhat ragged.

Cole tried Hamilton's phone. Voice mail. "Hey, Frank. Cole here. Please give me a call as soon as you know anything. Thanks."

The message probably wasn't necessary, but it also wouldn't hurt.

His mom's eyelids drooped as Cole started the car. Her head bobbed before they were off the prison grounds.

Media trucks and news people formed a ribbon along the roadway on both sides of the gate. Cole didn't want to stop for traffic, for fear reporters and camera people would rush the car and demand a statement.

He glanced quickly both directions. He wouldn't have to stop. Traffic was light. He eased toward the gate, gauging his opening, then jammed the accelerator to the floor. A few minutes later they were on the highway.

~

"Execution goes awry. Details after these messages." The newsman sounded almost giddy.

Cole wished he could turn up the radio. He couldn't. The women were still asleep. It was okay, though. He was sure if he missed something, he'd catch it later. This had to be the lead story on the evening news everywhere in America. The story had probably already gone viral on social media.

Outside, mature trees flanked both sides of the highway. The pavement changed from black asphalt to a lighter gray concrete with the addition of a fourth lane on his side of the interstate. Probably ten or fifteen minutes to Indy. At least it wouldn't be rush hour.

The weird little musical news theme played.

"The government failed in its attempt today to execute convicted Christian hate-speech criminal Kiley Evans," the newsman said. "Members of the media assigned to witness and cover the event reported Evans was strapped down, with the procedure under way, when executioner Wendall Schultz refused to administer the drugs to carry out the execution.

"Witnesses said Schultz used the J-name before they heard what sounded like a gunshot inside the death house. Terre Haute Warden Brice Hunter was splattered in what appeared to be blood, according to the witness reports.

"Schultz was taken to a local hospital. His condition is not known at this time. Bureau of Prisons officials said Hunter was placed on administrative leave while the bureau investigates.

"In Washington today, President Gonzalez praised Argentinian leaders . . ."

What? No information on what's next? Guess they don't know any more than we do.

His mom stirred and opened her eyes.

"Kiley's going to go free," she said sleepily.

"I hope you're right."

"I know I am. I know it in my knower."

~

As Cole had expected, Kiley was the lead story on the networks that evening and on primetime news commentary shows. One headline read, "Was God watching over her?"

Talking heads filled split screens on news channels.

"The government has a duty to carry out the sentence. They have a signed warrant and an order from a judge," a man said on a Fox News broadcast.

"Absolutely not," the man on the other side of the screen said. His voice had lost the polished professional tone that most politicians and others accustomed to being on TV use. The man sounded as if he were chewing out a twelve-year-old who'd been caught smoking behind the garage. "The government had its shot. To subject Kiley Evans to this again would amount to cruel and unusual punishment. And as far as I know, some parts of the Constitution remain intact and unmolested by the Gonzalez Administration and the Supreme Court."

The attorney general and a death penalty opponent squared off in one debate, with the attorney general proclaiming, "These Christians deserve a punishment worse than death. They're a menace to society."

So, those would be the legal arguments. How long would it take for all this to play out?

Cole turned down the volume and tried to pray, but exhaustion overwhelmed him.

The ringing phone jarred him awake. He didn't recognize the number.

Do I take this? Is it some reporter?

Better take it. I can get rid of them if I need to.

Rodney's voice came from the speaker. "Cole, I hope you understand what happened today."

Is he using a burner? Trying to avoid being recorded?

"Honestly, I'm not sure. I didn't know if you guys were there to kill her or help her."

"Definitely to help her. We did everything we could to stop the procedure and whispered prayers over her the whole time we were with her. But I sure didn't expect Wendall to do what he did."

"Yeah, that was pretty unbelievable. What's his condition?"

"He didn't make it."

"Oh." Cole could hear the surprise in his voice. Why had he assumed Wendall would survive a gunshot wound? "Wow, I'm so sorry, Rodney."

"Yeah, it's sad for us, but he's with the Lord now. He accepted Christ just last week."

"Wow, I'm so thankful, I can't even put it into words. I really don't know what to say."

He was reminded of the Lord's sacrifice and overwhelmed with a fresh wave of thankfulness for both Wendall Schulz and for Jesus.

"Don't say anything, just keep preaching," Rodney said.

"So, what's up with the warden?"

"Nothing, yet. He'll probably lose his job, but I bet he isn't charged with anything."

"That would be the way the world works right now, wouldn't it?"

Should he ask the next question? Would it be dangerous if someone was monitoring the call? It probably didn't matter at this point. Rodney had already said they prayed over Kiley as they strapped her down. "Are you, Joe, and Dennis okay? Has there been any blowback?"

"No, they just took statements. And it wasn't like we had any control over Wendall. We didn't even think to suggest he not go through with turning on the drugs."

"Well, I'm glad you guys are okay."

"I'll try to keep you posted, but it would probably be best if we laid low for a while."

"Gotcha," Cole said. "I'll keep you guys in my prayers. Reach out again when you're ready to resume our meetings. And take good care of Kiley."

"Will do, brother. You be safe."

"Well, even if I'm not, God's got this. To live is Christ, and to die is gain, right?" Cole said.

"Yep. I'll stay in touch as much as I can," Rodney said.

3 8

THE TALKING HEADS HAD been right. The attorney general wanted a new execution date, but Frank Hamilton and Jennifer Michaels had found an attorney in Indiana to try to get the sentence thrown out.

Briefcase in hand, Sabrina Jackson stood next to Frank Hamilton inside the railing in the courtroom. African American, tall and slim, she carried herself with the same confident air Frank Hamilton and Don Fisher did. Hamilton had said he'd contacted her through a Christian legal defense network. He'd said she came highly recommended.

"Sabrina, this is the client's brother, Pastor Cole Evans," Hamilton said.

Cole reached across the railing. Her handshake was firm but brief, and she gave fleeting eye contact. Her body language screamed that she wanted to get to her spot at the defense table.

"Good to meet you," she said. "Frank has briefed me thoroughly, and I've read the government's reports on what happened at the prison. I won't stand here and promise you the moon, I'm just going to make our case as well as I can and leave the rest in the Lord's hands."

"Do you know anything about the judge?" Cole asked.

"He's new. I only know what I've read. Not enough to know which way he might lean."

"I appreciate your honesty," Cole said.

She nodded and stuck out her hand for another handshake.

She moved with purpose toward her spot, opened her briefcase, and organized her materials in front of her.

She's in the zone, all business at this point. I like her.

Cole looked around the room. The glitz had worn off. Federal court. Been there, done that. And the T-shirt is faded with holes in it. It was sad.

Courtrooms had symbolized our democracy's greatness. Now they felt like places where the strong preyed upon the weak.

Olivia slid into the seat beside him. "Hey there, how are you doing?"

"Cautiously hopeful."

"Me, too. I've been praying like crazy. Didn't sleep much last night."

"Me, either."

Kiley wasn't in the courtroom. She hadn't been let off The Row.

"How sad. The gallery's only half full. People were much more interested in seeing Kiley convicted, sentenced, and executed than they are in seeing her freed," Olivia said.

"Human nature, I guess."

Everyone in the room rose and sat as the judge took his slightly elevated perch. The judge's thinning blond hair exhibited a few streaks of silver, and his blue eyes pierced.

Cole couldn't interpret the man's poker face. *I guess a good poker face is a job requirement.*

The U.S. attorney almost sneaked to his spot behind the podium. Of average height and build, and with short but unruly strawberry blond hair, the man fidgeted and looked around, like a child looking up and down the street before crossing.

"If it please the court, the people's position is that an order already exists for an execution, and the government now has a duty to carry that out," the young lawyer said. As he spoke, he repeatedly rubbed his thumb across the hem of his suit jacket. His words dribbled across the room. They seemed they might not make it all the way to the judge's bench.

How timid and weak! This guy's as persuasive as a wet tissue. Where'd he learn, or not *learn, how to deliver an argument?*

Cole leaned forward. He picked apart the attorney's performance. Words like "mealy-mouthed, restrained," and "downright wimpy" came to mind.

The realization almost snuck up on him.

Wait a minute! This guy's one of ours! *He's a believer!*

That's awesome! Thank you so much, Lord! Thank you! Now, please Lord, give Sabrina Jackson the words to wrap this up and free Kiley.

"This matter isn't about the government's duty," Sabrina Jackson began. Her delivery was quiet but confident. "It's about whether the United States brutalizes its own citizens, even those it intends to execute."

She started to pick up steam.

"Your Honor, I'm sure you'll agree that we're a nation that prides itself on being humane in certain situations. We stopped public hangings over a century ago because we realized they were inhumane. They'd become a circus, and botched hangings sometimes kept the condemned in their final agony far too long. As a nation, we realized even the condemned deserve to die with dignity. Today, our execution protocols reflect that. We desire dignity for the condemned, and dignity for their families. I'd even go as far as to say dignity for the nation, as we avoid yielding to our baser nature and morbid curiosity. Even in our execution protocols, we're a people who take the high road."

Her voice was strong and impassioned.

"Your Honor, I'm sure you're aware of the *Kemmler* decision. The court ruled the punishment of death is not cruel. The court couched its definition of cruelty in the terms of 'inhumane and barbarous.'" Sabrina Jackson made air quotes. She looked at her yellow legal pad for a beat, then continued. "Chief Justice Fuller wrote that cruelty is 'something more than the mere extinguishment of human life.' It's my client's position, Your Honor, that the government in this case is proposing to undertake exactly that, an irreversible action that would be more than the mere extinguishment of human life."

What's the judge thinking? She has his attention.

"Furthermore, in the 1945 *Frances* case in Louisiana, an electric chair malfunctioned, and Louisiana's governor issued a new death warrant. The court ruled that the execution originally was not carried out due to an 'unforeseeable accident,' and the second execution attempt went forward. Key in that case was a lack of intent on the state's part to inflict unnecessary pain.

"In the case before this court, the attorney general's own words point to the government's desire to inflict as much pain as possible on Christians. If it please the court . . ." she continued.

The judge nodded, and the video began.

I saw this! This is perfect!

The attorney general's visage took up the left side of the split screen, a death penalty opponent's face filled the right.

"These Christians deserve a punishment worse than death. They're a menace to society," the attorney general said.

When the video ended, Sabrina Jackson resumed, "My client was as prepared as any human being can be to accept capital punishment. But death didn't come. Now, Your Honor, as much as is possible, I'd like you to try to place yourself on that execution table. See those green wall tiles in the execution room. Feel the leather gurney under you. Feel and smell the straps that hold you down. Feel the mildly uncomfortable sensation of the IV in your leg. Imagine who's behind the windows to the observation rooms where the witnesses are watching. Stare at the ceiling lights as you wait for your life to ebb away."

Sabrina Jackson stopped. Her words hung in the air.

"Now, Your Honor, imagine you have to endure that a second time."

Stillness hung over the courtroom.

The judge stared at his hands resting on the bench.

"It doesn't matter *why* the execution wasn't carried out," Sabrina Jackson said. Her voice was again quiet but strong. "It matters that allowing a second execution attempt would be barbarous and inhumane, something more than the mere extinguishment of human life. And it would be carried out by a government intent on causing as much harm as possible, beyond the mere imposition of a death sentence."

Cole felt the quiet, heavy and uncomfortable.

The U.S. attorney stared at his table.

Awed expressions hung on every face. Even though there was more to be said, Cole knew the proceeding was over.

It was another five minutes before the judge rapped the gavel and stood up.

≈

People brushed past, and media members jostled for spots in the crowded hallway. Cole pushed his way through the mob and shut the huddle room door behind him.

"Well, we'll know in a month," Sabrina Jackson said. "The government has thirty days to file whatever they're going to file. But honestly, after talking to the other side, I think this is over. I don't expect any appeals."

Cole couldn't dial back his smile.

"I'll let you know as soon as I hear anything," the attorney said. Her joy seemed genuine. Cole got the impression Kiley's case meant something to her.

Was it appropriate to hug her? Probably not. Cole stuck out his right hand. "Thank you, Sabrina. I can't wait to hear."

~

Cole hadn't slept in days. Sabrina Jackson had called two days earlier to tell him the case was officially over. A guy at the prison had said it would take a day and a half to process Kiley out of the system. Now, the early fall sunrise peaked over the horizon. They sat with the car windows open, allowing in the morning cool. Olivia gave his knee a gentle squeeze. His mom sat quietly in the backseat. The prison was quieter than it had been a few months earlier. Bureau of Prisons officials had agreed not to disclose the time and location of Kiley's departure. That information would be released to the media after the fact. Guards silhouetted in their towers kept silent watch.

The prison door opened, and Kiley emerged. She wore the same jeans and white top she'd worn the day her ordeal began. They hung looser now and were out of style. She looked pale but elated, squinting at the morning light. She seemed different, harder in a way Cole couldn't explain.

She was halfway down the sidewalk by the time he made his way around the car.

"You going to buy me breakfast, or what?" she said.

Her bony hug was brief but intense.

Somehow everything was different, but everything was the same. America no longer enjoyed religious freedom. But Cole knew he'd lift up the name of Jesus regardless.

Epilogue

THE CHURCH HAD FLOURISHED since news coverage of the botched execution. The elders had found four additional isolated meeting spots, and Cole and three other New Hope pastors led services three times a week at all times of the day and night.

As the sun crept over the horizon in St. Jonas, Cole searched for Scriptures about deliverance. He meditated on sections of Psalm 34. *I sought the LORD, and he answered me; he delivered me from all my fears . . . This poor man called, and the LORD heard him; he saved him out of all his troubles . . . Taste and see that the LORD is good; blessed is the one who takes refuge in him.*

Cole's phone whistled the arrival of a text.

Who could want something this early?

Frank Hamilton: Brice Hunter is in jail, charged with murder.

Brice Hunter? Brice Hunter? Oh, the warden.

Me: Guess that's where he belongs.

Frank Hamilton: Yeah, even though he deserves it, I feel sorry for his family.

Me: I guess we forget about prisoners' families. Sometimes they're as dysfunctional as the prisoners, but other times, they're victims, too.

Frank Hamilton: Yeah, especially kids.

Me: Thanks for the update.

Frank Hamilton: Sure. Golf Saturday?

Me: Absolutely.

∽

Olivia was talking. Was he dreaming? Yes. No. Yes. Dreaming.

He rocked from side to side. What was happening?

"Cole! Wake up!" Her voice was hushed but insistent.

The yellow-green numbers on the clock swam into view. 2:34.

He tried to make his mouth work to ask what was wrong.

"Cole! Someone's at the door!"

The sentence bolted him upright.

"Who in creation—?"

"I don't know. Just go!" Olivia was at the edge of anger.

The cuffs of his pajama pants hung over his heels as he shuffled down the hallway. He rubbed the sleep from his eyes.

The image was distorted through the peephole.

John Porter? What in the world? This better be good.

"Pastor Evans, I'm so sorry to bother you in the middle of the night. This couldn't wait."